D0840762

First paperback edition: August 2022

ISBN: 979-8-9863886-0-1

10 9 8 7 6 5 4 3 2 1

YA HEY

PAUL BENSON

Telosery

CALIFORNIA

Part One

CONTROL

Chapter One

THE END

I found out I was depressed the old-fashioned way: I tried to kill myself. And when I failed to enter the gates of heaven to an afterlife unburdened by the corruptions of earthly life—*true happiness*—I instead realized that I'd reached rock bottom and needed to get professional help.

It was two in the morning, and I was lying stiff on my side, wearing nothing but my boxer briefs. My bedroom window blinds cast bars of light over me, a prisoner unable to break free. I was staring at the little blue pills strewn across the rug, wondering if they would be the last thing I'd ever see. I tried so hard to cry, to release the pain through salty tears, but nothing would come out. I'd swallow air and then puff out my cheeks, over and over and over again, trying to build up pressure to force the tears out.

But nothing. I just lay there in shame.

I moved my eyes to the left and saw the translucent orange pill container sitting on its side in the corner of the room. Its capless opening stared me down like a knowing oculus. Twenty minutes had gone by since I had taken the container, tilted my head back, and poured all the Adderall pills into my mouth like I was finishing a pint of beer. I swallowed and swallowed and swallowed, until I choked and out came at least twenty pills that were supposed to be part of my death sentence. But at least twenty made their way down. I was sure of it.

As I waited for my mind and body to go to sleep—*forever*—I began to feel heavy, like I was sinking into the ground. Every time my apartment's radiator turned on and hissed, my head would ache and my vision would scramble. I couldn't move my arms or legs, even when I closed my eyes and concentrated all my mental energy on making them do something—anything! I was trapped inside my body. I lay there wondering if I was in between life and death. Would there be purgatory? I hoped not. I just wanted relief. I just wanted everything to be over.

Then my arms and legs started shaking, and sharp pain pierced my stomach like someone was stabbing me from the inside out. My vision became blurry, and the room was spinning, slow at first and then faster and faster. *This is it*, I thought. *I'm finally leaving this hellish world behind! The white light at the end of the tunnel will come next, and then I'll begin my long walk down its path.*

But then, the room stopped spinning and the beige walls came back into focus. *Fuck! I'm not losing consciousness. I'm just having a bad trip that'll end soon and return me back to where I started from.*

And then, shame.

Oh, the shame!

I felt the shame of knowing that I had almost ended my own life, that I couldn't understand that my life wasn't that bad. I felt the shame of knowing that people loved me and cared about me, that there were people and things yet unknown worth living for. Most of all, I felt the shame of not pulling through for my mom and sister, for being too weak to finish what I had come to Washington to do.

The shame!

Feeling and realizing the shame made it even worse. I not

only felt that I'd disappointed my family, but I felt that I'd disappointed the world. I had failed every single person, every single creature and living thing, because I was too weak. Now I felt shame squared to infinity. I was worthless. I was pathetic. I was ashamed.

Shame!

Shame!

Shame!

My eyes darted up to find the clock on the wall, its ticking second hand the only thing I could hear. I strained my eyes to figure out where the hour and minute hands were. All I saw were blurs of black shapes and a big silver circle floating right in front of me. I think it was three or four in the morning, but I couldn't say for sure. All I knew was I couldn't even kill myself right, and now here I was.

I coughed on my spit, felt a sting at the back of my throat, and looked down. There were little white bubbles underneath my nose like a foamy ocean wave had crashed ashore. I blew through my nose and mouth—in and out—in and out—in and out—so I wouldn't choke to death. That's not the way I wanted to die. Only a pathetic, worthless person dies like that. I just wanted it to be over. I just wanted to sleep.

I moved my eyes to the right and stared at my bed. It looked like my sheets and blanket were melting off the sides. I wanted to be on top of it, curled up under the covers where I'd be safe and warm. I stared at the bed, imagining what it would be like to be in it, wondering why I'd taken it for granted all my life. It looked like a skyscraper from my vantage point, so tall I'd have to scale its sides to reach its peak.

I closed my eyes and imagined myself getting into bed. I concentrated on moving my limbs, on bending my arms and legs so I could get off the ground and stand on my own two feet again. The muscles on the back of my neck tightened and my head shivered. I could hear myself squeal in distress, summoning what little control I had to force my body to move. I knew I could will myself into bed. All I had to do was keep trying.

Don't give up, Mike. You can do it.
But nothing.

• • •

I strained to open my right eye because my bedroom was awash in light. I guess I survived to the next day. I was still on the floor and my body still felt heavy, but now I was so parched I wanted to drink from the Potomac. I lifted my head, felt a tug on my cheek, and heard a ripping sound. My face stung like a hot iron had branded me. I glanced down and saw a puddle of drool and white stuff on the rug. I traced a line of drool up to the corner of my mouth and wiped it away. *I guess I can use my arms again*, I thought.

I bent my legs and pushed my arms against the floor to get up. Then I took a few uneasy steps, bent over, and picked up my phone. I pressed the home button, and the screen zoomed into focus. I didn't care about all the unread emails and texts and notifications that littered the screen. I had survived a suicide attempt, for godssake! I needed the day to pull my pitiful self together and get back into the semblance of the twenty-two-year-old guy I was supposed to be.

Standing on my own two feet made me feel unsteady and nauseous. I ran across my bedroom and down the hallway and hurled myself over the toilet. I vomited violently all over the toilet rim, the bathroom floor, and myself. *How appropriate*, I thought. *Only a person as pathetic as I am would throw up on himself.* The shame I had felt the night before was resurfacing. Only this time, my nostrils and throat stung from the acid that had just burst from my insides. Now, shame tasted like vomit.

I turned around to close the bathroom door, then I turned the lock and heard a satisfying *click*. I was safe now. I stepped over the pool of vomit, leaned into the bathtub, and turned the faucet counterclockwise. The sound of the water was deafening to my ears, like rushing rapids carving a path through land. I leaned against the wall, waiting until I saw steam rise from the tub, and then pulled off my boxer briefs. My head ached so much I could feel my temples pulsing with blood.

I grabbed onto the towel bar to steady myself as I stepped into the safety of the tub's four walls. I turned on the shower, sank into the tub, and let the water wash over me. I realized that I didn't even bother to close the shower curtain because I could hear water splattering all over the bathroom floor. But I didn't care. I was focused on the warm water raining down on me, washing the vomit off my chest and legs. It felt so good.

I curled into the fetal position and closed my eyes. Fast-moving streams of light filled the darkness in my head. I thought about everything that had happened in my life, everything that had brought me to this moment. I wondered if my dad even cared about me. Then I lost control and cried out, "God, why have you forsaken me?!" And then the tears came, rushing out of the breached dam of my eyes.

I opened my eyes and stared at the tub floor as streams of yellow and brown water flowed toward the drain, the filth washing off my body. I lay there on my side until the hot water ran out and turned lukewarm. I thought about my mom and sister. I felt so much shame. *How could it come to this? Didn't I do everything right? I did everything I was supposed to do! I did everything the adults told me to do!*

I knew what I needed next: help. I walked into my bedroom, wearing only a towel, and took a seat at my desk. I opened my laptop, clicked on the internet browser icon, and went to Google. The cursor was blinking, waiting for me to give it a query. I typed into the search bar: *suicide help*. A little label said there were 412,000 results in .59 seconds. I clicked on the top result: *Georgetown Student Health Services*.

The phone number was conspicuous, with extra-bold font surrounded by a red rectangle that flashed and announced it was open twenty-four hours. *I guess this is it*, I thought. I picked up my phone and dialed the number, and a young woman answered on the other end.

"Hello, Georgetown Student Health Services. How may I help you?"

"Hello," I said, my voice cracking. "I...I need to see...I need to talk to a counselor."

"Sure, I can schedule something for you!" she said. "When would you like to come in?"

I paused. I didn't want her, a complete stranger, to know that I tried to kill myself last night. And yet I needed to communicate the urgency of the situation.

"I...I need to see someone *today*, if possible," I said.

"Are you in any danger right now?"

"I am not."

"OKaaaaaay...well, we have *one* counselor available for walk-ins, but she is only available for a specific type of patient. Like, for a specific type of patient, like, *focused on life*."

I gulped. I knew what she was implying.

"I...I think I am that type of patient," I said.

I knew she could sense my shame. I wanted to hang up and go to bed and curl into the fetal position again. I didn't want this life of mine anymore.

"Hey, ya!" she said.

Her voice and tone turned bubbly, as if she had just earned a gold star for scheduling a Code Blue patient.

"Since you're *suicidal*," she said in a whisper, "I can literally schedule you to see Margaret Dymphna today at three! You'll get a confirmation email with all the deets!"

"OK, thanks."

As I ended the phone call, I glanced at my computer screen to see the time. It was almost two, which meant I only had an hour until I'd have to admit out loud that it had all gone wrong. My stomach started trembling at the thought of confessing my life's failures to a professional. I felt such shame.

I got dressed, grabbed my coat, and ran out the door. I walked down Thirty-Sixth Street, checking the map app on my phone every few paces to make sure I was heading in the right direction. My hands and arms were shaking as I watched the pulsing blue dot, me, move closer to the static red pin on the screen.

When the blue dot touched the red pin, I stopped and looked up. Across the street was a small, two-story Federal row house with yellow clapboard sides. It had a narrow front door that was painted a glossy forest green. A sinking feeling formed in my stomach. *I should just run home now! Why would anyone care to hear about my problems anyway? No one will ever know. No one will ever care. I am worthless.*

But I needed answers because I was out of options. I ran across the street, took a deep breath, and opened the door. A small and crooked wooden staircase greeted me. A sign on the wall to my right said *Counseling Upstairs*. I turned around to close the door and then began a slow walk up the staircase. Each step I took caused the floorboards to squeak, announcing my entrance to all who dwelled there. My hand was clasped so tight against the wood banister I could feel my nails making indentations.

When I got to the top, I turned left and saw an older white woman waiting for me. She had silver hair and was wearing a blue kaftan that had white lilies printed on it. She was standing still, her arms limp and crossed near her waist.

"Hello, are you Michael?"

"Yes, hi. Yes. I'm Michael Morris."

"Wonderful!" she said. "Welcome! I'm so glad you're here. Come in, come in."

She gestured with her hands for me to walk into another room that was behind her. As I entered, I saw two chairs—the wide upholstered kind you see in coffee shops—positioned across from each other. But there was no coffee table in between. This wasn't a place to relax.

"Sit, sit," she said as her hands made a sweeping motion.

I took off my coat and scarf and sat in the chair on the right. My hands and arms were still shaking, which embarrassed me, so I took my coat and laid it over my lap. I tucked my arms underneath to hide my humiliation.

She took her seat and said, "Michael, I am *so* glad you had the courage to come here. Getting here was the hardest part, and you did it. You did it, Michael. You did it."

She was smiling, but it was one of those upside-down smiles that would be a frown if it weren't for the warmth showing on the rest of her face and in her eyes. I didn't know what to say back. I just stared at the ground, waiting for her to say something else. I was so nervous.

"Tell me about mom," she said.

"Uh, well, she's a teacher," I said, my voice cracking. "She lives in California."

She gave me a knowing stare. Her eyes were a piercing blue.

"And what about dad? What does he do?"

"Umm, he's a construction worker—freeways. He has to travel around the state a lot to go to his job sites. He, uh, he's not really around. My parents are divorced. My dad's an alcoholic and...um, he's got other problems, too, you know."

"Thank you for sharing, Michael," she said. "Any siblings?"

I didn't understand why she was interrogating me about my family. I was here for one reason and one reason only: *me*. I had tried to kill myself last night, for godsake! Did she not get the memo?

"I have a younger sister named Jess. She's a junior in high school. She lives in California with my mom. I don't really talk to them—you know, my mom and sister—very often. I probably should...I'm just so busy with grad school, you know, and starting my second semester and then having to look for a job soon...and I'm working so much for my internship, I don't really have any free time, you know?"

"Thank you for telling me about your family, Michael," she said. "Now *I* want to tell you something."

She paused, and I braced myself. I clasped my hands together under my coat and squeezed tight.

"Your mother and father and sister love you *so* much. They do, they really do." She gave me another upside-down smile and then continued. "You don't even realize it because you are so far away. But they think of you all the time. They miss you. They want the best for you. They love you so very, very much."

I didn't know what to say. Chills moved through my body, starting in my core and moving outward to every square inch of my skin. I wondered if I was still cold from my walk over.

"Are you religious? Did you grow up with any faith tradition?" she pressed.

"I mean, I guess I'm kind of spiritual. I was raised Catholic, but then I went to college and kind of forgot about it, you know? I only go to church when I'm home for Christmas or Easter. But I still remember all the things to say and do during Mass, though. It never leaves you, you know?"

I smiled, satisfied with my answer.

"Oh, wonderful, Michael! Just wonderful."

She adjusted her position in the chair, uncrossing and re-crossing her legs. As she moved, a flash of light reflected off her chest. It was a gold chain with a small cross on its side, now resting precariously against her collarbone.

"I want you to do something for me. Will you keep an open mind with what I'm about to request of you?"

"Yes," I said.

I noticed I had stopped shaking. She made me feel calm.

"Do you remember The Lord's Prayer?"

"Yes," I said. "I used to pray it every day as a kid. But one day I stopped—maybe in college? I dunno."

"OK, very nice. I want you to think of The Lord's Prayer not as a religious prayer but as a personal chant, to calm and center you. Don't think of it as a prayer to Jesus or to the Christian God. Think of it like a yoga chant or a mantra, a tool for what they are calling *wellness* and *self-care* these days."

I didn't understand what she meant. I gave her a puzzled look.

"I want you to use it—I want you to use The Lord's Prayer. Every time you get sad, say it. Every time you think everything's going wrong, say it. Every time a thought of self-harm crosses your mind, say it. Every time you feel gratitude, say it. Every time you feel alive with life, say it. Every time you are filled with love, say it. Just say it. Say it! Say it! Say it!"

She pierced the air with her right hand, scrunched into a tight fist, with every *say it*.

"I understand," I said.

"Good. It will calm you. It will center you. And it will cradle you in hard times. It will be the most powerful tool you will have at your disposal. Do not underestimate it, Michael. Do you understand?"

I nodded in excitement. Then she turned to her right and picked up a pen and notepad.

"Now, Michael, I am going to refer you to a wonderful psychiatrist. She is going to help you in ways that I cannot."

She scribbled down a name and phone number, ripped the top sheet of paper from the pad, and then reached forward to hand it to me. I looked down, turning it right side up, and read: *Dr. Romainine Bailey, Howard University Hospital, 202-555-0331.*

"When you get home, you're going to call that number and make an appointment. OK?"

"OK, I will," I said.

She stood up, and so I did, too. I put on my coat, wrapped my scarf around my neck, and then followed her out of the room. I walked toward the staircase and turned around to say goodbye.

"Thank you, Margaret. Thank you so much!"

In that moment, after our session, I felt so known. It wasn't as scary as I had made it out to be. I really was thankful for her.

"Goodbye, Michael. Please contact me if you ever need anything, day or night or middle of the night. I mean it!"

"OK, I will."

And then she reached forward and grabbed both of my hands. She pulled them toward her, squeezed them, looked me dead in the eyes, and said, "Remember: just say it."

She let go and I turned to walk down the stairs. When I opened the door, a rush of cold air hit me and a shiver went down my spine. I started my walk back up Thirty-Sixth Street, following the red brick sidewalk all the way home. And then, for the first time in a long time, I prayed.

Our Father, who art in heaven,
hallowed be thy name;
thy kingdom come,
thy will be done
on earth as it is in heaven.
Give us this day our daily bread,
and forgive us our trespasses,
as we forgive those who trespass against us;
and lead us not into temptation,
but deliver us from evil.
Amen.

Chapter Two

THE DIAGNOSIS

I was supposed to show up at Dr. Bailey's office, which was across town in Shaw, thirty minutes before my scheduled appointment time of two thirty. I looked at my phone and it was one thirty. I tapped open the transit app to see when the next bus would arrive. *Crap!* It said two minutes. I grabbed my P.W.K.—my phone, wallet, and keys—and rushed out the door to catch the bus.

I was feeling better after meeting with Margaret last week but still felt so sad about the whole situation. I was ashamed that I had tried to kill myself. But I also felt proud of myself for being smart enough to get help. Why couldn't I just be an irresponsible victim who didn't overthink his personally sanctioned death? I didn't understand why things were *happening*, things I didn't plan to happen.

I got off the bus at Seventh Street and walked north to the hospital entrance. The neighborhood was so different from Georgetown. There were groups of people hanging around the bus stops with no intention of getting on a bus. The sounds of horns honking and bus doors beeping open and people talking on their phones filled the air. I passed a corner used-phone store that was playing rap music really loudly, and I saw a small group of people my age dancing on the sidewalk. The song lyrics were so violent I wondered if it was even legal to play it in public.

When I turned into the hospital driveway, I started to feel nervous. I couldn't believe I was about to walk into a psychiatrist's office. I couldn't believe that my life had become what it was, that I needed mental health care from professionals, and that I was *here*.

I was ashamed.

I couldn't tell my mom or sister or any of my friends about any of this, not even Adam or Matt. I promised myself that this would be my personal battle, my own internal war to fight and win. I would fix this problem on my own and then get back to searching for love and purpose so I could become the man I was supposed to be.

I walked through two sets of automatic doors and into the hospital lobby. Two black security guards were sitting at a reception desk; they looked up at me but didn't say anything. I just kept walking.

I hurried down the hall and tried to avoid making eye contact with anyone. I noticed that everyone I passed was black. I was the only white person around. I felt insecure, like I wasn't supposed to be there. I wondered why Margaret referred me to Howard instead of the Georgetown or G.W. hospitals, which were in the white parts of the city.

"Hello, sir," said a doctor when I turned a corner. "Welcome to our hospital."

He smiled at me with the most radiant white teeth I'd ever seen. I just waved.

"Good afternoon, sir," said a nurse who passed me. "I hope you're having a wonderful day!"

She had long, thick braids that went down to her butt. My eyes widened and I smiled.

When I got into the elevator, my hands and arms started

shaking just like they had done when I was about to see Margaret. It all felt so surreal. A week ago, I was getting drunk with my friends at a bar, and today I was in a hospital on my way to see a shrink. I stared at my reflection in the shiny metal doors. I hated myself.

The elevator dinged and the doors opened. I got off and walked down a windowless hallway that seemed to go on forever. When I made it to the end, there was a sign on a door: *Romainine Bailey, M.D., Department of Psychiatry.*

I turned the doorknob and walked in. There were four people seated in the waiting room. Three were black and one was white. *Phew! I'm not alone*, I thought.

I walked up to the reception desk.

"Hello, sir. Do you have an appointment?"

"Yes."

"What's your name?"

"Michael Morris."

"OK, Mr. Morris. Please fill out these forms and bring them back to me when you're done. You can take a seat over there while you wait."

"OK, thanks," I said.

I sat down and spent the next ten minutes filling out the forms. Some were the standard medical forms and privacy disclosures and patient waivers so I'd never be able to sue. But there were also questionnaires that asked me to rate my levels of happiness, sadness, anxiety, and depression over the past two weeks.

After I had finished filling them out, I looked down and noticed a pattern: I was really sad and really depressed. It looked like I had filled in all the bubbles in a single column on a school test card in an act of defiance, that there could be no possible way it was the same answer to every question. But in my case, it was all true.

I took the clipboard and all the papers back to the receptionist. Then I dropped the pen in a coffee mug and went back to my chair. I sat still, not a single part of my body moving, while I waited to be called. I avoided eye contact with the other patients, afraid to reveal the depths of my despair. I felt such shame.

"Mr. Morris!" yelled the receptionist.

I took a deep breath, walked to the doorway, and stepped through. The receptionist guided me to another door, knocked on it, opened it, and said, "Dr. Bailey, Mr. Morris is here to see you."

"Please come in," said a voice.

I walked in, and the metal door began to close behind me, its hydraulic hinge making a slow, gassy sound. There was a middle-aged black woman shuffling through papers on top of a seafoam-green metal desk. She was wearing glasses and had colorful fabric twisted in a ring on top of her head. She was Ethiopian—or maybe Kenyan? She didn't look up at me.

"Hello, I'm Dr. Romainine Bailey. Take a seat," she said.

The door clicked shut, and I sat down and waited for her to say something else.

"Michael, please tell me why you are here."

"Well…you see, I…I tried to commit suicide last week. I was just feeling, you know, really down on life…and hopeless. And it didn't work out! You know, I messed up. So I went and saw a counselor at Georgetown to, uh, talk about it and she, um, told me to come here, to see you."

She didn't say anything. She just wrote furiously on her notepad. Her pen was hitting the paper and clipboard so hard it made a dull echo that filled the silence between us.

"Yes, I received your case file from Ms. Margaret Dymphna. Tell me about your work life."

Case file? I gulped. I felt ashamed, like a criminal.

"I just started working my first real job—well, internship— about four months ago. I'm also in grad school—studying political science. Before that I was in college in California. I'm really busy all the time and, you know, studying for my classes and trying to plan for my thesis next year and then finding a real job, I think…I think it all took so much out of me. And, you know, living in the city is hard…everything is hard here! And I think the stress and pressure—the pressure I put on myself—is part of the problem, to be honest. You know?"

"Romantic life?"

"Uh, I'm single. I haven't been on a real date in a while."

"Family life?"

"Umm, my family lives in California, my mom and little sister. My parents are divorced…dad isn't in the picture."

Every time I'd answer a question she would flip the page in such a camp way that it made me want to laugh. But I had to fight the smile trying to crack through my stoic face because this was a very serious situation.

"Social life?"

"I have a lot of friends. I like to go out to the movies and to the bars one or two nights a week."

"Drugs?"

"I don't do drugs. I, uh, smoked weed a few times in college at some house parties, but that's it. It's not my thing."

She lacked the warmth and personal concern that Margaret had had for me. Margaret had made me feel human. Dr. Bailey made me feel like a specimen.

"Sex life?"

I was startled by her question. I didn't know what to say, so I didn't say anything at all. She looked up, but her head didn't move—only her eyes, peering over the top rim of her glasses, which were bright yellow and in the shape of a cat's eyes. She prompted me with her hands to talk. I hesitated at first but wanted the interrogation to be over, so I rambled off random things.

"Well, I used to have a girlfriend back in college, and we, uh, we would have sex, you know—"

"Did you ever have trouble maintaining an erection?" she interrupted.

"Umm, maybe? I mean, there were hookups all throughout college, and, you know, after parties when I was drunk and, uh—"

"Any other sexual activities?"

"Well, I've been watching porn since I was in middle school, which they say is normal for sexual development. And since I don't have a girlfriend right now, you know, I, uh, you know, *masturbate* more than I'd like to. So, you know, I guess I don't really have a sex life, you know?"

"How often do you watch pornography and masturbate?" she asked, her head now fully vertical, her eyes staring me down.

"Umm…maybe every other day? No—more like a few times, or a couple times a week. Maybe once a week. Yeah, like once a week…or month? I don't really keep track. Is this…is this, um, really necessary for my, you know, diagnosis?"

I knew that she knew that I was lying, answering her question like I answered the question from my dentist about how often I flossed. In that moment I realized a sad truth: I watched porn and masturbated almost every day, sometimes multiple times a day. And I'd been doing it for almost fifteen years, ever since some kid on the playground told me what my penis was capable of.

"Thank you. That is all."

She continued to write like a madwoman. What could she possibly be taking notes about? I didn't even say that much!

"Michael, I am diagnosing you with major depressive disorder."

A sinking feeling hit the pit of my stomach. Did she just say I was clinically depressed?

"OK," I said.

"To correct an imbalance in the number of neurotransmitters that are released in your brain, I am going to prescribe you medication that will help balance your dopamine, serotonin, and norepinephrine. It will also help with your anxiety, which is the flip side of depression. They go hand in hand, as is evident in your questionnaires."

I was mortified that I was being put on medication. Had my life really gone so wrong?

"I am also diagnosing you with sexual dysfunction."

She paused and looked up to gauge my reaction. My skin instantly turned hot, first on my face and then on my neck and shoulders and then down my back and arms. I'd never felt such a strong burning sensation ever before in my life. I wondered whether I would need to go to the emergency room on my way out.

"There is a nascent field of scholarly study into what some researchers are now calling Porn-Induced Erectile Dysfunction, also known as P-I-E-D. I think you may have this disorder...as do *all* men these days..." she said, her words trailing off.

She looked down and started scribbling notes again.

"What? I don't understand, Doctor," I said. "I have what? I thought I was just sad and unbalanced, you know, *chemically*. I'm not here for sexual health stuff. Those—those things I said, they weren't the full picture. I'm not that person! Erectile dysfunction? I'm twenty-two years old!"

I started making faces because of how absurd it sounded. Then I shook my head back and forth in disbelief. I'm not this person she thinks I am. She's wrong! She can't do this to me!

"Michael, our emotional health and mental health are deeply intertwined with our physical health. Everything is connected. Our bodies and minds were not made to watch videographed acts of unrealistic sexual intercourse while self-stimulating our genitalia. It is anathema to human sexuality. From what you indicated, pornography and masturbation have been a regular part of your life for a long time. You likely use porn as a coping mechanism to deal with disordered emotions. You need a course correction."

I was stunned. I was ashamed. I wanted to die. First, she came after my mind. Then, she came after my manhood! How could she possibly know? I didn't even tell her that much!

She was writing my prescription on her official Rx paper pad, signing her name at the bottom with dramatic flair. I could hear the ballpoint pen roll against the paper and see the deep grooves it was making because she was pressing so hard. I wanted to disappear.

"You will take 150 milligrams of Wellbutrin each morning for one week. Then, you will increase your dose to 300 milligrams by taking 150 milligrams each morning and each evening. Do you understand?"

I nodded.

"I am starting you with a sixty-day prescription. You will come in to see me every sixty days for evaluation and, if needed, a prescription renewal. Thank you, Michael. You may leave now."

I couldn't believe it. I thought I'd be lying across a velvet-upholstered chaise lounge chair, my forearm resting against my forehead while I discussed my relationships with my mother and the ensuing Oedipus complex that must have resulted and ruined me for life. Or maybe we'd get into my id and ego and my attempts to avoid reforming either.

But Freud and Jung were irrelevant today. What mattered were the drugs. It was so cold and clinical. She didn't care about my feelings or my life. Her job was to medicate me, to numb the pain with legalized drugs. I couldn't believe it! I was in and out of her office within ten minutes.

Chapter Three

CALIFORNIA ORIGINS

It wasn't supposed to turn out this way. I thought I had done everything right. I thought I had done everything they had told me to do, everything the world had told me to do. I thought that leaving California for the East Coast, where all the important and special people I saw on TV lived, would be my ticket to success. It had to work out, didn't it?

I guess you could say I come from an average American family. I grew up in inland Southern California, also known as the "Inland Empire," which sounds greater than it is, like some Emerald City lined with yellow bricks. But San Bernardino, where I'm from, is no Oz. We aren't Los Angeles or Orange County, where palm tree-lined streets, expensive cars, and silicone breasts are the telltale signs of The California Lifestyle. We're just kind of ordinary, a place for middle-class families, Mexicans, and everyone else who can't afford to live near the beach.

Unlike most American kids who are nothing but mutts, I can at least claim some ethnic heritage from my late grandparents, which made me proud. My mom's mom, Grandma Bertta, was

Finish, and her dad, Grandpa Bruno, was Polish. My dad's mom, Grandma Irma, was Lebanese, and his dad, Grandpa Ryan, was English. They had all achieved the American Dream in their adult lives, but I had always hoped that it would be *me* who'd establish a family legacy worth writing about.

My mom, Marie, is a special education teacher—well, she *was* a special education teacher before the Great Recession. That means she works with Autistic kids, kids in wheelchairs, kids who are deaf and blind, kids with behavioral problems, and anyone else the public education system deems incompatible to learn alongside all the ordinary kids. She was good at her job because she loves everyone no matter their lot in life.

My dad, Ryan Jr., is a construction worker for Caltrans, which is the state organization that builds and manages the labyrinth of freeways across California's landscape. I always thought there was great honor in his profession, a working-class man performing manual labor five days a week to put food on the table for his wife and kids. Except we ate most of our TV dinners from the couch—and he was a deadbeat who wasn't around anymore.

Then there's my younger sister, Jessica, who started her junior year of high school when I left California and started my first semester of grad school in Washington. She's quiet and arty, but full of opinions she'll only share with people she knows well and trusts. I've always felt responsible for her, like she was my kid, even though I'm only six years older. I guess it's because I've always been the only man in the house and knew I had a role to fulfill.

Then there's me. I've always known I was different from everyone else, someone who figured out the rules of the game. My entire life I've known what was going on: the made-up social practices, the adherence to religious rituals, the contrived conversations, the predictable political theatre, the makeups and breakups of human relationships, the annual rituals of conspicuous consumption, and the feelings (oh, the feelings!).

And yet, I've also known I couldn't get by in life without

being a participant. So I promised myself that I would do the bare minimum. I would avoid the drama of life. I would only do what was necessary to fall in love and fulfill my destiny. Because it's love and destiny that would make me the man my father could never be.

To be honest, I didn't expect to make it through college without falling in love with someone special and knowing my purpose in life. I practically expected the clouds to part and God to reach down to me, his chosen son, and hand me what I needed. But now, I was feeling insecure and uneasy about not having either. Did it really have to be this hard?

What I knew for sure is that I'd have to do everything on my own. I couldn't rely on anyone for help.

• • •

I'll never forget the moment when I realized the house of cards had started to fall. It was June 2009 and I had landed at LAX, returning home from my spring semester abroad in the United Kingdom my junior year of college. My mom came to pick me up and take me home, back to San Bernardino, where I had to figure out a plan to finish college and get a job.

The sound of the tires on the freeway was so dull. I kept waiting for the cars in front of us to start weaving in and out of traffic, to start honking their horns and showing some signs of life, like the cars and mopeds and buses in London. Instead, all the cars stayed centered in their designated lanes, like lines of ants on a mission to nowhere.

"So," my mom said, "how was it? Did you have a nice time?"

A nice time? A nice time! A NICE TIME!!

She didn't understand. No, she could never understand. All the people I had met and all the places I had traveled to and all the things I had done. It wasn't some ordinary thing, my semester abroad. It was a Life-Changing Experience, for godssake! How could she diminish it and reduce it down to something ordinary and just *nice*?

"It was fine," I said.

I was staring out the window, looking at the strange Southern California landscape that felt so alien to me. I had never noticed before how brown everything was—including the sky. They said it was the beginning of a drought. Everything looked so dead and lifeless compared to Europe. I missed the rolling green hills and lush gardens and flowing rivers and bustling food markets. I missed the sense of history and purpose and place and tradition I had felt when I had lived in the U.K. I missed tracing my roots to the places my family had come from. Now I was going back to a place where I'd never belong.

"I need more money because I spent all my student loans for the year," I said. "Do you think you could write me a check? I need to put my deposit down for my new apartment for senior year."

There was a long silence. My mom was tapping her thumbs against the steering wheel and scrunching her face while I waited for a response.

"We don't have any money, sweetie," she said. She searched for what to say next. "Honey, while you were gone, I filed for bankruptcy."

I was stunned. I didn't know what to say. How could this happen to us? I was only gone for six months, for godssake! Did she do something reckless, like gamble away her retirement or life savings? Did my dad stop paying child support for Jess? I thought things like this, things like what you see on TV and read on the internet, only happened to *other* people. But not to *me*, not to *my* family.

"I don't understand," I said.

"Well," she said, "right around when you left for Europe, the school district furloughed me until who knows when, and I only had so much in our savings account to live off. We just have so many bills, Michael! We're still paying off your sister's medical bills from when she broke her wrist and the cost of our utilities—don't even get me started on how much they're ripping us off. Water and electricity are becoming too expensive in this state! After they furloughed me, I had to switch my health insurance—Jessica and I's insurance—to the state plan, which is triple what I was paying when I was working. And, you know sweetie, I wanted to keep supporting you in Europe. I thought we would be able to survive something like this because we've owned our house for so many years—you know, the court let us keep it, no strings attached, after your father and I divorced—but the real estate market crashed and we lost all our equity and, you know, it's going to be OK. God will protect us."

I went numb. She was talking but I wasn't hearing anything. To be honest, I had forgotten about the financial crisis and the Great Recession that they said was almost as bad as the Great Depression. *I* wasn't living in a recession, so I guess I had just blocked it out of my mind.

"You can move back in with us," she said.

I couldn't imagine anything worse. A man does not move back in with his mother. There could be no outward signs of defeat.

"No, it's OK," I said. "I'll just take out extra student loans this year."

I reached into my backpack and pulled out my iPod. I worked to untangle the white wires and then put the earbuds in my ears. My thumb traced circles on the touchpad until I found the song I wanted—the same song that played in all the clubs in all the countries I had just been to. I pressed the play button and closed my eyes. The music transported me back to where I wanted to be, to soothe the emptiness I was feeling.

Could it really be the next Great Depression? It didn't seem possible. The world was too big and complex for it all to come to a grinding halt, for people like my mom to lose it all. Didn't the people in charge know any better? They must have plans they're working on to fix things, to make it all better, to make it all go away.

My mom pulled the car into the driveway and turned the engine off. I sat there, staring at the brown garage door. Here I was, back to where I started from. And now, I had to figure out a new plan.

• • •

By September our house foreclosed, and my mom and sister moved into a one-bedroom apartment off a busy street where people raced their cars in the middle of the night. My mom was collecting $450 a week from the state for unemployment, but it would only last for twenty-six weeks. After that, all she'd have left to live on was the $819 a month she got from my dad for child support for Jess, plus the money I'd give her from working a second job during my senior year of college. If my dad hadn't stopped paying alimony all those years ago, or if my mom had had enough money from her job to keep fighting him in court, then there would've been enough. But there wasn't. We were broke.

It was a total wipeout. The Great Recession claimed its dominance over me and my family and our neighbors and even a rich family we knew who lived in a big house on a hill in the nice part of town. When I graduated from college, there would be no jobs, not for me and not for any of my classmates. What a rip-off! How could the people in charge do this to us? I knew they didn't like Millennials, but this was just plain sadistic. I didn't know what to do.

One night I was watching President Obama talk on TV about all the young people moving to Washington to help fix our country. He said anyone could make it in America as long as you worked hard. In that moment I had an epiphany, the kind you get when you're doing something banal like watching a pot of water boil and something deep within you stirs. It's like Barack Hussein Obama II was talking directly to *me*, Michael Johnathan Morris, and giving me instructions for my life. And what he was telling me was that *he* needed *me* to move to Washington, D.C., where love and purpose would be waiting for me. I didn't know what I'd do once I got there, but I would at least be in the place where it would happen. I just knew it. I could feel the conviction course through my veins. Duty was my destiny.

That moment set in motion a new plan to figure out how to get to the East Coast. All the online job boards with listings for San Bernardino were empty anyway, and the unemployment rate was in the double digits. But in Washington, there were thousands of jobs and internships listed online. It's as if it were on another planet where recessions didn't happen. All I needed to do was hope for some dream gig that would connect me with someone with influence, and then the rest would work itself out. I was destined for greatness.

I spent months browsing the internet to figure out a way to make it happen, researching every possible thing about Washington. I learned everything I needed to know about the city on a hill that I'd help make shiny again, and got first-hand accounts of the life I was meant to live. In fact, I learned everything about life from Google, online chat rooms, pornos, and YouTube. I learned nothing from my parents or teachers or coaches or anyone else with a fancy title.

Based on my extensive research, I found out a few key things: Washington is a competitive place, where only top talent can survive. Washington is a serious place, where only things that matter drive the day. And Washington is a powerful place, where people and institutions make decisions that trickle down to ordinary people all over the country and the world.

And guess what? I was and wanted all of those things! It's like Washington was made just for me. I was meant to move there and fix things so something like the Great Recession could never happen again. So Mom and Jess would be OK again. So I could become the man I was meant to be.

Since I couldn't possibly interview for jobs across the country, the next best thing I could think of was grad school. I didn't really want to keep going to school; another two years after undergrad would total nineteen consecutive years of being a student. But by staying a student, I could get student loans to not only pay for school but to pay for rent and food, too. It would be the quickest way to get to Washington, with no job interviews required. Plus, bachelor's degrees are cheap nowadays. Everyone has one, so they mean nothing.

I just needed to figure out what I would study. I didn't want to get a J.D. because the thought of being an attorney, of having to do research and write briefs for the rest of my life, made me want to vomit. And I didn't want to get an M.B.A. because they basically teach you how to be a white-collar criminal, which is not virtuous enough for me. Instead, I decided I'd need to get a master's degree that would prepare me to lead our great public institutions. So I chose political science. (Though I never understood why they called it "political science" instead of "political arts." What the hell was the science part?)

I would become great by moving somewhere where great people lived: Washington, D.C. And I would apply for grad school as my ticket to get there. Things were always happening on the East Coast. All the action and drama that you read about every day on the blogs happens on the East Coast. And all the people and their houses you see on TV shows and in movies are on the East Coast. It was where I belonged, where I could become someone that would make my family proud.

I searched on Google for lists of the best universities. I decided I would apply to just one school, the only school that the internet said was the best: Georgetown. Going there for grad school would make me competitive and open up doors to opportunities I knew I deserved. When I'd get there, I'd finally find love and purpose so I could become the man that my loser dad wasn't.

But the clock was ticking. I only had two years until the child support checks would stop coming. There was no room for error. I had to be perfect.

Chapter Four

EAST COAST ARRIVAL

I got to Washington—or D.C., as the locals call it—in August, three months after I graduated from college. I focused all my time and energy on getting each and every piece of my new life in place to make certain I'd succeed. Item number one was housing: I found a room in a second-level garden apartment north of Georgetown's campus. Well, actually, my bedroom was a former living room. The landlord had installed one of those plastic accordion doors you use for a bathroom in an RV. It sucked, but it was all I could get—and all I could afford.

Before I found my apartment, though, I had to go through the humiliation of auditioning to be a roommate for a bedroom in a group house. I was drawn to the idea of living with a bunch of strangers who would become my best friends. We would come home from our long days at school and work, and banter about politics and local affairs. We would walk down the street to the local coffee shop, *our* coffee shop, that wasn't part of a chain, and we would live The City Life, *together*, just like people did on TV shows and in the movies.

I started my search to find this life in the online housing

classifieds on Craigslist. The listings were straightforward enough: *1 bedroom available in 4-person house for $1,200.*

When you clicked on it to read the details, there would be a list of all the house's amenities: *washer/dryer, furnished living room, granite kitchen countertops, central A/C and heat, monthly cleaning service.*

But at the very bottom of the ads, like it was the fine print, is where it got weird: *Must commit to making a house dinner once a week—no excuses. Must be socially extroverted but know when to stop talking to give your roommates emotional space to recharge. Must be non-binary and queer friendly. Must be active in a cause that is greater than yourself.*

I learned very quickly that everyone had their own political agenda in this town—including entire houses. And they preferred to keep it that way by only letting people who were just like them live there. You *must be* something in order to be accepted.

I showed up to my fourth, and last, audition at an old row house in Adams Morgan, a hip neighborhood with bars and restaurants and Latinos on the other side of Rock Creek Park. It was a few miles from Georgetown's campus, so it wouldn't have been very convenient, but that's what made it *cool*. I would have cachet.

I trudged uphill on a sidewalk with too many broken sections until I got to the house. The outside of the tall, narrow row house was made of brick colored a dark gray, with sharp vertical paint lines on either side where it attached to its neighboring houses. What greeted me was a black iron staircase that led to a front door made of glass. Inside this glass door was a mudroom, its floor and the bottom half of its walls made of white and green penny tiles, and then another door, only this one was made of wood so you couldn't see in.

"Hi, I'm Mike!" I said to the three people who greeted me at the glass door.

I was nervous, already insecure about whether or not I had been enthusiastic enough in my opening line. I needed to make sure I showed that I *wanted* this house, that I wanted to be the chosen one. I needed to be perfect in order to be picked.

They ushered me in and we stood in a rough approximation of a circle in the living room. I glanced around and marveled at the thick white baseboards and crown moldings that framed dark brown wood floors and walls painted light gray. It looked just like the houses I saw on TV as a kid. It was clear I wasn't in San Bernardino anymore.

No one was doing anything or saying anything, so I started talking. "I'm from California, and I'm starting grad school at Georgetown, where—"

"What are you studying?" one of the chicks interrupted before I could even finish.

"Umm, poli sci."

"Oh, my god!" she said. She had a look of disgust washed across her face. "Political science is *so* traditional. I feel like you *should* have studied something more postmodern or interdisciplinary. I feel like the world is *so* tired of traditional disciplines that do nothing to advance the rights of the oppressed."

She had no idea how excited, how *passionate*, I was about political science. I loved learning about elections and public polling and the West's central project of figuring out the best form of self-governance. She made me feel small.

"Well, umm," I said. I had trouble finding what to say next. "I get a kick out of the *Communist Manifesto*!"

She shot darts at me with her eyes.

"Aaaaaaanyway," she said. "Follow me, and I'll give you the *grand tour*." She sarcastically used her fingers to make air quotes as she leaned her head back to communicate how unexcited she was about me.

Nope, I thought. *Not doing this!* I didn't move across the country to audition like some B-list actor trying to make it in L.A. These people should be auditioning for *me*, for godssake! *Don't they know that I'm special, that I'm going to change the world?* I tuned out the rest of the tour and left as fast as I could.

I spent the subsequent two weeks with my laptop inside a

bookstore on M Street. I'd refresh the Craigslist website every minute, all day long, waiting for a new posting to be published. If I found something I liked, I'd open up my email window and draft a cover letter that outlined why I was the most qualified person to live there. Most people didn't even have the courtesy to respond. But for those who did, I would make appointments to see places all over Georgetown, walking with my five-pound laptop and everything else in my backpack through the sweltering summer heat, all just to find a place to sleep. It was the sweatiest housing search of my life.

And then, one day, I finally found a place. The posting's title was simple enough: *Looking for chill guy in Georgetown.*

Because I thought I was pretty chill, I went for it. I met up with the poster, a guy named Jud, and he walked me through the apartment. The place was pretty spare and the kitchen didn't have more than a few mismatched plates, coffee mugs, and pots and pans. The walls were painted a horrid beige color—or maybe it was water damage to the plaster. The kitchen and bathroom had off-white linoleum with little green diamonds in between the embossed grout lines. The place was rundown, but it was functional.

I knew I couldn't pass it up. We went into the kitchen, and I pulled my checkbook out of my backpack to write him a check for the first month's rent. There was nothing else for me to sign. He had a lease in his name for a one-bedroom apartment, even though the landlord was charging rent for the price of a two-bedroom. I paid $680 a month for my share.

Jud turned out to be a fun roommate, even if I thought he was a little weird. We went out together at least once or twice a week, to a bar or a club or a house party. He loved to listen to rap music and repeat all the lyrics *verbatim*—and also did some rapping himself. It was weird that he liked rap music so much, this small white kid with a mop of curly black hair on his head and glasses that looked like they were at least ten years behind trend. He'd perform as a *gangster rapper* every night when he got home from his unpaid internship on Capitol Hill. I didn't mind it most nights—only when the bass was cranked up and rattled my desk.

"I identify with the *struggle,*" he said to me one night while we were standing in the galley kitchen, the only place to socialize in our apartment.

He emphasized the last word as he maintained eye contact with me to make his point. Or to see how I'd react, to see if I'd give him permission to keep going where I think he was heading.

"What do you mean?" I said.

"Well," he said. "I've always felt beaten down, like the kids from Brooklyn...like some *ni—.*"

"OK!" I said. "That's enough! I get what you're sayin'."

I laughed nervously, unsure what anyone was supposed to say to a proclamation like that. It made me feel uncomfortable to hear him say it out loud instead of saying "the N-word" like he was supposed to. But it wasn't the first time some white guy had said it to me. It seemed like everyone was listening to rap music these days and repeating the stuff they heard. I thought there might be something wrong with me because I *didn't* like rap music.

"Yeah, yeah, yeah," he said. "You may think it's funny, some Jew from Long Island who raps like he's from the projects. But I'm serious, man! I have really struggled in my life. And being a Jew ain't easy either. I fucking love black people! I fucking love rap music! All my homies know it. They love me because I *identify* with the same struggle."

He giggled as he walked away to go back into his room, to play a new rap song on his CD player. I retreated to my living room-turned-bedroom and slid the plastic door shut.

• • •

Item number two was friends: by the end of my first week of classes, I had become fast friends with two guys who were each in one of my three grad seminars. They would prove to be my most trusted advisors, my confidantes whom I would turn to as I navigated the choppy waters in search of my future wife and career.

There was Adam. He was on my level, enjoyed the same music as I did, liked to have intellectual conversations for sport, and was from the westside of Los Angeles, which is way cooler than San Bernardino.

Aesthetically speaking, Adam was everything I wasn't but wanted to be. He was tall, tan, and muscular with sculpted facial features that gave him a celebrity appearance. His angled jaw emphasized his perma-stubble, while his perfectly coifed light brown hair added at least two inches to his overall height. He was the type of guy whose looks were arresting to anyone who crossed his path. Naturally, his good looks meant he bedded a lot of women.

He was a fuckboy.

I'm not sure why Adam liked my company. After all, attractive people hang out with attractive people, ugly people with ugly people, fat people with fat people, and weirdoes with weirdoes. But I eventually realized that we had become friends for intellectual reasons, which is kind of pretentious and a little insufferable, but extremely logical.

"There are definite racial undertones to the Republican response and criticism of Obama," Adam would argue, as he—as *we*—often did in between classes.

After class got out, we'd go buy a six-pack of craft beer from a bodega near Georgetown's campus, sit on the rooftop of one of our classroom buildings that faced M Street and had a sweeping view of the Potomac River, and drink and dialogue.

"I mean, these Tea Party people aren't flat-out calling the guy the N-word. Perhaps the N-word is the base, subconscious feeling that is the id to their resentment toward him," I would retort.

"That may be so, but I think these people are actual racists. They know they're racists! They're just afraid to be openly racist because they know we—the educated, professional class—will socially shame them if they are."

"Yeah, man. These people are still getting over losing the Civil War. The things they say about Obama is their new states' rights—it's just coded language for the ugly truth: they hate him because he's a black man living in the White House, their house."

We would nod in agreement, satisfied with how swift we had reached resolution.

And then there was Matt. He was potentially smarter than me but definitely not as charismatic. He mostly liked to troll me with his philosophy-101 arguments about everything we weren't allowed to debate during our grad seminars.

Morally speaking, Matt was everything I thought I was. He was tall, thin, and pasty with a round head that made him look like the kid next door. His blonde hair was parted down one side and combed the other way, while his clean-shaven face communicated his daily discipline. He was the guy who was in the background, but the one you were always glad to find out later was in the room. He was the type of guy you'd call in a crisis or turn to for guidance when it seemed like the world was going to hell.

He was a Boy Scout.

We'd go to the library or to lectures in between classes and then discuss every possible controversial topic that we could argue about.

"Abortion is murder," he would say. "The Nazis would be impressed with our swift categorization of the uselessness of the unborn to the state. It's the same logic they used to exterminate Jews, gypsies, homosexuals, blacks, artists, resistance fighters, deviants, and the crippled and mentally ill. Ours is the second American genocide."

He was unfazed at the intensity of what he uttered.

"OK," I would say, my voice stern. "First of all, pro-choice and pro-life is a false dichotomy. You can be pro-choice from a classical liberal democratic standpoint and also pro-life from a moral standpoint—at the same time."

"But you can't, Mike!" he would protest. "You either believe in life or you don't! You either believe in murder or you don't! There are limits to individual freedom, but we are too stupid as a society to even talk about it."

There was one small problem, though: he was a Christian. Like, a *real* Christian. The kind that goes to church every Sunday and reads the Bible. His was a framework incompatible with the grad student-cum-cosmopolitan life I was now living in D.C. He was such an outlier I had no idea how he existed in grad school, where everyone was liberal and thought the same way about everything.

Matt was my earnest friend, and Adam was my cool friend. I was glad to have them both around, my voices of reckoning whom I'd turn to as I figured out how to make it in D.C.

Chapter Five

SMART PHONES

And item number three: an iPhone. I had to wait in line for two hours at the store, like a congregant queuing for communion, to get the thing that everyone said would change my life. But I wasn't like those other people, those people who'd camp out overnight on the sidewalk in front of the store, waiting for the new model to be released like it was a new book of the New Testament. I was just a regular guy trying to keep up.

I convinced myself to get an iPhone after watching an unboxing video of the new model on YouTube. For twelve uninterrupted minutes, I watched enthralled as some guy took a new phone out of its box, plus all the accessories and plastic and paper packaging, and narrated his thoughts and feelings in real time. I could hear the nuanced sounds of the packaging ripping and crinkling, like it was right up against my ear, which weirdly excited me. It was tech porn.

I knew I was at the right store because its entire façade was made of glass. When it was finally my turn, I walked up to one of the doors and pulled on the giant stainless steel handle. When I crossed the threshold into the store, I looked out and saw a cathedral of tech. The floors, walls, and ceiling were all stark white, like the store was from some futurist world where there was no filth. It even smelled like the future, fresh and feathery with no trace of grime or cleaning chemicals. There were rows of maple wood tables full of computers and phones—and crowds of people surrounding them, examining them like they'd discovered the fountain of youth.

A salesman wearing a royal blue T-shirt, black jeans, and white sneakers walked toward me.

"Hi!" he said. "How can I help you?"

"Hi," I said. "I'd like to buy an iPhone—the basic model, whatever's cheapest."

"Wonderful! You're making a great choice," he said. "Is this your first time?"

"Yeah."

"OK, great," he said. "The phone is $599, but you can get it for only $199 with a two-year contract. The basic plan includes 450 minutes and 200 megabytes of data per month. Plus, you'll have really fast internet with 3G speeds!"

"How much does texting cost?"

"Texting's free!" he said. "It's taking off like crazy."

"Uh, sure—yeah, the cheapest option," I said. Then I reached into my pocket and pulled out my wallet. I slid my credit card from its slip and handed it to him. "Here you go."

"Oh, not yet!" he said. "Walk this way and we'll get you checked out at the register, and then we'll get your iPhone set up."

I followed him toward the back of the store where there was a giant TV screen playing a loop of close-up shots of all the gadgets. They seemed to be floating through outer space, except the background was white instead of black, and every time the edge of a computer or phone would turn, a flash of light would burst. *Slick marketing*, I thought.

"Which color do you want?" he asked.

"What are my options?"

"Black or white."

"I'll take the black one."

"OK," he said. "Your total is $246.94, which includes taxes and an activation fee."

"Oh," I said. "I didn't know there'd be more charges. Is there any way you could waive that fee? I'm pretty tight on money, you know. I'm a student."

"Unfortunately not," he said. "It's how the carriers make their money."

I grimaced and then handed him my credit card and watched as he swiped it through the terminal. I cringed at the thought of money being taken from my bank account.

"Please wait here while I run to the back to get your phone," he said. "Here's your credit card and your receipt. Your card's on file now for future purchases."

My stomach was knotted in anticipation. I knew this phone was going to change my life. I just knew it.

When he came back, he placed it down on the counter with a reverence usually reserved for a baptism.

"Would you like to do the honors?" he said.

"You mean unbox it?" I said.

"Yeah," he said. "This is your moment. This is *your* iPhone 4."

I couldn't believe it. Unboxing was actually a thing! I felt giddiness like a kid on Christmas morning. The anticipation of finding out what was on the inside made my stomach tighten and rise up.

I stretched out my right arm and placed my palm on top of the rectangular box. Its edges were soft, the cardboard matte. I tightened my fingers around the sides and slowly lifted. I could feel the tension between the inner and outer boxes, the air trying to find a way to escape. I heard the faint sound of the pressure being released.

And then, it was there. I stared at the black rectangular object recessed into a white contoured bed. I could see my reflection in the glass, my face in awe at the creation I was staring at.

"Well?" said the salesman. "Take it out!"

I reached over and put my index finger into a little recessed space. Then I lifted it out of the box. It was so shiny but so cold. I pulled on a single tab that had an arrow printed on it and peeled off the protective layer of plastic. I could hear the static crackle as I lifted.

"Are you ready?" he said.

"Yeah, I think so," I said. Then I looked up at him and said, "I'm ready."

He pressed a little button on the top of the black rectangle, and the screen lit up with an icon of an apple that had a bite taken out of it. It was alive. I felt a rush of excitement course through me and had to control the trembles.

Then it went dark again.

He grabbed my hand and guided my index finger to the circular button at the bottom of the screen like a father showing his son the way. He looked at me and nodded. I pressed my finger down until the block of black glass and plastic came back to life. A background picture of water drops that looked real, with the time superimposed, filled the screen.

"Wow," I said. "That was such a rush!"

"Yep," he said. "They all look at me like I'm crazy until they experience it for the first time. We've entered a new era of humanity with this device."

"Yeah, no kidding!"

"Just wait for the next software update, which will have tethering. It's going to be a game changer."

"Wow!" I said. "How much will I have to pay for the update?"

"Oh, the software updates will be free," he said. "Like I said, we're entering a whole new era. They're going to push all kinds of updates to your phone—like *magic*."

I wasn't sure how I was supposed to feel. How would I know when they wanted to change what was on my phone? Wouldn't they have to ask for my permission? It didn't make any sense.

"Anyway, go ahead and play around with it," he said. "I

have to run to the back again to get your SIM card and activate your phone number."

I slid my finger across the screen's slick surface to unlock it. What greeted me on the other side were colorful little boxes with illustrated icons that revealed their utility. They were called *apps*. These apps were the digital versions of all the single-utility things I already owned. There was a music app to replace my iPod, a calculator app to replace my old T.I. 89 from high school, a camera app to replace the digital camera I had traveled throughout Europe with, a banking app to replace having to go to the ATM to deposit my checks, and a reminders app to replace all the little paper lists I'd write for things like groceries. I had even heard there was a maps app that would be released soon to replace the expensive GPS my rich friend handed down to me after he bought a newer model.

It really was magical. It felt otherworldly—like some alien technology from a society far more advanced than ours. I couldn't believe my eyes. Everything was so smooth and slick. The apps were so colorful and had beautiful animations. But it wasn't as smart as you'd think—it kept autocorrecting *fucking* to *ducking*.

With *my* phone, I was finally ready for D.C. I was ready to compete in this town and make it on my own.

• • •

Now it was late September, a month into my first semester of grad school, and the text messages were flooding in.

> Maybe
>
> yeah, I'm a maybe too
>
> I dunno I literally feel like
> death

I was in a group text message, a feature that came with my new *smart* phone, with a bunch of friends from school. It was a new phenomenon—like a group email chain—except in my pocket, incessantly buzzing against my leg, with no way to stop it.

> i might b able to make it! ill
> let u know…

> 50/50…

> I'm double-booked tonight,
> so maybe?

Ours was Generation Maybe and they didn't care about their inability to commit. They were always waiting for something else, something better, someone more interesting, to come along. But for me, I always said yes because I was always glad to be invited.

> R we doin this or wut?!

I was mesmerized by my new phone's virtual keyboard. There were no buttons, for godssake! When you'd tap a letter, it would pop out at you to signal you had selected the right one. It was amazing.

> Yeah—Rhino it is. Be there
> at 10.

Jud and I pre-gamed at home, drinking whiskey and cola until we were both drunk. Then we went our separate ways and promised to meet up later. I walked south toward M Street to get to Rhino, a bar-slash-club. After paying a ten-dollar cover, I walked in and scanned the room to find people I knew. The floors, walls, and ceilings were black, so I could only see faces when the lasers and lights would illuminate the smoke that was hovering over all the bobbing heads on the dance floor. I felt resistance with each step I took, my shoes sticking to the floors because of all the spilt drinks.

I walked over to the bar and elbowed my way to the counter to order my favorite clubbing drink: Red Bull and vodka. It was classy-trashy and made me feel like I could conquer any dance floor and go all night. I kept scanning the room, trying to find anyone I knew. Did they all flake out on me? I felt nervous at the prospect of being stood up.

As I turned around to walk back to the dance floor, I noticed a pretty blonde standing to my right, waiting to order drinks. She was staring straight into the mirror of the bar's back wall while fidgeting with the phone in her hand. I wondered if she was a Georgetown undergrad—or maybe even a G.W. student. George Washington University, down Pennsylvania Avenue in Foggy Bottom, was a striving university full of rich kids, New York Jews, and oil-money Arabs. Maybe she was a G.W. undergrad who would totally be turned on by dating a Georgetown grad student. I had to find out.

"Hey," I yelled over the music.

Hers eyes shifted their gaze toward me.

"You havin' a good night?" I said.

"Uh, yeahhhhhh," she said.

"So, tell me a bit about yourself," I said. "You go to Georgetown or G.W.?"

"Neither," she said as she cracked a smile. "I'm a working professional!"

"Nice!" I said. "Cheers to that!"

I moved my glass toward her, but she didn't have a drink to meet me in the middle.

"What do you do?" I asked.

"Well, I'm *originally* from North Carolina and went to Dartmouth and majored in French literature. But it's my *passion* for Latino immigrants that brought me to D.C. to work as an assistant director of an NGO that rescues victims of sex trafficking across the Rio Grande river on the Texas border."

"But what about the rest of the border?"

"Oh, there are other organizations that focus on other parts or problems with people who cross the border looking for a better life here in the U.S. I really like that our mission is so focused. It helps ensure I can do the best job possible and have a *real* impact."

She didn't answer my question. No one in this town ever answers the goddamned question!

"Cool," I said.

"I, uh, I think it's my turn to order. Nice to meet you!" she said as she turned her face away from me.

I took that as my cue to leave her alone. I turned around and walked toward the dance floor, scanning it some more to see if I could find any of my friends. Or, more importantly, to see if I could find Her.

I spotted a petite brunette with a big butt who looked like she was having fun. There were no guys dancing with her, so I decided I'd give it a try. I walked up to her, yelled "Hey!" over the booming bass, and started dancing. She didn't pull away, which was my invitation to stay.

I leaned forward and said, "I'm Mike! What's your name?"

"Amy!"

"Nice to meet you, Amy!"

I was so hot and sweaty from dancing but so was the rest of the crowd. I held my drink up in the air with my right hand while I put my left hand on her lower back. I looked over at the DJ, and he had his hands in the air, like he was pushing on an invisible ceiling. Every time the bass would drop, everyone's hands would go up just like his.

I kept grinding against her on the dance floor. It's the only thing I knew how to do. I gyrated my hips back and forth against her upper right thigh, her right leg between my legs. Then I pressed my fingers into the spot where her glutes meet her spine, to see how she'd react. She leaned forward, which meant she wanted me. *Yes! Finally!* Maybe we'd have sex all night and then wake up and talk about our dreams in the morning. Then we'd go to brunch and fall in love over omelets and cappuccinos. I just wanted someone to talk to.

I grabbed her hand and pulled her through the crowd, through the throngs of sweaty boys and girls and into a back hallway that led to the bathrooms. Then I pinned her against the wall and started making out with her. The feeling of her tongue swirling against mine instantly gave me a boner. I leaned in and pressed my crotch against hers. She yelped and turned her cheek, her hot breath beating against my ear.

I leaned into her ear and said, "Let's get out of here!"

She backed up, made a coy face, and then leaned into my ear and said, "I'm not one of those girls."

I backed up and pulled her hands out toward mine. I smiled, made flirty faces, and stood there, waiting for her to change her mind. I was so drunk. Everything seemed to happen in slow motion, but I felt so good.

"Come on!" I said. "We're having fun! You're so beautiful. Let's make tonight the best night we've had in a long time!"

She smirked and then paused. "Give me your phone," she said.

I was confused about why she wanted it. I reached into my pocket, pulled out my new iPhone, and handed it over. She gestured for me to put in my passcode. Then she tapped the contacts app and added a new entry.

Amy it said. Then she typed in her number and tapped save.

Wow, I thought. I guess this is how you get a girl's number in the year 2010! My heart was racing, I was so excited.

"I have to go peeeeee. See you back on the dance floor!"

She disappeared through one of the doors, and I never saw her again. I tried to find her again on the dance floor or by the bar or near the entrance, but nothing. Why do people disappear like that? It's so ill-mannered.

I stumbled out of the club and sat on the curb, watching drunk people get into cabs. I texted her.

Hey

I never got a text back. I think this is the new phenomenon they called *ghosting*. How rude!

I texted Jud to see where he was. He immediately texted me back.

Yo, yo, yo I just left
Third's…meet for jumbo
slice?

On my way

When I got to the pizza place, Jud was already eating his slice, which wasn't really a slice but more like a medium-sized pizza in the shape of a triangle. It was huge! "Jumbo slice" was D.C.'s preferred drunk food—cheap, greasy, gets the job done—sold by different pizza shops all over town. I handed a five-dollar bill to the cashier, and he handed me my pepperoni jumbo slice, which was hanging out of its cardboard box. Pizza was my favorite food in the whole world. Every time I bit into a slice, I felt a small burst of calm. It didn't matter if it was cheap frozen pizza I made in my microwave or fancy Neapolitan pizza with ingredients imported from Italy and cooked in a wood-fired oven—I ate it all, and I loved it all.

"Yo, homeboy! This pizza is stupid good!" Jud said as we started walking north to get home. "Did you come up empty tonight? There was this chick who was *so* into me, but then she made up that she had a boyfriend and ran away like a little kid! I was so close, man!"

Unlike me, he wasn't a good conversationalist. In all the time we lived together and hung out, I never really figured out to talk with him.

"Yeah, same thing happened to me," I said in between bites. "Sucks."

He was giggling while he ate his pizza and doing a sort of tap dance in fits and spurts as we stumbled our way home to our apartment. I was focused on getting the right combination of crust, cheese, and sauce in each bite. I looked up and saw him kicking over urns and statues and plants that were on the stoops of the townhomes, the very expensive houses where important people lived.

"Jud!" I yelled. "You can't do that!"

"Yes, I can!" he shot back.

"No, you can't!" I said. "These houses have cameras with twenty-four-hour security. You'll get arrested."

"Nah, the po-po won't come after me," he said. "I'm white."

We both giggled and then threw our empty pizza boxes in the gutter. Then we turned into one of the alleys and peed in whatever unlit spaces we could find. There was garbage strewn about and giant rats scurrying from trash can to trash can. It was all so gross, the backstage of Georgetown.

Chapter Six

DUAL LIFE PLAYBOOKS

"You've gotta look a certain way if you wanna make it in this town," Adam said.

We had taken a student shuttle from campus to Dupont Circle, and now we were walking toward K Street in downtown. Daylight savings time had just switched over on Sunday, so it was dark out even though it was barely five o'clock. He was walking so fast, and I was trying to avoid the metal bollards in the middle of the sidewalk. I hit my knee on one of them last month, which caused a big purple bruise that took two weeks to go away. Now I hated them, those three-foot-tall metal posts all over the city that were police-state perimeters in disguise.

"I think I dress fine!" I said. "I've got all the basics—you know, T-shirts, jeans, a dress shirt, black pants I wore to my high school graduation."

"Jesus Christ, man—you've got nothing," he said. "You've entered a different league in D.C. There're rules you gotta follow, guidelines to abide by. In this town, you gotta dress for the job you want—not the job you have."

I didn't understand what he meant. Couldn't I just apply for the jobs I wanted and be selected based on my merit? And I didn't understand why we had to come all the way across town when there were lots of clothing stores in Georgetown.

"I think it's up here—lemme check."

He pulled out his phone and pinched the screen to zoom in on a map.

"Yep, another left and then we're there. Walk faster!"

Out of nowhere, the sound of sirens blared, and a line of police on motorcycles with flashing blue and red lights raced down the street. A long line of black SUVs followed, with windows rolled down for the barrels of the machine guns. And then two limousines with little American flags on their hoods waving in the wind, followed by an ambulance. It was exhilarating, and also a little terrifying, to see a motorcade—in real life!

"Was that the President?" I said.

"Probably," he said. "I couldn't care less. He's just a puppet."

"Anyway—Adam, we're still in school. And I'm working an unpaid internship, you know. I'm pretty sure I don't need new clothes right now. Plus, I don't have *that much* money—just some left over from my loans and some savings from my jobs back home."

"You're wrong," he said.

"Why'd we have to come all this way? Aren't there stores on M Street we could've gone to?"

"No," he said. "You need clothes from where the power players work and play. K Street is where it happens. All the lobbyists and lawyers and political operatives work down here—and they all get their clothes from this store."

Adam pulled open the store's front door, and I walked in. A black security guard dressed like a cop, with the toolbelt of weapons and everything, nodded his head. Then Adam zoomed by and gestured for me to follow him all the way to the back of the store. I never knew a clothing store could smell so good, like a mix of new car and freshly laundered linens. We passed rack upon rack of sport coats, suits, and dress pants. I'd never seen so many options for blue, gray, and beige in my life.

And then we got to the wall. It was where all the dress shirts were displayed, lined up in perfect rows from floor to ceiling. The white shirts were on the left and the dark blue shirts on the right, with a gradient of colors in between. They were in little cubbies lined by shiny mahogany wood trim, on display like it was a museum of textiles. I was hypnotized.

Adam opened his arms and said, "Welcome to the rest of your life. This is where you'll find the D.C. uniform."

He turned around and pulled out a light blue shirt from the wall. Then he yanked out little metal pins and clips, followed by pieces of cardboard and tissue paper, and tossed them all on the floor.

"See these five little pleats?" he said as he pointed to one of the shirt's cuffs. "They matter more than anything in this town. You'll have status once you start wearing these bad boys. And see these buttons? Made of pearls."

I pulled on the tag hanging off the shirt and brought it to my face. It said it was eighty-eight dollars. For a dress shirt! Never in a million years did I think clothes could cost so much. Adam came from a rich family, the kind that had a second home for summer vacations and didn't have to check the prices on things they bought at the store.

"I don't know, man. That's a lot of money for what looks like a regular dress shirt," I said. "You can't even see the pleats anyway. And do I need pearl buttons? I dunno. Do they have a sale section or something?"

I looked up but Adam was gone. I turned and saw him leaning against a wall near the fitting rooms, so I walked over.

"Hey, should I try it on?"

"No, not yet. You need to get measured."

I didn't know what he meant, but I didn't want to ask because it would make me seem even lamer than I already felt. So many things were new to me since I got to D.C., including being in a fancy clothing store. I felt like a fish out of water.

"I thought shirts just came in small, medium, and large, you know. At least, that's how it was at the stores my mom took us to back home, you know?"

"Nah, man. This is next level. This is proper men's sizing. When your clothes fit like a glove, you feel like a million bucks and can conquer anything you want—including the ladies."

He winked and then pulled out his phone and started scrolling.

There was a middle-aged man standing on a raised box that was carpeted with the same navy blue diamond pattern as the rest of the store. He was surrounded by five floor-length mirrors, which provided 180 degrees of self-reflection. He was staring at himself, turning different ways, adjusting his pants, pulling on his shirt cuffs.

"The cut of this shirt is not as flattering as I would expect. There must be something better," he said as he looked at the salesman with a forced smile. "Could you please think about other options you have? I have to look my best…I know you understand."

I recognized his voice. He was a bigwig news anchor, the kind that read the national news every weeknight to millions of Americans with no trace of a regional accent. I felt giddy, like seeing a celebrity in the flesh.

"Hey, Adam," I whispered as I elbowed him. "That's that guy from cable news! Can you believe it?"

He looked up, stared at the man, and said nothing.

After the salesman came back and handed the news anchor a stack of white dress shirts, Adam waved him down to come over to us.

"Hi. My friend needs to get measured—top to bottom."

Before I knew it, the salesman whipped out a plastic measuring tape and was holding it against my body. First, he wrapped it around my neck and then across my shoulders and down my arm. Then he squatted and wrapped it around my waist, hips, and legs. He cleared his throat and tapped on my foot to spread my legs wider, and then he measured my inseam, from my crotch all the way down to my ankle. It was the first time someone's hands were *down there* in a long time, which was somewhat thrilling.

"Sixteen thirty-three for shirts, thirty-three thirty-two for pants, and forty-regular for jackets," said the salesman. "May I help you with anything else?"

"Gotcha, nope," Adam said. "Thank you very much!"

Adam led me back to the wall of shirts and picked out three: one white, one light blue, and one medium blue. Then we walked over to the racks of pants and he picked out two: one light khaki and one dark khaki. Then he took me to the racks of sport coats and picked out one: navy blue with gold buttons.

"Alright, you're good to go!" he said. "Here's a red tie. It's the only one you need. It communicates power and dominance."

"But don't I have to try everything on?" I said.

"Nope," he said. "They'll fit perfectly now that you know your measurements."

I didn't want to argue with him because I trusted him. He dressed like people you saw on TV, after all. He knew what he was talking about. I was mesmerized by his confidence in all matters of life, including clothing.

We went to the register and I fiddled with my thumbs while I watched the price on the register go up with each beep of the scanner. The salesman wrapped each item in tissue paper and put an embossed sticker on the seam. I'd never seen anyone do that before, not at any store I shopped at back home.

"Alright, sir. That'll be $685.26."

I gulped as I handed over my credit card. I knew I needed these clothes to make it. I had to dress like I wanted it. What choice did I have?

As we walked out of the store, Adam said, "One more thing—do you have boat shoes?"

"Nope. Don't own a boat."

"Doesn't matter. Get a pair—stat!"

• • •

"You have to know the right things if you want to be taken

seriously," Matt said.

We were walking across Georgetown's grassy quad on our way to a bookstore on M Street. There were students lying out on blankets, groups sitting in circles studying together, and some guys playing frisbee. I kept hearing the cawing of a crow, so I looked up and spotted a black bird perched at the peak of one of the neo-Gothic buildings made of stone. Its stained glass window panes were glistening in the afternoon sunlight, and the vines that softened its hard angles were rustling in the breeze. It was idyllic—Georgetown's campus—like the way a university campus should be. Not like my ugly state college back home with buildings that looked like they were copied and pasted from a strip mall.

"I don't get it," I said. "I know a lot. I got good grades in school. And, you know, I made it *here*."

"Doesn't matter," he said. "You need to get a *real* education in order to compete in this town. And you ain't gonna get that here. This place is just for the socialization of the elite. Sorry, you're not part of it."

"That makes no sense!" I said. "This is one of the best universities in the world! I made it here based on merit. Why are you here then?"

"Credentials. I've been forced by our economic order to get a master's degree that I don't need as a requisite to get the job that I want. It's all bogus!"

We laughed and continued our way through the neighborhood, down a street with old trolley tracks set in cobblestone and past all the fancy townhomes and their manicured gardens. I was in awe of the old trees whose canopies created vaulted ceilings of yellows and oranges, the telltale sign of my first autumn. Then we hurried down The Exorcist Steps as a shortcut to M Street, trying not to fall down.

"There it is," Matt said. "The biggest bookstore in all of D.C. Come on!"

He gestured with his arm and I followed him into the store. When we walked in, I looked out and saw row upon row of bookshelves, with escalators in the middle that went up to two more levels. There were oak wood tables in the aisles with stacks of books displayed like little city skylines. The entire place smelled of paper fresh off the printing presses.

"Alright, here we are. This is the section that's going to turn you into a real scholar," he said.

I looked up at the *Philosophy* sign. I had no clue why we were there.

"OK, where to begin," Matt said as his fingers traced the rows of book spines. "I think we'll start with the Greeks and then move on to the Middle Ages. And I do wonder about the utility of the religious writers. Hmm..."

I stood there, unsure of what to do or say. His lips were pursed as he tilted his head to read the titles. And then before I knew it, he started pulling books off the shelf and tossing them my way.

"Here's Aristotle, Plato, and Hobbes. I assume you read Homer in high school?"

"Uh, no."

"Are you kidding? Where the heck did you go to school?"

"Uh, a public high school," I said. "We read other stuff, I guess."

He let out a heavy sigh and turned back toward the bookshelves.

Matt came from a stable family, the kind where everyone was happy and knew the roles they had to play. His dad was a family doctor, and his mom stayed at home to raise him and his four younger siblings. He'd tell me about his private school experiences where he was part of clubs, like chess and debate, and traditions, like canoeing races and celebratory feasts. It was all foreign to me. All I could claim from my childhood were the free breakfasts and lunches the government had given me during the school week.

"What are you guys reading in your international relations class?"

"I dunno. Mostly modern stuff. Everything after World War

II."

"Ugh!" he said. "That's so myopic! I wish you'd take political theory courses with me. Then you'd have a better grounding for all that crap they're shoving at you."

I didn't know what he meant. I *liked* the books and articles I had to read for class. They were challenging, but they were also relevant to the problems I'd one day get paid to solve.

"Alright, my friend, here's Dante, Cicero, Plato, and Machiavelli," he said. "And, I think for you, you'd benefit from reading some of the religious guys, so here's Augustine and Pascal. Oh, and Aquinas! One is *not* a learned man until one has read him."

I was forming a pile on the floor. He kept throwing books behind his back, not even turning around to aim them in the right direction.

"You also need Locke, Smith, and Kant. And maybe Tocqueville, too. Our democracy *is* crumbling before our eyes, to no one's chagrin…"

A man dressed in black turned a corner and walked toward us. He stopped halfway down the aisle to scan the rows of books and then continued on his way. As he passed us, he made eye contact with me and then looked down to fumble with the stack of books and papers he was carrying. He had a little white square in the middle of his collar.

"Can I assume you've read the Bible?" Matt said.

"Negative."

"This is madness! It's *the* foundational text of the entire Western canon—of all of Western civilization! I can't believe how uneducated our educated are."

"Sorry, man. I'm just, you know, a regular guy. I don't think most people these days read this stuff."

"And that's precisely the problem."

He was silent for a few moments as he scanned the shelves before turning to me again.

"What about the moderns? Did you read Mill or Marx in college?"

"Nope," I said.

"Seriously?" he said. "What did you major in again?"

"Communications."

"Why would anyone major in that? How useless! I can't believe it's even offered."

I let out a forced chuckle but felt a little offended. What's wrong with learning theories of how to communicate? It was a highly rated program at the state college I went to.

"I thought it sounded interesting when I picked it from a list," I said.

"You picked it from a list? Is that what your guidance counselor advised you to do?"

"I, uh, I didn't have a counselor. I just did it on my own, you know."

"Seriously! What's happened to our public education system? When even the universities stop teaching history and philosophy and start handing out degrees in *communications*. Geez Louise!"

He shook his head and then turned back toward the books. I wandered to the end of the aisle, looked across the store, and spotted a different section, a better section that would probably be more useful to me: *Self-Help*.

"Hey, can we go to the self-help section?" I said.

"Are you kidding? Those books are all made up! They're written by simpletons who think life is black and white and can be boiled down into basic platitudes that look good on a book jacket."

"Oh, OK," I said. "Well what about the nonfiction section? Maybe I need some books with some firsthand accounts of, you know, people who led our country or went to war or whatever."

"No," he said. "It's too soon. All those books are vanity projects and legacy building. We need another hundred years to figure out what these people actually did to us."

I was taken aback by his confidence. He just knew so much—about everything.

"OK, I think this is enough," I said.

He looked at the stack of books that came up to my knees.

"Great!" he said. "I'll pay for half and help you carry them home."

"Really?" I said. "You don't have to do that, you know."

"Oh, I know! But I want to," he said. "You've got great potential. All you need to do is read the stuff that matters, and think deep about it. Who knows? Maybe it will lead you to prayer."

I didn't know what to say back, so I said nothing. Buying all these books to make my life better was one thing. But praying about it? I didn't even believe in a god.

Chapter Seven

GRAD SCHOOL DREAMS

I walked down a flight of stairs that led to an underground door that led to The Tombs. It was a pub a block from campus where students and professors hung out, the type of place where people had conversations that would affect the rest of their lives. Inside was a tableau of preppy East Coast themes: framed illustrations of rugby and football games on the walls, pictures of collegiate rowing and lacrosse teams in the wood booths, and waiters and waitresses who wore bow ties. It was dark and cozy with wood paneling and brass accents. And it smelled damp, like so many old buildings I now frequented.

"What do you think I should do professionally?" I asked my professor.

"Well, Michael, many of my students do indeed go into international development after they graduate," he said. "Some of them go into nonprofits, but there is so little money in that sector and it's not prestigious enough for most, especially those with Georgetown degrees. Of course, a think tank would be terrific for you, but that's not an avenue available to you until much later in your career, once you have professional credibility and esteem among your peers."

Figuring out what I was going to do for the rest of my life was on my mind. Professor McEnery, a superstar in the field of international relations in conflict zones, had emailed me with an invitation to meet. I had never been invited out for drinks by professors during undergrad. But this is how they did it on the East Coast, and this is how it was done at Georgetown. This is what an *elite* education looked like.

"What about government jobs?" I said. "Does anyone go work on Capitol Hill or for the White House?"

"Some," he said. "Those jobs usually require prior campaign experience to demonstrate loyalty to the politician—or connections through family networks. You must know the right people, nurture the right relationships, and be willing and ready whenever opportunity arises—no matter the *financial implications*." He paused and looked into his drink. "What *you* should consider is working for a premier federal agency, like the State Department."

My eyes widened, and I leaned forward. It's like he was continuing what President Obama had told me, that my country needed me. This was my next clue!

"Have you ever considered becoming a diplomat?" he asked.

My heart started racing at the thought of me, a kid from San Bernardino, becoming an international bon vivant. It's the type of job, the type of career—the type of purpose!—I came to D.C. to find.

"No, not really. I mean, yes—yeah, I've considered the possibilities. You know, I think I could do the international thing. Yeah. Yeah!"

"Joining the Foreign Service is very prestigious," he said. "You would lead an international life and be challenged intellectually. You must be adaptable to different social, cultural, economic, and political contexts. It's not for everyone, but I think you've got what it takes."

"Well, yeah. Awesome! I think I should go after it, if you

think so. What else can you tell me about it? It sounds like an exciting life, being a diplomat and all."

He chuckled and then took a drink from his pint glass.

"It *is* an exciting life, I'm sure. However, the work is demanding, and the hours are long. And, of course, there will be sacrifices. Many diplomats don't have families. In fact, many don't even marry. Those that do, choose to sacrifice so much in order to serve our nation."

My chest tightened at the idea of having to sacrifice, of not being able to have everything I wanted. I quickly finished my beer and grabbed the pitcher to pour myself another round. Then I drank half the glass before speaking up again.

"What other advice can you give me?" I said. "You know, like how can I prepare myself to be the best candidate? I want to be the best at everything I do."

"You should start preparing for the test now. And I mean now!" he said as he tapped his index finger on the bar top. "It is my recommendation that you should make an appointment with the career center to talk specifics with one of the advisors."

"Great!" I said. "How much will it cost to meet with one of them?"

He let out a deep staccato laugh and then said, "It's included with your tuition, Michael. Everything at Georgetown comes as a package deal!"

He finished his pint and poured himself another. I wanted to keep up, to be like him, so I did the same.

"Do you want some *real* advice, Michael?" he said. Then he leaned in toward me and lowered his head. "The type of advice I wish my professors had given me when I was your age?"

I was spellbound. His words made me even more excited about all that my future had in store for me. We were talking about things that mattered because we were in a city that mattered with people that mattered. Pretty soon I'd find my purpose and then my wife—and then I'd be set for life.

"D.C. is like a prostitute," he said. "You come to this town to get what you want—then you leave her on the curb. Nothing more, nothing less."

I smirked and then laughed nervously. My throat tightened a bit at the brutal honesty of his remark.

"Wow," I said. "That's one way to look at it." I paused, and then added, "But isn't D.C. amazing, with all the smart people and their ideas converging in one place to make the world a better place? I find it so exciting, you know, to wake up every day in this city!"

He frowned, drank all of his beer in one pass, clanked it on the bar top, and wiped his mouth with his shirt sleeve.

"Wide-eyed kids like you say things like that," he said. "The streets of this town are paved with broken dreams, and underneath those streets run the sewers of corruption. It's all just a mirage, this so-called city on a shining hill."

I couldn't believe it. I thought he was the greatest professor I'd ever met, so brilliant and renowned and, I don't know, *professorial*. He wore tweed sport coats that had suede elbow patches, for godssake! Maybe he was just drunk and didn't mean what he said.

He stood up and pulled on his belt and then straightened his shirt and tie.

"Well, this was such fun, Michael." He grabbed his sport coat from the hook on the post and put it on. "I always enjoy having a drink with my best students. You have a good night— see you in class next week."

As he walked away, he patted my shoulder and then squeezed it. Then he disappeared down the hallway that led to the exit.

I ordered another pitcher of the cheap house beer and drank it as fast as I could. I slumped onto the bar top, my elbow and hand propped up to provide a home for my head. Why would he say those terrible things about D.C.? What was he trying to tell me? I didn't understand, but it made me feel disappointment. I still liked him, though. And what he had told me about joining the Foreign Service made me hopeful for my future, but I was unsure about his comment about having to know people to get the good jobs. I don't know *anyone*. But President Obama had said that if I worked hard I could make it. I knew I could do it. Plus, I had voted for the guy, so it had to work out.

I felt my phone buzz in my left pocket and pulled it out.

Nothing. *That's strange*, I thought. I could have sworn I had felt it vibrate against my thigh. But there were no new emails or texts.

I got up and went to the men's restroom. There were guys peeing at the two urinals, so I went into the only stall. I could hear the urinals flush and smell the soapy water running in the sink bowls. I closed the door and started peeing. But then I started to grow hard, so I grabbed my phone, tapped on the browser app, and opened a new incognito window.

The most amazing thing about my smart phone was that I could watch porn—in the palm of my hand, in any place. There was no more clunky laptop to worry about, no sign to those around me of the perverted things I was about to do. Now I could watch porn in a toilet stall on campus, while standing in a bus shelter, or even while running along the Potomac. I could summon millions of titillating images and videos with just a few taps of my thumbs on the virtual keyboard.

I was drunk and sad about what Professor McEnery said. So I did what I always do when I feel out of luck: I jerked off to all the women who always say yes to me. The two-dimensional ones that come alive on my little screen. The ones who moan with every stroke. The women who never let me down and always get me off.

All I had to do was wait for the videos to buffer.

• • •

It was Thursday night and I was sitting at my desk, toggling between the window with my research paper and the window to the world: the web. The Iraq War had recently ended, and all the important people were writing news articles and opinion pieces that seemed to blanket the internet. I had kind of forgotten about the war, to be honest. It was just something that'd been in the background for as long as I could remember, its quiet hum a white noise of life in America.

Grad school was both so much harder and so much easier than undergrad. Harder, because we had to write twenty-five-page papers and read so much every week and have questions and answers to fill hours of Socratic discussion. Easier, because we only had to take three classes a semester and we weren't concerned with all the campus life stuff the undergrads did and we knew our disciplines pretty well.

What was stressing me out now, at the end of my very first semester, was whether or not I was good enough for Georgetown. I wasn't one of the kids who had gone to an Ivy League school for undergrad and gotten a full ride to come here for grad school. Nor was I rich like all the international kids, whose parents paid their tuition and sponsored their study abroad adventures in America. I came from nothing and took out tens of thousands of dollars in student loans to get my Georgetown degree.

But was I good enough? I thought so, but still I battled unsure feelings.

I had met with one of my professors earlier in the day, distraught and embarrassed because I didn't think I could finish my final paper for her class. I expected her to lash out at me, to call me weak and unprepared for the rigors of Georgetown. I expected I'd need to pack up my stuff and move back to California with my tail between my legs, ashamed that I'd been found out at last.

Instead, she said with such nonchalance, "You're fine. At least you're not Chinese."

I was so confused.

"What…what do you mean?" I said.

"My Chinese students turn in the same papers every semester, right on cue. There's a whole underground system—including Communist leaders who come to campus to watch their every move. They're under the eye of Beijing."

"But…but," I said, "isn't that cheating?"

"Of course it is!" she said, throwing her hands in the air. "But the university—*all* universities in this country—turn a blind eye. We need their money."

I couldn't believe it. Why was life so unfair? Why were there so many double standards? Why did money seem to explain why things were the way they were and why people were who they were? *Fuck the Chinese*, I thought. *What a bunch of Communists!*

I threw my notebook and books into my backpack and left her office in a rage. I walked across the quad and stood at the front gates in the pouring rain without an umbrella. I hailed a cab home, but because I didn't have any cash and the D.C. cabs didn't take credit cards, the cabbie drove up and down Wisconsin Avenue, running the meter, looking for the glowing lights of an ATM so I could withdraw cash to pay for my one-mile ride home. What a crook!

Now I was distracting myself by browsing the internet and making a new playlist in my music library. I had to burn a bunch of new CDs I had bought onto my laptop, then I had to manually go through all 5,000 of my songs and drag and drop the ones I wanted in the playlist. I was watching a video on YouTube about how to plug my phone into my laptop to start syncing the playlist. I glanced at the iPod sitting on the other side of my desk, dusty and dead. I hadn't really stopped to think that I wouldn't need my iPod anymore now that my iPhone did everything it could do—and more.

I looked down at it. I felt sad, staring into its blank gray screen, wondering if I was supposed to say a few words or thank it for its service. That iPod had gone everywhere with me, all throughout Europe when I studied abroad and everywhere I went when I lived in California. I wondered what would happen to it. Where would its plastics and metals and battery end up? Was I supposed to take it back to the store so they could cremate it with all the other iPods at the end of their lives? There were no answers. I opened my desk drawer and put it next to my old camera and my old cell phone, a little brick with a rubber key-pad and a square black-and-white screen.

I clicked the trackpad to move the last song into the playlist and leaned back, satisfied with my work. I right-clicked on *New Playlist* and typed in a couple words: *Mike's music*. I stared at it and then hit the delete key. *Hmm*, I thought. *I need something catchier, something clever, something cool.*

I typed: *Songs of the century.*

Nope! I hit *command+z*, and it disappeared from the screen.

What about something pun-y, like a double entendre? My fingers were resting limp on top of the keys, ready to type something brilliant.

I typed: *Music notes on life.*

I stared at the screen, unsure if this was it.

Nope!

Then I decided to just call it what it was and typed: *Life Soundtrack.*

It was fitting because my life had finally started when I had gotten off the plane at National Airport last summer. My child-hood was just a waiting game, and college was just a warm-up. Studying abroad in the U.K. was a stepping stone. Now I was here, in D.C., at Georgetown, ready to fulfill my destiny and find everlasting love. All my favorite songs would be the score to the movie I called my life—and I was its protagonist, its boy hero who would become a man who changes the world with my life partner by my side.

I unplugged my phone from the laptop, put in my earbuds, and jumped onto the bed. I scooched onto my back, held my phone over my face, opened up my Life Soundtrack, and tapped play.

Music enveloped me as I opened my apps and scrolled through endless feeds of pictures, videos, news, blogs, political rants, and memes. It was hard to quit. If I wasn't careful, I'd sometimes fall asleep with my phone wedged between my neck and chest. My phone now provided all the distractions I could ever want or dream of. Everything I used to do some other way was now done on my phone. It was a small miracle and a big shame, my smart phone.

I went to the app store and downloaded a new app called Instagram that everyone and their moms were talking about. It was like Facebook, but only pictures. With a few taps and my email address, I created an account, and the app came to life. I decided my account name would be @mikemorrisdc1988. The app uploaded all my contacts from my phone and prompted me to become friends with everyone so I could follow their feeds.

I started scrolling through all the pictures, a never-ending vertical feed of images of food and animals and babies and places and things. There in pictorial form were people from high school, friends from college and grad school, musicians and artists, and politicians and pundits. All the pictures had faux vintage filters applied over them to make them look weathered and old-timey. It was all a simulation.

I tapped on someone's profile and scrolled through her pictures. Her name was Caitlin and we hadn't talked in years, not since high school. Now that I followed her, I liked that I could be a voyeur to her life—without her ever knowing. According to her feed, she was already married and she and her husband had just moved into a house they had bought. *Aren't they a little young?* I was still in school, for godssake!

I tapped on one of her picture's comments, which were always the best part, from someone with the username @socaltiff33. It took me to a profile, which was full of pictures that were light and airy, like they had all gone through the same post-production process of sitting out in the sun for a few days. Her profile description read: *wife to daniel | mom to sara and silas | follower of jesus | romans 5:3-5.*

I scrolled through her photos, a reverse-chronological record of her life on visual display. She was beautiful, with sandy blonde hair and bleach white teeth. Her husband looked Mexican, was always dressed in black, and never showed his teeth. One of her kids was a baby and the other a toddler, and they were always dressed in striped shirts on top and white diapers on bottom, with fringed moccasins on their feet.

They were so beautiful and so perfect. They were everything I wanted. I loved them so much. I decided they would be my Instafamily.

Chapter Eight

DUTY AND LOVE

I rushed out of my downtown office because I needed to get a haircut. It was a crisp night in November, a sign that my first winter on the East Coast was coming. I had been working an unpaid internship all semester at an association that focused on international development in emerging energy markets. I didn't actually know what it all meant or how I was supposed to play a part in the global system, but I kept my head down and did a ton of research so the paid fellows and experts, who all made six figures, could put their name on my work and get the prestige they sought. I was just glad to be a part of the place.

I would be meeting with a former Foreign Service Officer in the morning and needed to look my best. I planned to wear the new sport coat I had bought and talk about all the things Professor McEnery and I had discussed over drinks. This would be the most important meeting of my life, the very beginning of my long career as a diplomat.

I usually got my hair cut from a barber near campus because he catered to the student crowd and his shop was convenient, but he closed at five. I didn't leave my internship until six thirty, and all the barbershops downtown were closed by then. So I Googled barbershops all over the city, and there was just one that said it would be open till eight. What luck!

I took the Metro north to Petworth, rode the escalator out of the station, and followed the blue dot on my phone. The barbershop was a ramshackle place on Georgia Avenue that didn't have the spinning red, white, and blue thing out front, so I missed it the first time I walked by. It was just a plain, square building with white wood paneling on the front.

After I found the entrance, I pulled open the door and heard a bell ring. As I turned back around from guiding the door shut so it wouldn't slam, I was met with a room of faces staring at me.

Crap! This is a barbershop for black guys! I panicked. I didn't want to walk out because that might offend them. But I also didn't want to stay because it was obviously not a place where white men came to get their hair cut. But I was also in a bind—I *had* to get my hair cut tonight to be ready for my big meeting in the morning.

"Hello, sir. Have a seat."

"OK," I said. And then added, "Thank you!"

"Alright, alright."

I sat there, my hands fidgeting and my left leg shaking, as all the men in the shop picked up where they had left off in their conversations. Some were talking about sports, some about local politics, and others about things I couldn't decipher. An old cathode-ray tube TV was mounted on a stand in the ceiling corner and was playing a college football game. The cheers of the crowd filled the room after a player made a touchdown, and one barber even clapped his hands. I started making a list in my head of the things I would talk about with my barber, making sure to leave out religion, sex, and politics so as not to offend.

"Young man!"

I was startled by the booming voice from a middle-aged barber who called me to attention. I jolted up in my seat.

"Marcus is ready for you," he said.

He pointed to a young guy, gesturing with the electric razor he was holding in his hand. Marcus couldn't have been older than me.

"OK, thank you!" I said as I stood up and walked toward the chair.

"Wassup, man?" Marcus said.

"Hey," I said. "I'm good, I'm good. How 'bout you?"

"Alright, alright."

I didn't know what to say next, so I didn't say anything. I decided in that moment I would only speak when spoken to.

"What type of haircut do ya want today?"

"Umm," I said. "How about a two on the sides and just shorten the top with scissors? And a round neck?"

I was usually more confident when answering a question. But I decided to answer his question with more questions in order to lower the tension that was palpable.

"OK, OK. Not a problem. That's cool," he said. "I can do that. So, you dunno how long you want the top? Ya just want me to do whatever?"

"Yeah," I said. "Just do whatever, you know—I trust you."

He pulled out an electric razor from a drawer, grabbed the clipper with the number two embossed on it, and slid the clipper onto the razor head. I flinched at the sound of the buzzer turning on.

He started buzzing the sides and back of my head. He didn't say a word, and neither did I. I could smell the mechanical mix of hot oil and metal as he made each pass. I think his hand was shaking because I could feel tremors against my head, but I wasn't sure. I was avoiding looking directly into the mirror so it wouldn't seem like I was watching his every move.

After he finished, he opened the drawer and pulled out a pair of scissors. I was waiting for him to grab a squirt bottle full of water to mist the top of my head, which is what every barber who has ever cut my hair has always done. But there was no sound of squirts, and I felt no mist land on my head. He just started cutting.

I finally looked at him through the mirror and saw beads of sweat on his forehead. The hand he was using to hold the scissors was shaking. He was so nervous.

"So, how about this weather?" I said, trying to defuse the situation. "That random warm day last Sunday was such a treat during this cold spell."

"Yeah, man," he said. "I hate the cold. It's messed up."

I could feel the tips of the scissors prick my scalp, which hurt. I tried not to move, to just suck it up. But he was doing it wrong! He was *supposed to* use his index and middle finger from his other hand to pull up the strands of hair, and then use his other hand to cut with the scissors. I don't think he knew what to do, which made me feel sorry for him. And then I felt guilty, like it was *my* problem that he didn't know how to cut my hair. But he was the one charging money for his professional services! I just wanted it to be over.

"Almost done?"

"Yeah, man," he said, and then paused. "I'll be honest with ya. I've never cut white hair before. It's different from black hair. It's just…so…I dunno…*flat*."

I could tell he was nervous about admitting this out loud, so I laughed to help relieve his stress.

"Hah," I said. "It's all good!"

It was a lie. It looked terrible! My side part was now lopsided with short, little hairs sticking up near the front. I turned my head, looked at myself in the mirror again, and added, "It looks great!"

He cracked a smile, which lowered my stress level. Then he took the cape off me and brushed away the loose hairs. I watched as my little hairs floated to the floor. I noticed there were some gray strands, which I couldn't believe. I'm only twenty-three, for godssake!

Then he led me to the front counter to pay.

"Twenty dollars," he said. "Cash only."

I hardly ever carried cash, but I had learned to always keep a spare twenty in my wallet for cab rides. I looked into my wallet and found one twenty-dollar bill. *Crap!* I didn't have enough for a tip. If he were any other race, I wouldn't hesitate to not give him a tip. The service I had received was awful. But this situation was different.

"Listen," I said. "I only have twenty dollars on me. How about I pay for the haircut now, and I'll come right back with the tip?"

He looked at me suspiciously. "Alright, man," he said. "Ya do what ya gotta do."

"OK, thanks for understanding!" I said. "I'm just going to run to an ATM and be right back. I promise! I'll be right back."

I rushed out and searched for ATMs on my phone. There were a bunch of little red pins that popped up on the map, all up and down Georgia Avenue. I walked to the closest one, two blocks away, so the entire ordeal could be over and withdrew a hundred dollars from my checking account.

When I got back to the barbershop, I walked up to him and gave him another twenty dollars. We stared into each other's eyes, reading the words inside that were not allowed to come out of our mouths. We had an understanding.

"Thanks again," I said. "Have a good one!"

"Alright, man! Yeah, cool! Thanks!"

• • •

I was feeling insecure and less confident than ever with my new haircut. What if my haircut was so bad it prevented me from taking on the world and meeting the love of my life? What if I looked so ridiculous nobody would take me seriously and offer me my dream job? What if that barber had ruined everything? I decided I needed to have a few drinks to ease my nerves before my life-changing meeting with the Foreign Service Officer in the morning, so I hopped on a bus to take me to where the movers and shakers lived and worked.

The bus made a loop around Dupont Circle and onto Massachusetts Avenue, a grand boulevard lined with fancy mansions that housed all the ambassadors and diplomats from other countries. They called it Embassy Row, and I was excited that I'd one day be on the *inside.* I'd get invited to the cocktail parties and dinners and important meetings to discuss things that mattered with important people. *I* would matter.

It was around ten o'clock when I walked into a bar on Connecticut Avenue. Its interior was an amalgam of random themes, with plasticky diner booths that stuck to your leg skin when you got up in the front room, a giant paper mache dragon enveloping the hipsters in the room next door, a space upstairs that had arcade games for the college crowd, and a tropical tiki-themed patio out back for the few people who smoked cigarettes in this town. For all the sheen found in the corridors of power in D.C., Dupont's bars were downright grimy. I liked it that they were stuck in time and that they didn't care about giving in to today's expectations. It felt authentic in a city full of charlatans.

I walked in and made a beeline to the very, very back of the front room, sitting down in my own booth so I could have some privacy and a clear shot of the people coming in through the front door. The only downside was that I was next to the bathroom, a dirty three-by-two-foot unisex stall with a plywood door, like the kind you see in Western movies. But this one had one door, not two. You could see the occupants' feet and head, hear their urine trickle into the toilet, and smell the various smells that restrooms are host to. It was disgusting, but it was authentic. It was *cool*.

I pulled out my phone and scrolled through my Facebook feed. Every five minutes or so I'd look up from the glowing screen and survey the room, waiting for Her to walk in and finally put an end to my misery. I tried not to look back down at my phone, to be more adult-like or something. But I felt so naked without it, like I was missing out on life. My phone was my safety blanket, an insurance policy against ever having to experience absolute silence or isolation. *This is what every single person without someone to talk to does, right?* As I swiped up again on the phone's smooth glass screen, I realized

I was simultaneously interested in everything and nothing at all. What a bore.

Just as I was losing interest in the goings-on of my one thousand or so *friends*, I heard the front door close with more than a click but less than a slam, followed by the careful *click-clack* of stilettos across the wood floor. It was the most intentional entrance I'd witnessed in a long time. I looked up and saw a woman around my age approaching a stool at the bar with the kind of confidence you only find in someone who lives and works in D.C. She sat down, crossed her legs, hung her purse on the hook under the bar top, and pulled out two phones.

She proceeded to perform what is a modern-day ritual in D.C. that instantly advertised her status as someone close to power. She took her iPhone out of her purse and laid it flat on the bar. Then she took her BlackBerry out and laid it directly on top of the iPhone. Then she used her fingers to perfectly align the square edges of each device so that they would cast one shadow.

The only people in this town who carried a personal iPhone and a government-issued BlackBerry—and needed to neurotically check both at all hours of the day—were Capitol Hill staffers and White House aides, those ambitious Type A achievers whose days were full of pleasing their narcissistic bosses. In this one move, I knew more about her than I could learn in a month of dating her. And now I wanted to know everything else.

I did that inconspicuous thing that guys do: I steadily eyed her from head to toe, tracing her every curve and feature. I didn't want to seem creepy, like I was salivating over a piece of meat with drool dripping out of the corners of my mouth. I was a gentleman, so I only stared when I was out of her line of sight. When she moved her head even the slightest, my eyes would dart away to the wall or to the bathroom or to my phone. But I couldn't stop staring at her. She was beautiful.

She took off her coat and uncovered a cream-colored silk blouse that drooped with extra fabric near her chest but didn't give anything away. It had a small slit in the back that wasn't a sexual tease as much as a small preview of her tender porcelain skin underneath. She had on tan tights and a formfitting navy blue skirt that ended just above her knees. *Conservative yet modern*, I thought. The stark contrast of the end of her light blouse tucked into her dark skirt emphasized her waist, which was an advertisement for the pricey lifestyle gym she surely belonged to and religiously attended each morning before dawn. Her legs were thin but shapely, with strong calves that led to petite ankles that filled the black stilettos perched on the rung of her stool. I wanted her so bad.

I know people go to bars to get laid, but I thought that this time maybe I could be different and find someone real. *Maybe she is that someone. Maybe she is real.* Maybe, even though she is smart and attractive and ambitious and probably the star of her congressman's sexual fantasies, she is looking for someone different. A guy who is smart and ambitious, too, but looking for more than a quick screw. *Maybe she's looking for someone like me.*

I imagined our life together. We would have a passionate, yet mature, courtship that would last three to five years before getting engaged and married. She would laugh at all my jokes and appreciate my witty banter and unique take on life. I would take her out for cupcakes and coffee and walks along the C&O Canal. She would come home after long twelve-hour workdays and tell me about the latest machinations of Congress. I would listen intently and advise her on how to maneuver the halls of the Capitol to advance both her and her boss's interests. Then we would watch just an hour of Netflix, nothing more because anything more on a weeknight would be gratuitous and nothing less because anything less would mean we took ourselves too seriously. Then we would make love for fifteen to twenty minutes because we had to wake up early. And we would wake up early and do it all over again the next day, and the day after that, and the day after that for the rest of our lives till death do us part. We would be madly in love. We would be soul mates. We would be happy.

I glanced down at my phone. The screen said it was eleven eleven. I had been staring at her and imagining our life together for almost an hour. Meanwhile, the room was filling up with stressed-out Washingtonians and yet she was still sitting alone, switching between furiously tapping at her iPhone and furiously typing on her BlackBerry. Back and forth, back and forth, her thumbs doing a modern-day dance.

Her presence was a mystery. Was she here solo, just a pretty gal at the bar waiting for a handsome guy to buy her a drink? Of course, guys don't do that in this town. We wouldn't dare approach a Millennial woman in a bar and offer to buy her a drink. Especially on a weeknight. Doing so would violate her independence as a woman and reinforce the patriarchy, no matter how chivalrous the act. In the hour she sat at the bar not one guy approached her, the prettiest gal in the room.

Were they—was *I*—subconsciously afraid of an intelligent, accomplished, attractive woman? Was it the fear of rejection? Was it an obsession over gender equality? Perhaps it *was* because of an obsession over gender equality and all the times my friends and I had been verbally slapped in the face by young women for being ourselves.

Frustrated, I fumed inside and wondered why there were so many boys in the room yet no men. In my anger, I decided I couldn't let an opportunity for love and happiness pass me up without at least trying. I had to at least try! I decided I was the only man in the room with a pair of you-know-whats who was ready to woo his future wife, the pretty gal sitting alone at the bar. She was obviously waiting for her knight in shining armor to rescue her from the doldrums of her D.C. existence. I knew I was the man to do it.

I took a final swig of my beer, set the glass down with a thud of confidence, and rose from my booth. I pulled my shirt down, my pants up, and my shoulders back and started walking over, emerging from the darkness of the back of the room.

As I started walking I noticed another guy also walking toward her, but from the opposite direction. He had the same confidence and determination I had. I made a mental map of how I would navigate through the people standing around with their drinks in hand, how I would get to her first. Then I saw the guy turn left toward the bar. My heart dropped.

He pushed his way through the crowd to the polished, rounded edge of the bar's oak top and leaned his left hand against it, displaying his nickel-colored watch, sky blue shirt's French cuff, and navy blue suit jacket sleeve. Then he leaned in, not to the bartender to order a drink, but to the pretty gal to give her a kiss on the cheek. *No! How could this happen to me? Of course she's taken! She's the prettiest gal in the room, for godssake!*

My heart sank into my stomach. It felt like I got dumped for no good reason because the other person is a selfish jerk who doesn't appreciate you. I put forty dollars on the bar top and stormed out in a stupor. I hailed a cab and took it back to Georgetown, back to my miserable life in my crummy apartment with my weirdo roommate.

When I got home, I rushed into my bedroom and locked the door. I kicked off my shoes and threw my P.W.K. on the floor. Then I took off all my clothes, grabbed my laptop, and hopped onto the bed. I opened my laptop, launched the incognito mode of my web browser, put my earbuds in, and typed in the URLs to all my favorite sites. I began to stroke myself, switching between all the videos I had playing concurrently in the little tabs I had opened and lined up. I just wanted someone to want me.

Chapter Nine

DESTINY AND DELIRIUM

"Mr. Morris!"

My head jolted up at the sound of the receptionist yelling my name. I had been slumped over in a chair for at least half an hour scrolling through all the feeds on my phone while I waited in the lobby of one of Georgetown's *modern* buildings—which was code for *ugly and soulless*. I can't believe architects got paid money to design such garbage.

"Yes, here I am!" I said as I stood up. I straightened my sport coat and then buttoned the top button, which is what Adam had told me to do.

It was Friday morning and I was at the Career Services Center. I needed to do what President Obama and Professor McEnery had told me to do. I needed to get ahead and start planning *now*, even though I hadn't even finished my first semester at Georgetown.

"Right this way, please," the receptionist said.

She led me down a long hallway and then we took a right down another hallway. There were rows of office doors made of frosted glass lining each side. We stopped at one of the doors, and she knocked on the metal trim while saying, "Ms. Ruiz, Mr. Morris is here for you."

"Thank you," said a voice from the room.

The receptionist stretched out her left arm and held the door open for me while her right arm made a motion to direct me toward a chair. I walked in, one hand holding my backpack strap over my shoulder, and stood there. Then the door clicked shut, and the receptionist was gone.

"Hi, Michael," said Ms. Ruiz. "It's so nice to meet you. Please call me Pamela."

She stood up to shake my hand, and then I put my backpack down on the floor and sat in the chair.

"It's nice to meet you, too," I said. "Thank you so much for taking the time to see me today. I've been looking forward to this for a long time."

"So," she said, "tell me about your ambitions and what questions you have about the Foreign Service."

"Well," I said, "I've known for a long time that I'm meant for a challenging career, like being a diplomat. I've studied international affairs and politics and am specializing my graduate studies in elections in emerging democracies. I know I have so much to contribute to my country…and to the world, you know?"

I stared and waited for her to start rolling out the red carpet. I knew she knew I was special, that I was meant to join the diplomatic corps and change the world. And before I showed up today, I did what Matt had mentioned to me: pray. I wasn't sure what god I was praying to or whether it would make a difference, but I thought it couldn't hurt. I prayed that my destiny would finally happen.

"Well, Michael, that is a *very* compelling case," she said. "I can tell that you've given this great thought."

There was a long pause as she sat still, staring at me with a confused look on her face. Then she continued, "I am happy to share with you all about my three and a half decades in the Foreign Service, or I could walk you through the requirements to apply to join. Which would you prefer to start with?"

"I would *love* to hear about your time serving our country, but since I'll be graduating next year I think it would be best if you could tell me what I need to do to get in," I said. "I want to be sure I'm ready to go when I graduate!"

She nodded her head and then swiveled her chair to the back side of the desk to grab a sheet of paper. She placed it on the desktop in front of me and pointed to a checklist with her pen. I leaned forward to absorb every word.

"This document outlines the eight steps of the process," she said. "It's very, very rigorous. You will need to register for the Foreign Service Officer Test as soon as possible, start studying *now*, and then sit for the exam in the spring. Most candidates fail the test, so do not underestimate it."

"Great!" I said. "I can do that. Do you have any tips or advice on how to prepare?"

She paused and looked at me. *Did I say something wrong? Was I coming off as too ambitious?*

"Michael, what is your second language?"

"Second language?"

"Yes, in order to be competitive, you will need to demonstrate fluency in a second language. Very few candidates make it through by just knowing English."

My throat tightened, and my heart was beating faster than it ever had before. My sport coat was tight against my stomach because I had forgotten to unbutton it when I sat down. I felt trapped.

"Wha—what? Fluency in another language?"

"Yes," she said. "You didn't know?"

I didn't want to seem like a fool, so I lied.

"Oh, right. Of course, of course!" I said. "It's Spanish. *Soy de California!*"

She smiled but looked skeptical.

"OK," she said. "Do you have any other questions?"

"Nope, not today! Thank you so much, Pamela!"

I took the piece of paper, grabbed my backpack, shook her

hand, and darted out of her office. I walked so fast down the hallway that I knocked over a plant. I turned to survey the damage but couldn't stand the thought of getting caught, so I kept walking.

I couldn't believe it. I felt so small, like I didn't matter. Why didn't anyone tell me about the second language requirement years ago? How could I have missed something so essential? It felt like all my plans for my life were unraveling. It felt like I wouldn't be able to pull through for my family. It felt like I was becoming a failure.

• • •

I escaped to Brooklyn the very next day to see one of my favorite bands play at some hip venue on the riverfront. I had bought the concert tickets ages ago and kind of forgotten about it until I looked at my calendar app last week and saw it blocked out, a little gray square to remind me that I had committed to doing something.

The first thing that went wrong was the Saturday morning bus ride to New York, which was supposed to be four hours but turned into a seven-hour ride from hell. Of course, I did everything right—printed my ticket, showed up early to Union Station, brought bottled water and nuts to snack on—and I still got bumped to the next bus because they had overbooked it. Then our bus got a flat tire, and we had to wait on the side of the New Jersey Turnpike for two hours until a mechanic showed up.

The second thing that went wrong was I couldn't find anyone to go with me. I had two tickets, hoping that by the time the concert happened I would have someone special to take. I had planned to have met Her by now so we could have a romantic weekend together in New York City. I would surprise Her with the concert tickets because I would know that the band would also be one of Her favorite bands. We would fall more deeply in love as I stood behind Her, my hands on Her shoulders, swaying back and forth together to the sound of the music.

But none of it happened how I wanted it to. I texted Adam and then Matt and then some other friends from school to invite them to come with, but everyone had somewhere else to be. I got so desperate, so desperate to not go alone, that I texted some of the less crazy chicks I had hooked up with. Not a single one of them responded back.

Now here I was, by myself, walking down South Sixth Street toward Kent Avenue to the park where the concert would be. Walking through Williamsburg was strange, like some fantasy land full of kids who were dressed as adults. I passed by stores selling artisanal foods and craft goods, men with handlebar mustaches riding fixed-gear bikes, and women wearing slouchy beanies while riding skateboards. And a lot of plaid shirts and tattoos. The people looked as plastic as the suburbs they had all fled from.

When I got to the park gates, I pulled out my two paper tickets, which I had printed out at the school library and folded into little squares. Then I opened one and held it up in the air to peacock that it was for sale. In no time at all, a white girl dressed in black skinny jeans, a black sweater, a black beanie, and black boots walked up to me.

"Hi!" she said. "How much?"

She wasn't wasting any time.

"Hey," I said. "Umm, well, let me see." I lowered my arm and looked at the ticket price, and then added five dollars in my head for the online service fee. "Forty-seven dollars."

"That's it?" She snatched the ticket out of my hand to inspect it. "Is this, like, even legit?"

"Yeah," I said. "I'm not here to make any money, you know." I paused and then added, "My friend who was supposed to come with me canceled at the last minute, so I just want it to go to someone who wants it—at cost."

I didn't want to look like a loser, like some loner who went to concerts all by himself.

"OKaaaaaaay," she said and then paused. "Is it literally even a real ticket? Or are you, like, messing with me? Why isn't the ticket, like, on your phone?"

"It's a real ticket. I guess I'm old school—I always print my tickets."

"Oh, my god!" she shrieked. "Who even does that anymore?"

I didn't know what to say. I just wanted her to go away. She was everything I hated about girls my age. She sighed like she was starring in a soap opera—again, for what felt like the millionth time—and then handed me fifty dollars.

"Keep the change," she said and then patted my chest like I was some chump.

I turned to walk toward a different entrance from the one she was going through to avoid the possibility of running into her again. I handed the attendant my paper ticket, he scanned it with a smart phone that had a laser scanner contraption attached to it, and I walked onto a vast lawn full of drunk and high people. I was sober.

I looked around and saw people rocking back and forth to the opening act. Puffs of smoke were rising above their heads, which practically gave me a contact high. There was a group of girls to my right who were dressed like a bunch of hippies. They were wearing turtle neck sweaters with fringe across their chests and bellbottom jeans and flower crowns in their hair. To my left was a group of guys who weren't wearing much at all—just jeans and hats on backward. I wondered if they were cold since it was late fall and crisp outside, but I guess showing off their torsos was more important than keeping warm. I was wearing khaki pants, a forest green sweater, and brown boat shoes.

After the main act started playing, the crowd grew denser, and I scanned around. Maybe She would be here, the person who would become my wife. Maybe She would bump into me during my favorite song, the both of us singing out loud without shame, until we opened our eyes and they met for the first time. We would have a moment, and the rest would be history. I hoped so badly for it to happen, to finally find love and be happy.

I looked up at one of the giant screens projecting video of the band on stage. I was so far away I was essentially watching the concert on TV. The band was an assemblage of folksy, indie bohemians who were smoking marijuana in between songs. One of them was wearing a vest like he was Sonny Bono circa 1976. They were a big band with musicians playing guitar, mandolin, keyboards, bass, violin, saxophone, drums, and even an upright bass, which the hipsters loved. I loved it too, even though I didn't identify with being hip. Their music was part of my Life Soundtrack.

The lead singer started clapping his hands, and so the crowd did, too. Tens of thousands of arms went up and clapped along to the beat. Some guy's elbow kept hitting my side, so I turned to see what was going on. He was flailing his arms around while little lights on the tips of his fingers changed colors and created ribbons of light in the air. He must have been high, maybe even on acid. He looked like he was having an awesome trip.

"Hey," I said to another guy next to me. "Can I have a puff?"

"Yeah, for sure man, for suuuure. Good vibes, good vibes," he said.

He handed me a joint and I took a few puffs, inhaling it as deep as it would go. I think it was weed, but I couldn't say for sure.

The first strums of the next song filled the park, and everyone started screaming and jumping up and down at what was to come. I knew exactly what the lead vocalist was about to start singing. It was *my* song. I closed my eyes and mouthed the lyrics along to his voice. I felt a rush of happiness course through me as the words and sounds washed over me. I opened my eyes and saw everyone else singing at the top of their lungs, their mouths and arms aimed toward to the sky.

The beat dropped and the crowd went wild. Fireworks exploded from the top of the stage, and lasers blasted from behind the band to create a ceiling of light over the crowd. Smoke in the air created little floating galaxies that moved in slow motion. Arms reached higher and higher into the air, trying to touch—

to *feel*—the lights. I could feel the bass inside my body, my organs booming to the beat. I was so elated, just like everyone else. I felt like I was on another planet.

But then I suddenly felt shattered. How could my favorite song—*my* song—be everyone else's favorite song, too? This wasn't even one of the singles on the album! I thought I was the only one who appreciated it and loved it.

The thousands of other people singing my song out loud, surrounding me with their voices, crushed me. I started to get tunnel vision, like the walls of the world were closing in on me. My heart was racing, and sweat was forming on my forehead. My breaths shortened, and my chest grew tight. I felt my face get hot and figured everyone around me knew something was going wrong, like I was being found out. I turned around and elbowed my way out of the crowd. I needed to get out ASAP.

I found the nearest Subway station and took it to Manhattan, where a bus back to D.C. was waiting on some random street corner near Penn Station. I didn't even have a ticket for this bus, but I didn't care. I boarded anyway and found a seat in the back. I sat down and stared lifelessly at everything around me. I was so small, so alone, so invisible. My eyes traced drops of water streaming down the window glass. I was jealous they got to disappear into the black abyss of the window flashing.

Who was I? Why was I here? What had I done to deserve this? This life of mine didn't feel like mine at all. This life of mine felt like someone else's, some poor soul's excuse for a life. This life I was living was not the life of someone who was becoming the man he was supposed to be.

It's as if there were things inside of me that needed to be released but couldn't come out. There was tension and stress and anxiety in every cell of my body. There was fear and longing and disappointment physically weighing me down, in every fiber of my muscles. I felt defeated. I felt unwanted. I felt alone.

When I got back to my apartment, I'd take the orange bottle of Adderall with the blue pills that had helped me survive grad school and my internship and everything else in my life, and try to end the pain once and for all. The pills that I'd buy every couple months off some guy who went by the name "K" that I met in the bathroom of a bar one drunken night when I first got to D.C. The pills I wasn't supposed to use. The pills that didn't fix any of my problems.

Fuck those pills.

Chapter Ten

BECOMING A MAN

It was the middle of June, and I had stayed in D.C. for my internship. There was no room for a summer break. I had finished my first year of grad school *and* survived a suicide attempt. It had been six months since I had started taking the pills—the ones legally prescribed to me that promised to fix all my problems. I liked the work I was doing so much for my internship that I had agreed to stay on past the spring semester even though they still wouldn't pay me. This was part of my plan to work harder than all my peers in order to get ahead. But it seemed like this was a dumb plan because I realized by May that everyone else was doing the same thing.

Most of my friends from school were also in town for the summer, except for the rich kids who went to their families' summer homes to vacation. For those of us who were less fortunate, we had to suffer each day and night with the D.C. heat and humidity, the air thick and inescapable like a swamp. We made it our ritual to go out on Friday and Saturday nights all summer long, where we sweated and complained about being sweaty but still drank and danced our cares away.

"Yo, Mikey," said Scott. "Want another round?"

"Yeah, thanks, man," I said. "I'll take another PBR tallboy."

"You got it!"

Some of us had met up earlier to see an indie band play at the 9:30 Club, but there were no hipsters at the concert, which meant the band was actually mainstream. Now we were at a run-down sports bar, our second or third bar since we had left the concert. This one was on U Street, which used to be a black neighborhood with jazz clubs but was now for everyone and every genre. The bar had cheap drinks and eats, and they only took cash, which made it *cool*. There was a main bar in the front room, a little room off to the side, and a whole upstairs area with a dance floor. It had options.

As for me, I was standing against a countertop in a bay window in the main room, my eyes scanning the place for pretty brunettes. It was dark inside, and the ceiling was low, just like a bar was supposed to be. A baseball game was playing on TVs mounted from the ceiling, but I didn't care. There was local sports paraphernalia hanging on the deep burgundy walls—Redskins, Nationals, Capitals, Wizards, and D.C. United—and an old jukebox in the corner. The setting was ideal. I hoped tonight would be the night I would finally find Her.

The place was full of two types of people that I had come to know well after a year in D.C.: Basic Brian and Basic Becky. Basic Brians were mid-Atlantic bros whose greatest stress in life was whether or not they were behaving macho enough. They wore navy blue gingham shirts with chinos and boat shoes and could go from working in a corporate office on Friday to hunting deer in the forest on Saturday. Basics Beckys were chicks who had college degrees but got all their validation from men. They wore expensive blouses and skinny jeans with brown boots that went up to their knees and spent their weekends traipsing through D.C.'s most photogenic neighborhoods.

I loathed the mindless existence of The Basics but mostly resented them because of their frictionless lives. They were happy and content, came from intact families, and had financial security. They weren't my people.

"Hey, man," I said to Adam. "Cutie at three o'clock!"

Adam discreetly glanced over to his right to check her out and then turned his head back to me.

"Nice!" he said. "Now go talk to her."

A pit formed in the bottom of my stomach, and I became nervous. *What if she didn't like me? What if I said the wrong thing? What if she said no?* Hitting on ladies at the bar was not something Millennial men were well versed in doing. Women just didn't want it. They liked to be in control of their lives.

"OK," I said. "Wish me luck!"

I became excited at the possibility that tonight could be the night, that she could be The One. I straightened my back, puffed out my chest, and walked toward her. *Just be cool*, I thought. *Don't overthink it*, I told myself.

When I got to the bar, I leaned my left elbow against the bar top and took a long look at her. She was absolutely beautiful, just my type. She was wearing a black V-neck T-shirt, light wash skinny jeans, and black ballet flats. Her outfit communicated that she was laid back and ready to fall in love with me.

"Hey."

"Hey," she said.

"How's your night going?"

"Fine," she said. "How's your night going?"

"Great!" I said. "But I think it could get better."

"Oh, yeah?"

"Yeah," I said. "And you might be the thing that makes it better."

"No, thanks."

And just like that, she turned her head away and picked up where she had left off with her girlfriend. I didn't feel devastated, just numb. I wasn't sure if the alcohol was making me feel numb, or if all my failed attempts at finding love were making me numb. Maybe it was a little bit of both.

I walked back to join the group, my head hanging low with another defeat.

"Yo, what's the capital of Florida?" Scott said. "Cassady *swears* it's Tallahassee, but I always thought it was Orlando. Or maybe it's Miami?"

"I feel like it's Orlando?" Priya said.

"I don't know, guys. If I remember from the fifth grade, Florida was *literally* one of the weird states with a weird capital city," said Keisha. "I feel like it's not, like, what you think."

"It's Tallahassee" said Anthony with confidence.

He held up his phone and waved it in front of the group to show us the Google search results page with his query. The group looked around at each other, unsure of what to say next. The conversation ended before it even began. It was kind of amazing, these smart phones with the internet in your pocket. You could get an answer to anything—anytime! It almost seemed wrong.

"Soooooo, anyway, Mike," said Adam. He turned his back to the rest of the group so he and I could have a one-on-one conversation. "No go?"

"No go," I said. "Didn't even have a chance."

I took a big swig of my beer, which was sitting on the counter waiting for my return.

"Like I was saying earlier," Adam said, "you gotta focus on what women want. You have to be the answer to the question they haven't even formed in their heads yet."

Finding women came easy to Adam. He was charming and good looking and taller than I was, plus so much more confident. I didn't have the charisma he possessed.

"What does that even mean?" I said.

"It means you gotta meet—or *exceed*—their expectations."

"Give me an example."

"OK," he said. "Remember when you told me about that chick who was getting ready to suck you off and then pulled your pants down and shrieked in horror at all your pubes?"

"Uh, yeah," I said, uncertain of the point he was trying to make. "It wasn't *that* bad, you know. You make it sound like a scene out of a horror movie!"

"Trim your bush! Trim your bush! Trim. Your. Bush."

He guzzled the rest of his beer and slammed it on the counter, convicted at his commandment to me.

"So did you?" he asked.

"No," I said.

"Jesus Christ, man!"

We both let out a guttural laugh, a telltale sign that we were wasted. Adam walked away, and I turned to stare out the window at all the people passing by. I didn't know how to be a man in a world where women had equality. Was I supposed to chase them? Were they supposed to chase me? Were we supposed to rationally agree on who would pursue whom? Whatever happened to women wanting to be *wanted*, to be charmed and convinced to fall in love by men with visions of what could be? Why didn't any pretty brunettes ever walk up to *me* and ask me how *I* was doing?

"Yo, dude! What. Do. You. Want?"

My eyes were heavy, my head spinning in circles. I didn't know where I was or how I had gotten there. Was I in the upstairs bar now? I couldn't say for sure. I think I drank too much.

"Hel-lo! Earth to white boyyyy," she said, waving her hand in front of my face.

There was a black lady with attitude yelling at me from the other side of a tall counter with a stainless steel top. She had boobs the size of watermelons, long braided hair with hot pink streaks, and pointy nails that sparkled under the lights. Her skin looked so smooth and shiny, like she had rubbed baby oil all over. She was mesmerizing.

"Hi, sorry," I said. "I'll take fried chicken, mac and cheese, and green beans."

All I really wanted was pizza. I guess I chose the wrong place.

"We outta' mac and cheese," she said.

"Oh," I said. "I'll take baked beans then."

"Order number eighty-eight," she said while ripping a page from her memo pad and handing me a little paper receipt—

without making eye contact.

"Thank you!" I said, oblivious to everything else going on around me.

I waited for my order for what felt like an eternity. I wondered where all my friends were. What happened to Adam? I looked to my left and then I looked to my right, but I didn't see anyone. I just saw a bunch of strangers standing around waiting for their food like me. They all looked so happy to be together, so happy to be talking and laughing with each other.

"Eighty-eight!"

I grabbed the to-go box, stumbled outside to the curb, and hailed a cab.

When I got home, I devoured my food and washed it down with one more beer from the fridge for good measure. Then I took off all my clothes and threw them on the bedroom floor and did what I always did when I failed to find love: opened my laptop and ended my night with all the women on the screen who always said yes.

• • •

I couldn't believe how alone I felt in such a big city. There were thousands of people around me all the time—walking by on the sidewalks, riding on the Metro underground, sitting on their couches on the other side of the apartment wall—and yet the feeling of isolation was material. I guess we all lived a cloistered life, set apart from each other in our little boxes arranged next to and on top of and behind each other. It made no sense.

Why did it have to be this way? It's not the life in the city I had seen on the TV shows and in the movies growing up. I thought friends would live with each other and next door to each other and down the street from each other—and would hang out with each other all the time. But my city life felt more like life abandoned. Everyone seemed to be just as alone and miserable as I was, and yet no one was doing anything about it. What a damn shame.

It was a Saturday afternoon and I was in my bedroom, the

door closed and locked. I could hear Jud's music through the walls, my windows rumbling with every drop of the bass. Every so often I'd hear him rapping about his oppressed childhood in Long Island or something. I didn't get it.

I was on my laptop at my desk, trying to finish a project for my internship. I was having trouble concentrating, toggling back and forth between surfing the web and running statistical models. I opened YouTube to play a song I had heard at a coffee shop the other day, but before I knew it, an hour had gone by and now I was watching a video of a cat slapping a human across the face.

I decided I needed to take control, to stop being a slave to work and the internet. I got up from my chair and walked to the corner of the room where a small package had been sitting all week. I leaned down to pick it up. On the sides of the brown cardboard box was a smiling mouth underneath one word: *Amazon*.

These days I ordered everything off Amazon. If I needed a can opener or toilet paper or school books or hemorrhoid cream, I'd order it from the app on my phone and, before I knew it, it would be waiting on my doorstep two days later. Buying things online was too easy. Now everyone in the city shopped online because no one had cars—or time. You never had to commute to a store and choose between just a few options and talk with strangers and get help from the sales associate. You could do everything privately, quickly, and efficiently—no people, no cash, no shame.

This little package had something special inside: a hair trimmer. I'd ordered it because Adam told me that I'd have better success with dating if I went bare—*down there*. In many ways, this made no sense. I liked my pubic hair. It made me feel like a man. If it wasn't supposed to be there, then why would it grow there? But in many other ways, this made complete sense. If I expected women to always be bare down there, then the fair thing to do—the *equitable* thing to do—would be to also get rid of my hair. Plus, women didn't like getting hair stuck in their teeth when they used their mouth down south. I would become a female liberator!

I grabbed the package and a men's magazine I had bought while standing in the grocery store checkout line last weekend and tiptoed to the bathroom. I quickly turned around and locked the door, jiggling the knob to make sure Jud couldn't get in. Then I opened all the packaging—the layers of cardboard and plastic, the zip ties and adhesives, the crimped plastic shells that were razor sharp—and plugged the trimmer into the wall outlet.

I turned to the feature story in the magazine, which was titled *How to Shave Your Junk the Right Way—And Have Explosive Sex!* I had never liked reading men's magazines because they made me feel insecure. They were full of toned and hairless guys with really white teeth, which made me feel like a fat, hairy schlep. Yet here I was, using it like a manual for my life.

I pulled my pants down, turned the razor on, and went for it.

"Ahh, fuck!"

There was blood streaming down my shaft and little black hairs were falling onto the vanity drawer fronts and scattering across the floor. I ripped a piece of toilet paper off the roll and blotted myself. Then I took another piece and put it on the nick, which was where my shaft met my scrotum.

Indignant, I grabbed the magazine and re-read the instructions: *Avoid painful nicks by keeping the razor guard on the trimmer and putting it on the shortest setting.*

I put the plastic guard on the razor head, and it clicked into place. Then I turned the trimmer back on and tried again. I could feel the vibration of the razor on my pubic bone. Every time it passed a patch of hair, the buzzing sound would go down a few octaves. It sounded like I was mowing a lawn, which I guess I was.

After I had finished, I turned sideways, backed up, and took a long stare at myself in the mirror. My penis looked *different*, and it did look bigger. What I really noticed was all my other body hair—*en totale*—for the first time ever. There was more hair on my chest and stomach than I had remembered, and there was now hair on my neck and even my lower back. *Wow*, I thought. *I am hairy like a man!*

I felt self-conscious, the same way I felt about my beard, which wasn't as full as other guys' beards. I had a beard because all the men now had beards. The lobbyists and financiers and even some congressmen were sporting beards these days. I knew because all the blogs were talking about it. Beards were in, and I needed to be in the club.

I grabbed my phone and started taking a bunch of pictures of my bat and balls. Then I opened my photos app and scrolled through the pictures, examining the different angles. *Hmm*, I thought. *That's not how it looks in the mirror. And that's definitely not how it looks when I'm staring down at it.*

I wondered if this was the same phenomenon as when you hear your voice on a recording: shock, awe, disbelief! And then, acceptance. Or maybe it's like the looking-glass self. Maybe you could never really know yourself, not like how other people know and see you—including your penis. *Whatever*, I thought. *If this is what it's going to take to get to the next level in the game, to finally get Her, then I have nothing to lose. Adam said it would work.*

I was a little nervous about putting *myself* out *there*—in the airwaves and on the cellular towers and probably on the internet, too. But I felt like I didn't have a choice. I started to text my dick pics to some old flings anyway, just to see if it would work.

Hey, long time no talk haha

A tingle went down my spine, a new feeling of thrill. I felt so…naughty? So…manly! I practically held my breath, waiting to get a text back. *Wow*, I thought. Sexting really was thrilling! Now I understood why everyone was doing it.

Gross. It looks like a
drowned rat

How demeaning! I would never say such a cruel thing to her if she sent me a picture of her vagina. If I did, she would surely label me a sexist or misogynist. What a misandrist!

> Hi mike…this is quite the
> hello…

Yes! I was getting warmer. Who knew it could be so easy to re-engage a good lay?

> Hot!! I want it inside me.
> When??

Jackpot.

Chapter Eleven

GRAD SCHOOL YEAR TWO

It was Halloween weekend, and I was ready for a release. I had just wrapped up writing all my midterm papers—fifteen double-spaced pages *each*—and emailed them to my professors. One was about the history of presidential power, the second was about the fallacy of public opinion polls, and the third was about a neo-Cold War coming in the 21st Century, an argument I had no problem articulating, but one that my classmates deigned. Grad school was exhausting, but it challenged me intellectually in a way college just hadn't. I was meant for it.

Georgetown's townhouses were decorated just like I had seen on the TV shows and in the movies growing up: bales of hay stacked on stoops, expertly carved jack-o'-lanterns flickering on stairs, and non-demonic skeletons hanging from windows and tree branches. The rich people who lived in these homes exclusively handed out name-brand candy—and not the miniature sized versions either—which isn't something I had experienced as a kid in San Bernardino.

I had never really liked Halloween because the costumes my mom bought me never looked like the costumes the kids wore on TV. But now I was an adult, I was in control, and I was at a house party dressed up as a dinosaur. A dinosaur! I was a stegosaurus who had opposable thumbs, which was essential for drinking my beer. I had gone on Amazon three days ago, searched for Halloween costumes, and picked the cheapest— and least offensive—option. A few taps and two days later, like magic, it arrived on my doorstep.

The party was mostly full of grad students, but there were some undergrads there, too. When I first walked into the house I expected to see a display of wealth and opulence. It looked like it was three stories from the outside, maybe even four with one of those secret bump-out floors with a rooftop deck. Instead, it was a ramshackle group house with cracks in the plaster walls and boarded up fireplaces in all the common rooms. I guess there was too much money to be made by renting the place to students who had no choice but to live in squalor.

I was in the kitchen, in the very back of the house past the formal living room and dining room and another room that I didn't know its purpose, when I stumbled upon a gaggle of wizards and witches. They were playing beer pong—or Beirut, as they call it on the East Coast. There were red plastic cups, which were full of cheap beer, arranged on a folding table like bowling pins. The teams were throwing ping-pong balls into the cups. I looked around and stared at the kitchen cabinets, which were made of off-white, or maybe yellow, laminate with little plastic handles. There were no granite countertops, and there was no chef's range. I walked over to the fridge, grabbed a bottle of beer, and twisted off the metal cap. I was already drunk because I had pre-gamed on whiskey and ginger ale at my apartment.

I wandered onto the back patio, scoping out the crowd to see if I would find Her. Maybe my future wife would be someone whose path had crossed mine many times before at social events on and off campus, but *tonight* would be the night where magic happened. I looked to my left and saw a group of people smoking weed. They were dressed as obscure and cultish pop culture characters and other forgettable personas. I turned around and made my way back to the living room.

The temperature was at least twenty degrees warmer in the living room because it was so crowded. I looked into the center of the room and saw a chick dressed like a black cat, wearing four-inch stilettos and dancing on the coffee table. Every time the beat would drop, she'd squat down and spread her legs open like a hooker and then lick the top of her hand like a kitty cat. I was mesmerized by her—and a little horny.

I kept scanning the room, trying to find Her. I knew the chances of finding my one true love at a Halloween party were slim, but maybe this party would defy convention. Maybe we *would* find each other and have a wonderful story to tell in the wedding section of the newspaper. The headline would be cheeky yet scintillating: *Dinosaur and Cowgirl Meet, Fall In Inter-Species Love.*

There was a DJ with a little table and a laptop set up in front of a grand fireplace with a pink marble mantle and surround. But there were no discs and no record player. He was more like a Digital DJ—all he did was add songs into the virtual queue on his laptop and click play. I recognized him from another house party last year. He was a hipster who wore tight jeans and ironic T-shirts and moonlighted as a DJ on the weekends, but wore a suit and tie and worked for the CIA during the week. D.C. was full of these types of people: smarties with hobbies.

I wandered upstairs to find a bathroom to go pee. I had held it for as long as I could to avoid breaking the seal, but now I was about to burst. I reached out to the wall to steady myself as I walked up the creaky staircase to the darkened upstairs. I could hear the house's window panes vibrating because the bass was so powerful.

After finding the bathroom, I turned around and closed the door, put my beer on the sink counter, and released what felt like gallons of urine into the toilet. When I was done, I washed my hands and then downed what was left of my beer bottle, tossing it in the trash can. It made a loud *clink* as it hit a pile of beer cans and bottles that had already reached the brim.

When I opened the door and walked out, some guy was waiting in the hallway. I figured he was in line for the bathroom. He was dressed like a cartoon mouse.

"Hey," he said. He was holding a wide smile, which was creepy because of the way his face was painted. "How's your night going?"

"Hi. Good," I said.

"I've been watching you all night."

"Oh, yeah? You like my costume or something?"

"No," he said. "I like you."

I didn't know what to say back. Was he hitting on me? Or was I just drunk and imagining things? Before I had a chance to respond, he leaned forward and put his hands against the wall, one on each side of my body. He was hovering just a few inches from me. My body went stiff.

"Ever been with a man before?" he asked.

I could feel the heat from his breath with each word he spoke, but I couldn't see very much of him because of how dark it was. I didn't say anything. Then he leaned forward, and I felt his lips touch mine. Before I knew it, his tongue was in my mouth, and I could feel his stubble scratch against my face. I didn't stop him.

He backed away and said, "You know you want it."

I didn't know what I wanted. I was drunk and lonely. I liked that someone—anyone!—wanted me. I could feel the erection grow in my pants, ready for whoever wanted to take care of it. *Don't pass up an opportunity to get off*, I told myself. *Just let go and be. It's a new era. There are no rules anymore.*

He led me into a bedroom and closed and locked the door behind us. I stood there while his hand rubbed my bulge, and he muttered dirty things. Then he dropped to his knees and pulled my pants down. I stood there, my top half dinosaur and my bottom half human, with my erect member floating in the air.

And then a warm, wet sensation enveloped me, and my eyes rolled back into my head. I could feel his tongue making swirling motions. He opened his mouth extra wide and breathed hot breaths onto me. Then he moved his head back and forth, consuming me whole with rapture.

I looked down, and he looked up. What I saw back was the face of a mouse with exaggerated, oblong eyes painted black and a smiling mouth painted red with laugh lines that didn't move. In that moment, I felt as if I was having an out-of-body experience. I could feel physical sensations, yet I wasn't alive inside.

"Mmm," he moaned.

"Yeaaaah," I moaned back.

I felt like such a man. Here I was getting serviced by another man, a man who couldn't resist *me*. The entire situation was absurd, a mouse sucking off a stegosaurus. Yet there we were.

In no time at all, his hands squeezed me tight, and I exploded in his mouth. He whimpered as he slurped, and I moaned louder than I ever had before. It was complete ecstasy.

• • •

It was now ten months since I had started taking the little white pills called Wellbutrin, one pill in the morning and one pill in the evening. Even though the pills were *allegedly* correcting a chemical imbalance in my brain, I stayed sad most of the time. And I was sad that I was sad, a kind of self-fulfilling sadness. Which made me even more sad and—worse—even more ashamed. How would I break the cycle? How could I possibly? The deep, dark hole I had dug for myself seemed to be getting deeper and darker. There seemed to be no way out. Being depressed was a real drag.

What most people don't understand about depression is that it's not a choice. Nor is there direct cause and effect, as if the human condition is something that can be understood exclusively through the framework of the scientific method. Depression is an illness, a thing that comes out of nowhere and infects you. No one decides to get cancer, and no one decides to get depressed. Now I had to figure out what had gone wrong, and why my life had stopped working out. I had to find a way out for the sake of my mom and sister.

If I had to describe depression in three words it would be this: nothing moves me. Not birds chirping or children laughing or the feeling of euphoria when the little hairs on the back of your neck stand alert like soldiers upon hearing the crescendo of an orchestra. Not winning small wins at work or getting laid by a great lay or the feeling of breakthrough when an idea comes barreling through your mind like a direct shot of lightning from Zeus.

Depression is the absence of all good feelings. It is the complete and total nonexistence of all the normal things that make life worth living for normal people: creativity, inspiration, friendship, family, joy, and happiness. Depression is a real bitch.

I had never wanted to be a cliché, to be one of those people whose life unfolded like a character in a TV show or movie. I didn't want to be depressed and start seeing a shrink and start taking pills. I didn't want to be so ordinary. Yet here I was. Lonely, sad, and depressed. But I couldn't fully understand my loneliness, sadness, or depression—to know what it was *actually* doing to me—because depression confused all my feelings! I could only feel the bad ones, only the ones that warped me. So how was I supposed to fix myself?

I'm not sure when my depression started. My depression was like a wild vine that years earlier had taken root and attached itself to my exterior, its shoots growing upward and outward at a steady pace until it had penetrated the small cracks in my façade. Once inside, it kept growing and growing and growing until it found and suffocated my soul. I was no match for its feral grasp. Depression was my master, and I was its slave. I was entwined in its death grip.

The shoots of the vine that had grown inside me were now creating new buds, whose sticky tendrils attached themselves to my soul. I thought the pills would kill off the vine, but they seemed instead to act as fertilizer. The vine continued to grow. Every time I would gasp for the air of life, its grip on me would tighten. I was smothered by sadness.

A typical week for a depressed person doesn't look that different from a typical week for a regular person. To the world, I was a functioning human. I woke up and got to class on time most days. I finished my assignments on schedule and delivered high-quality work for my internship. I ate enough food to sustain me. I still went on my late-night runs to relieve my stress. I went to happy hours—a weeknight requirement in D.C. if you wanted to make it in this town—and socialized to stay part of the professional-class scene. I paid my rent and bills on time. I still showered and brushed my teeth and trimmed my fingernails and toenails. I did all the normal things that all the normal people do.

But in reality, it was exhausting. It was a charade of happiness I had to perform to the world to mask my deep sadness inside. The worst of it was on weekends, which was like depression on steroids. Weekends were sixty hours of soul-shattering darkness. Last weekend and the weekend before and the weekend before that till my memory serves me no more. Every weekend was just like the last: a pit of despair.

Every weekend would start when I'd wake up around noon. I would open my eyes, realize I was still alive, and say to myself: *fuck my life*. I would pick up my phone, check the time, realize I had slept more than twelve hours, and sigh a great sigh of self-pity. I would close my eyes and try to force myself back to sleep, to escape my reality, to go back to my dreams of happiness and weightlessness.

Sometimes it worked, but sometimes it didn't. When it did work, I would sleep for hours more, the clock ticking into the early evening. When it didn't work, I would go through a cycle of irrational self-reasoning.

Why are you just lying here, Mike? *I am here because I am pathetic.* Why don't you just move your legs and get out of bed? *My legs won't move; they do not want to leave this bed.* Why are you inside when life is happening outside? *I like it inside; it is safe inside.* Why don't you just choose to be happy and end this insanity? *My sadness is not a choice; it infects me and it won't go away.* Why are you so pathetic? *I am not worthy of the joys of life; there's something wrong with me.* But don't you have to eat or go to the bathroom or take your pills? *My body doesn't want to do any of those things; I am dead inside.*

Then I would feel extreme guilt for my self-loathing, knowing how self-indulgent it was in a world tarnished by greater suffering than my own. I knew there were starving children and thirsty mothers and slave laborers and contaminated homes and natural disasters and child molesters wreaking havoc on earth. I'd try to rationalize, to make relative, my own suffering in an attempt to rid myself of it. But it never worked. My intellectual contortions just made me sadder, more ashamed, and angrier at myself. I wanted to die.

Then I would turn to my side, the sound of ruffling sheets the only sign of life, and stare at the floor. I would concentrate really, really hard. I would think about what it would be like to get up and out of bed. I would imagine myself standing on my own two feet on the rug in my room. I would close my eyes and concentrate on willing myself to make it happen. I would squint my eyes harder and clench my jaw, trying to make something— anything!—happen.

But it was no use. I never had the strength or the willpower to get out of bed. I would just stay in a permanent state of grogginess, cycling through hours of sleep and panicked moments of wake. I was a forlorn human, abandoned by the world because I wasn't strong enough.

Our Father, who art in heaven.
Our Father, who art in heaven.
Out Father, who art in heaven.

Just say it. Just say it. Just say it. I did what Margaret had told me to do, but it was no use. I just couldn't get out of bed.

And then darkness would come. It was nature's signal to me that I had squandered an entire day, a day I would never get back. The sun would not wait for me, and now the moon was taunting me, reminding me of my sickness. It would go on and on and on, until the weekend would end and it was time for class on Monday. And then another five-day-long weekday charade would begin, with Mike Morris a master performer.

Chapter Twelve

THE MCSPECIALS

It was a frigid Friday night, and the wind was cutting my face like shards of glass. I was walking up the Eighteenth Street hill to Adams Morgan on my way to a "Friendsgiving." It was some new holiday I'd never heard of before, made up by urban Millennials to help with the guilt of abandoning each other to go home to their real families, back to where they came from, for real Thanksgiving. I was just happy to have received an invite from this group of friends, because they were *cool*. More than a year into my D.C. adventure, and I was still having trouble making friends. I didn't know what I was doing wrong.

I was mesmerized by all the leaves blowing sideways toward me. The glow from the streetlamps created a tunnel of light, and I could barely see what was just a few steps in front of me. But I found the row house thanks to the flickering flame of its gas-lit lamp and the round bay windows that jutted into the garden. I looked in and saw the people as though they were little characters inside a snow globe: talking, laughing, and drinking but silent to me, the outside observer.

When I walked in, I handed a pricey bottle of red wine to

Alexandra, one of the hostesses. She was ethnically ambiguous with translucent-looking skin and black hair that was styled in a pixie cut. And she was so thin like a movie star. She looked just like her Facebook and Instagram photos come to life (which I had stalked before coming over). I felt a small thrill seeing her in the flesh for the first time.

I put a pink box of cupcakes on the dessert table. These were the *it* foodstuff of D.C., the status symbol of the urban palate. I had spent seventy-two dollars on two dozen bespoke cupcakes, not because I wanted to and not because I could afford to, but because I *had* to. I didn't have real kitchen supplies to cook anything homemade, not even a dish for a casserole, and I knew that regular pastries from the grocery store would be socially unacceptable. Most of all, I needed these people to like me because I'd be like them one day: beautiful, rich, and powerful.

"Oh, my god!" Alexandra squealed as I set the box down. "Love it! These are literally the *best* cupcakes in the city? I cannot! These, are like, sooooo amazing? I'm literally dead."

I had no idea what she was trying to communicate, but she was smiling, so I knew it must be good. I wasn't sure why lots of things seemed to be phrased as questions these days even when they weren't. But I was happy with her reaction—with her acknowledgement—of my considerate contribution.

I turned to walk into the living room. It was an old row house, so the wood floors were crooked and creaky. The light gray walls stretched higher than you'd expect, with intricate crown moldings and trim painted a bright white. The fireplace had a stone mantle and surround, but there was a flat-screen TV mounted above, which kind of ruined it. I had never seen such an impossibly thin TV before in my life. It was neat, but I longed for a fire to be burning on this cold night instead of staring at moving images.

"Yo, yo, yo!" someone shouted. "What's up, Mike?"

"Hey, guys," I said as I waved.

There were a bunch of people I knew from school, but most

of the people I didn't know. These ones looked older, so I assumed they were Georgetown alumni or other people with real jobs. Everyone was sitting or standing in the living room, eyes on the TV, imbibing and laughing and looking cool. They were watching YouTube videos, which were beaming through the air from Alexandra's laptop to the TV. *What is this black magic*, I wondered. It was hard to keep up with all the new technologies that seemed to launch on the regular. Sometimes it felt like I wasn't paying close enough attention to what was going on in the world.

"Aaaaaanywaaaaay," said a guy named Max. "Fail! This bitch needs to check herself!"

He was a flamboyant, white gay man whose commentary on the videos was dominating the room. He talked like he was a sassy black lady, the ones you'd encounter at all the front desks in D.C.—and everyone loved it. It's like he was the royal jester.

"Oh, you're such a hater," said Alexandra. "The woman *obviously* didn't know the table wasn't legit."

"Giiiiiirl, she knew," he said. "Oh, that bitch knew!"

They were bickering back and forth about a fat woman who fell off a table while singing. Alexandra and Max personified the gay boy-straight girl relationship that was common in the city, which is not a combination of people I had ever known growing up.

"OK, well, watch this one," he said, before then beaming a new video to the TV from his phone. "This is literally cray!"

"That is v wild," she said.

It was a video of a hippo pooping. I discreetly pulled my phone out to Google what "v" meant. It meant *very*. That's all it meant! I didn't understand why she didn't say the entire word. After all, it's just two syllables.

I walked to the kitchen to get another beer from the fridge, then came back and found a spot on the sofa. It was the same dark gray sofa that was in every twenty-something's apartment. I leaned over to put my beer on the side table and realized it was the same square black table that was in every twenty-something's apartment. Then I looked down and saw the same black-and-white rug that was in every twenty-something's apartment. The tyranny of IKEA and its basic design across America was really a new style all its own: Generica.

We ate off paper plates and drank from red plastic cups. We pretended like we were *of the people*, like we couldn't afford to eat off real dinnerware or use metal cutlery. But it was all performance, intentionally created to be casual, comfortable, and ironic. And I loved it! I felt like I was on the inside, part of the cool kids' club.

Of course, we still ate bougie food—the expensive cupcakes with organic frosting, the fancy green bean casserole made without the can of condensed soup, the turkey deep fried on the back patio because we could. There were wood cutting boards with varieties of imported cheeses and crackers and charcuterie, and the fridge was stocked with all kinds of sparkling water but nothing flat. This was the culinary lingua Franca of the urban set, and I liked it so much I never wanted to go back to eating the slop I was fed as a kid. My new life tasted amazing!

I looked around the room and saw a multi-cultural tableau. It was two-thirds white people, but the rest looked like they were hand-plucked by the ACLU. Every non-white person was an archetype of urban liberals' diversity dreams: there were two flamboyant gay guys, one white and one black; two obese women, one white and one brown; two lesbians, both brown; a black chick with an afro; and a gaggle of internationals from both hemispheres who spoke no fewer than ten different languages and who most definitely worked at either the World Bank or the International Monetary Fund.

I wondered where everyone came from, what their stories were, and how they had gotten to D.C. I wondered if anyone was like me—you know, a regular guy from a regular place where people don't have extra money but did have real problems. None of these types of people exist in San Bernardino. My only exposure was in high school when the majority of the girls' basketball team turned lesbian for a semester. But most were back to straight when they got back from summer break. Now I was feeling like an outsider, like an alien who had dropped into some parallel world with different people and language and rules and views.

"Fuck all the haters," said a woman named Brittany. "I am body positive. I will *not* be shamed by the white patriarchy into believing that I am *less than* just because I'm a curvy girl."

She was obese. Very, very big. I was actually concerned for her health.

"That's right! Get it, girl!" Max said as he snapped his fingers into four points in the air to draw an invisible Z.

"White, cisgender, heteronormative men have fucked up the world, and I'm not taking it anymore!" she said. "We gotta tear down the patriarchy and build a more socially just and environmentally conscious world where we have proper representation, equality, and equity. When women run the world, there'll be no more problems. Fuck all the white men who've ruined my life!"

"Preach! Preach!" he said as he fanned himself with his hand.

I gulped. I was a white man. I hadn't ruined her life, had I? I felt attacked but mostly confused because I didn't understand half the words she had said. I looked around and noticed everyone was still smiling, waiting for her to say something else. I guess they understood everything. I looked over at Brittany. Now she was quiet, pensive but seething.

"Aaaaaanywayssss, did you guys see the meme Ingrid posted to my wall?" Alexandra said.

"Oh, my gaaaaaaawd, yes girl!" Max shouted. "The little baby was all like, 'Char-lay bit my fin-gah!' I cannot!"

Ugh, I thought. I hated inside jokes! I hated when people talked openly about posting things on Facebook. It's like social media was some alternate reality, an intangible place you were peer-pressured to care about. It made me feel even more insecure than I had been feeling a few minutes ago when Brittany said all those mean things about white men; plus, I was unsure of how to engage in conversation. I clenched my hands around my beer bottle and started to zone out. I wasn't sure I belonged.

I stared across the room at a crack in the wall. In that moment, I imagined myself shrinking down to the size of a dust mite so I could crawl through and escape the party. Even though all these people fit the bill for the characters I had created in my head for the life I would one day live, I was left feeling empty inside. They seemed on the outside to be how I thought people were, the way I thought people should be. But in reality, I think they were all insecure and angry and didn't care to get to know me.

Mostly, I couldn't get past the feeling of loneliness in a room full of friends in a city full of people on a planet full of humans. How could it be possible to feel so alone with so many people around? Here they all were, the people I aspired to become. They were the Millennials who flitted through the city like it was a playground, moving into neighborhoods like urban colonizers. They were overly educated, saw no need for religion, only believed in science, and traveled all over the country and world like life was a never-ending sightseeing tour. They were the ones who made at least six figures as members of the professional creative class, the ones who ate, drank, and fucked their way through life without ever putting down their smart phones. They represented everything I thought made for a good life, but now I was unsure.

What a bunch of McSpecials!

Now I was starting to hate them. And more than hating them, I hated myself—because I feared I was becoming one of them. What if I wasn't actually special? What if I was special just like everyone else thought they were special? What if I were as generic as all of them? What would my mom think of these people? What would my mom think of my new life here?

I got up and snuck out of the party without saying goodbye to anyone, which is something you can do when no one's paying attention to you. I walked down the block and stood on Eighteenth Street, waiting for a red cab to start heading my way. I looked over and saw a chick holding her arms out and over her head. The LED light next to her phone's camera was turned on, and she was making different faces, from smiling to pouting to biting her lip, while she craned her neck forward. She was alone, taking pictures of herself. I'd never seen someone do that before, and she had no shame. I couldn't believe it.

I raised my arm to hail a cab I saw coming my way. I slid into the backseat and told the cabbie, "Thirty-seventh and T, Northwest." I pulled my phone from my coat pocket, tapped on the browser app, and opened an incognito window. I typed in the URL to my favorite porn site, made sure the volume was on mute, and started watching videos. Then I reached under my coat with my other hand and unzipped my fly. I stroked myself all the way home.

• • •

There was only one person who ever left me voicemail: my mom. I remember when I was a kid you had to call yourself by dialing your own landline number and then key in a special code to retrieve your messages. Now, on my smart phone, I could scroll through a list of missed calls and tap the ones that had left me a voice message. It was too easy.

I tapped my mom's contact card to call her back.

"Hello?"

"Hi, Mom."

"Oh, hi, sweetie! It's so good to hear your voice," she said. "What're you doing?"

"I, umm, I'm just finishing some homework," I said.

It was a lie. I had just finished jacking off to some videos, and now I was lying naked on my bed, too lazy to get up and clean myself off.

"That's so nice. I know you work so hard, sweetie. Do those people at George University even know how smart you are?"

"It's called *Georgetown*, Mom! I've told you this a million times," I said. "And, no. Everyone here is really smart. I guess I'm just part of the crowd."

"Don't you say that!" she said. "You were always the smart-est boy in all your classes. You're being modest, Michael."

I didn't know what to say. To be honest, I didn't really know how to have a conversation with my mom now that I was a grown up. She always asked dumb questions and talked about stupid things. It always felt like a waste of my time, time I could be using to *accomplish* something.

"Anyway," I said, "I'm just returning your call. Did you need something?"

"Well, no," she said. "Yes, well—yes, I called about noth-ing, and then I remembered I did want to talk with you about something."

"Did the school district get back to you?" I said.

"No, honey. They're not hiring me back. I think this is the end for me. I'm only fifty-seven, but in their eyes I'm too old. They're only interested in hiring the young people fresh out of college."

"Sorry, Mom," I said. "Don't worry about it—I'll take care of you."

"That's very sweet of you, Michael. But I was thinking I could get a job at the grocery store or maybe even the ice cream stand until Social Security kicks in. Wouldn't that be nice?"

"Sure, yeah. That'd be nice," I said. "Is there anything else?"

"Well, yes," she said. "It's about your father."

My stomach sank as low as it could go. I felt tightness at the back of my throat. Why would she bring him up? He's a lowlife, for godssake!

"OK," I said in a stern voice. "*What* about him?"

"Well, I just…I just wanted to make sure you knew some things about him," she said. "You're turning into such a fine young man, and I know all men, all women—all of us, each one of us made in the image of God—we all have our struggles."

"OK," I said.

"Your father had a drinking problem that I didn't know about until after we got married," she said.

"Yeah, I know, Mom. And then he went to A.A. and nothing

changed and yadda yadda yadda. I've heard his sob story a million times."

"Michael, there's more to the story," she said. "There's *always* more to the story."

My face became hot, and I held my breath.

"Wha—what is it...about *him*..." I said, the words barely escaping my mouth.

"Well, Michael, we're all human. Life isn't as simple as you think it is when you're a little boy. And your father, he was a good man. I think he still is, or at least I hope he still is. He does struggle, I know."

"OK," I said.

"Addiction is a terrible, terrible thing, Michael. After your father became sober we were in such a good place. We were so happy—our marriage, of course, but also with you. You brought us so much joy, and your father, after he stopped drinking, finally noticed you. He loved watching you explore the world as a toddler, asking all those questions. You never stopped asking questions, Michael. Did you know this? Did I ever tell you about this? You could be exhausting!"

I laughed as tears started to form in my eyes. I tapped the mute icon so she couldn't hear me.

"And, so, what I wanted to tell you, Michael, is that there *were* happy times in those early years...before the divorce. Together, as a family. But addiction is just such a terrible, terrible thing."

"OK," I said. I knew she was trying to tell me something else but was having trouble getting it out. "What is it, Mom?"

"Michael? Michael?" she said. "Michael are you there? There is your mother. Michael, this is your mother speaking!"

I tapped to unmute myself.

"Sorry," I said. "I think my phone accidentally went on mute."

"It's OK. I'm glad you're alright," she said. "Anyway, what I wanted to tell you, is that after your father defeated his alcoholism, he found other addictions to replace the drinking."

"Wha—what kind of replacements?" I said.

"He started going to the Indian casinos and gambled away all the money he worked so hard to earn. That, ahem, *hobby* led to other things." She paused while she cleared her throat. "You know, Michael, it's not so easy. Once you're on a certain path in life it can be really, really difficult to get back on the right one. Your father became addicted to gambling, and then he became addicted to...*sex*."

I shot up in bed and leaped off. I put her on speakerphone while I leaned over my desk, my hand steadying my body that now felt like gelatin.

"What?" I said. "A gambler? And a sex addict?!"

"Yes, it is sad, isn't it?" she said. "He met all sorts of women at the casinos. I guess it's where people go to find that kind of thing to, you know, cope with the pressures of life."

She was so nonchalant about it. Wasn't she mad? Wasn't she pissed off? Wasn't she angry? He screwed her—he screwed us!

"I hate him," I said.

"Hate who, Michael?" she said. "That's a very strong word. I don't like hearing it come out of your mouth. You're my son!"

"Why are you telling me this stuff, you know? Why are you telling me all this bad stuff...you know, *now*...like it matters more or something?!"

"I understand it's hard to hear, but I always wanted to tell you and your sister...eventually. You deserve to know the truth. I thought now would be a good time, now that you're on your own and pursuing your goals. And you're growing up so fast; you're becoming a man. I want you to understand the struggles men have, Michael. I don't want you to become like your father!"

I was stunned. Did she know? There's no way she could possibly know.

"I won't. I'm already more of a man than he ever was," I said.

"Have you ever struggled with the hard parts of life?" she

said.

"No," I said. "I'm a strong person, Mom. I can manage everything on my own."

"Well, that's nice to hear, sweetie," she said. "I just wanted you to know. I read online that some of this stuff can be genetic."

"OK," I said.

"Are you coming home next month for Christmas?"

"No, I can't. I'm sorry," I said. "I'm just so busy with school and my internship, and, you know, I don't have much money left over from my loans."

"It's OK, sweetie. I know you're working very hard."

"I only have a semester left, then everything will start to work out. I bet I'll land a high-paying job with all my Georgetown connections. Then we'll have lots of money. Don't worry, Mom—it'll work out!"

"OK, sweetie. That sounds so nice," she said. "I just don't understand why you couldn't have gone to graduate school in California. There are lots of great universities here!"

"I already told you—Georgetown is one of the best. All the best schools are on the East Coast. It will guarantee certain things for me."

"Alright, Michael. Whatever you say…"

"Hey, Mom. Is Jess around? I want to say hi."

"Sure, sweetie. Here she is," she said. "I love you, Michael. Please call once in a while! I don't like that you work all the time and don't leave any time for your family."

"OK, I will," I said.

I heard muffled sounds and hands sliding against the receiver.

"Hey, Mike, what's up?"

"Hey, Jess. How's it goin'? Listen—you make sure Mom knows that there's nothing to worry about. I'm going to take care of you guys. I'm almost done with grad school! I only have a semester left, and then I'll get an important job and make lots of money. You guys have nothing to worry about."

"Whatever you say, Mike," she said. "I don't know why you think you have to take care of us. I'm going to college soon, and then I'll get a job, too. You're not the only one who can make money, you know."

"You're not listening to me, Jess!" I said. "I'll take care of you and Mom! Why won't you accept that?"

She didn't say anything back.

"Jess? Are you there?"

"Yeah," she said. "Listen, I have to get back to my homework. If you ever cared enough to ask about how *my* life is going, then maybe I could tell you that I love my history class and I met a guy I really like!"

And then she hung up.

Part Two

SURRENDER

Chapter Thirteen

USURY AND FREEDOM

A month before graduation, I got a letter in the mail informing me that my student loan repayment would begin six months after receiving my degree. The grand total for my Georgetown master's degree, which consisted of ten classes and two research seminars, was $65,000.

I kept staring at the number on the sheet of paper. Its ink made it feel so *real*. It was a big number to stomach, but I hedged that it would be worth it and I would soon be making millions of dollars. After all, I needed this degree in order to fulfill my destiny and make lots of money. I had to do whatever it took to provide for my family.

There was also the $33,000 in student loans I owed for my undergraduate degree. I had forgotten about *that* balance because the government had so kindly put those repayments on hold while I was piling on more debt for my grad degree. In total, I would soon be paying back $98,000 plus interest for what was my generation's mortgage. And did I really have a choice? There were no jobs to be had in 2010 when I graduated from college, when the Great Recession was happening. I *had* to go to grad school.

The stress of my impending loan repayments added urgency to my job search. My original plan to join the Foreign Service, advance America's interests abroad, and become a renowned and respected diplomat had gone to hell. I still couldn't believe no one had told me that I needed to start learning another language, not a single professor or advisor or responsible person. I thought I had done everything right! Yet here I was.

What was crystal clear to me was that I wouldn't be able to afford my rent, food, phone and internet, utilities, Metro and bus fares, health insurance, and student loan payments—plus money I needed to send home to my mom and sister—with a normal starting salary of $50,000. I'd need to make as much money as I possibly could or else I'd end up homeless or back in San Bernardino living with my mom. I was aiming for a cool $80,000 to start, maybe even more since I had two degrees and was now in the Georgetown network.

I considered other public service jobs in D.C. because I still wanted to do something good and contribute to something bigger than myself, just like President Obama had commanded me and just like Professor McEnery had told me. *I could become a journalist*, I thought. The news media's public service mission was a worthy one. I could start out as a beat reporter, work my way up to a front-page investigative star, and then maybe transition to reading the news on cable TV. But then I found out you can't just become a journalist. Nowadays, you have to start out by managing a Twitter account and fact-checking real journalists' work, which I thought was beneath me. Plus, I wasn't Jewish.

I even considered staying in school—forever—and continuing on toward a Ph.D. All my professors loved my term papers about modern electoral politics. I even got a runner's up award for my thesis on political branding for a consumerist electorate. But then I realized that being a student for life would be economic suicide. I'd be living on poverty wages and working as an indentured slave while my student loan balance would just sit and grow with its capitalized interest. Ph.D. degrees were now only for rich kids, the Chinese, and minorities—and I wasn't any of them.

So I browsed the online job listings and saved a bunch of jobs that sounded interesting, like *advancement relations coordinator* and *assistant policy strategist* and *engagement manager*. I updated my resume, highlighting my tony master's degree, and submitted it along with my online applications to at least twenty jobs. I figured I'd get a ton of calls back. The recruiters would know I was too good to pass up, that they *had* to hire me. All I had to do was wait.

While I waited for all the calls to schedule my interviews, I still hoped that by graduation someone would recognize my specialness and tap me for an amazing job. Maybe a professor would contact a bigwig friend and tell him or her that a star pupil was ready to make his professional debut. Maybe I would get lucky, and fate would have me randomly run into a who's who of Washington, and our ensuing conversation would lead to great things for me. Maybe I would get hired by a startup and, with my talents, be running the company by year's end.

A week before graduation, I got one email back from a political consulting firm. I did a phone interview and then an in-person interview where I met with the partners and they asked me a bunch of hypothetical questions. I had no idea what the company actually did or what I'd be doing, but it was the only company to offer me a job. The salary? A measly $42,927—per year!

I couldn't say no. I had to take the job. I had no more student loans to live off. I *had* to start making money to send home to my mom and sister. It was a real shame that money was the deciding factor and not the firm's mission or my personal ambitions. This was not how I had planned it would be. This was not how I had wanted it to be. But this is what it was.

My career situation went in the face of what the world had been telling me. All the online think pieces said that in order to become successful—to become someone who does big things—you have to hustle. But I didn't understand how I was supposed to hustle when I was so overleveraged.

I'd watch money-losing startups turn into billion-dollar companies and wonder, *Why not me?* I'd read about average people starting lame blogs and getting rich quick off display ads and wonder, *Why not me?* I'd watch child CEOs make rookie mistakes, their inflated confidence no replacement for wisdom, and feel bad about myself. And don't even get me started about all the rich kids who were described as *gifted entrepreneurs*, who put their *blood, sweat, and tears* into their always success-ful companies. By now I'd learned that if you're ordinary but rich, it always works out. They had access to networks, to peo-ple, and to capital. I had access to nothing.

Maybe there was a certain amount of fearlessness and level of shamelessness that was required in such endeavors. Maybe these passion hustlers had some secret sauce that couldn't be bought by a middle-class kid from San Bernardino. *But I am smart! I am talented! Where's my reward?*

I tried not to care. I knew my professional life would work out because I *am* special. By now I was eager to stop being a student and start being a professional. I was ready to fulfill my destiny—to transform the world with my gifts. And I had to start somewhere.

So I began my career as an analyst at the firm 50 Stars Political Consulting, LLC.

• • •

My lease with Jud came to an end, and I decided I was too mature and ambitious to live with someone like him, so I didn't renew it. Now was the time to assert my independence, to live like a real man. Plus, I never really knew the guy, which was amazing considering we had lived together for two years.

"Mike, you're starting a new season of life. See, things are getting better!"

Matt was so happy about it, about everything. It was a Saturday, and he was helping me move across town to

Columbia Heights, a neighborhood full of other young professionals like me. I didn't own very much furniture—just a mattress and box spring, a desk and chair, and a small couch and side table—so I avoided renting a moving truck and opted for a cargo van instead. The fatal flaw in my plan was that the van necessitated six roundtrips between the two apartments instead of one. I guess there were still things in life to learn.

"Yeah, I'm happy to open up a new chapter, you know?" I said as I lifted a box into the van. "I thought I was really stuck—like, actually stuck living with some white guy who thinks he's a black rapper. But now that it's all over and I never have to see him again, I just feel sorry for him."

Moving in the middle of summer sucked. Moving in the city sucked even more. We were dripping trails of sweat as we walked back and forth between the van and apartment. We also had to deal with angry drivers honking and yelling at us to move the van, which we had to park in an alley because there was nowhere else to go.

My new apartment was in an old pre-war building made of unpainted red brick, which was becoming rarer these days. There was a black metal staircase with intricate ironwork that led to the main entrance. I was on the second floor in the middle apartment in a building with three floors and fifteen apartments total. My 525-square-foot dwelling was cozy. There was a rectangular room you walked into, with the front door in the middle of the wall, and a galley kitchen straight ahead. To the left was the bedroom, and through the bedroom a bathroom.

I liked Columbia Heights. It was full of hipsters, gays, dogs, blacks, and Latinos. It felt more like California than posh Georgetown because it was so ethnically and economically diverse. It reminded me of home whenever I heard people speak Spanish at the bus stops or smelled spicy food cooking as I walked passed the row houses. Plus, there was a lot of weed everywhere. People even puffed while driving, which kind of concerned me. But I could never say anything about it lest I be labeled an old fogey.

As we were making our last trip from the old apartment to the new one, Matt turned to me and said, "You know, Mike, I hope this entire ordeal has taught you something important about life."

"Oh, yeah, what's that?" I said.

"That even though people may disappoint you and not live their lives according to your standards, you still have to accept them as human. We're all flawed, including Jud. You can't use these moments in your life to run away from people."

"Yeahhhhhhh, that makes sense in theory," I said. "But it's another thing living it in real life, you know? It was *so* painful to live with him. I felt like I was in jail, like I was robbed of my freedom!"

"Well, maybe that was the whole point?" he said as his eyebrows rose up and his forehead wrinkled. Then he stared at me while we were waiting at a red light.

"What do you mean?"

"What I mean is there's a plan for everyone's life," he said. "And I know you're going to roll your eyes and say that what I'm about to say is cliché, but it's really true." He paused. "Your suffering, being held against your will, has brought you closer to God."

I laughed out loud, and then the light turned green and he gunned it.

"What does that even mean?" I said. "Closer to god? He's not here, he's not my friend, he's nowhere to be found! He's some invisible guy in the sky!"

I turned toward him and tightened my smile. He didn't say another word.

After we had finished unloading the last of the boxes, we took off our shirts and threw them on the living room floor; then we slumped against the wall until we fell to the floor. We were exhausted. I opened the music app on my phone, scrolled to my Life Soundtrack, and tapped shuffle. We sat there together, satisfied by our work, as the air conditioning hummed and the song played through my phone's speakers. Its notes and lyrics echoed across the room. I felt such relief.

"Mike, there's only one way you'll find true happiness and stop being sad all the time, and His name is Jesus Christ."

Matt was so sure of himself.

"Oh, really?" I said.

He couldn't help it. He loved lecturing me!

"Sure! I know you think I'm a *cah-ray-zee* Christian, but I'm serious. The Bible has answers to all of life's great questions and wisdom for all of life's great dilemmas. People of faith are the happiest, most stable people I know. And that's a fact."

"But it makes no sense," I retorted. "All I see on TV are a bunch of self-righteous Evangelicals who just want the world to end now so they don't have to deal with all our human problems. It's reckless, Matt! They're reckless!"

He looked down and didn't say anything. I think I hurt his feelings, which made me feel bad. Sometimes I felt like living in D.C. was rubbing off on me. I automatically had strong opinions about everything and always felt a need to voice them—just like everyone else in this town. We were conditioned to dominate everything and everyone at all times.

"So, here's the thing," I said. "I know all about Jesus and his life on earth and the miracles he *allegedly* performed—I went to Sunday school as a kid, you know."

"Uh, huh…annnnd?" he said.

"And—so, for *me*—it's just so outdated, you know? Like, I like the values of Christians and Catholics, doing charitable things and good things for the world, but the whole organized religion thing, to *me*, seems like a thing of the past. We don't, you know, need it anymore. We've evolved."

"Oh, but we need it more than ever!" he said as his eyes widened.

"What do you mean?"

"There is no shared truth anymore," he said, and then paused. "But there *is* truth out there—non-relative truth, inconvenient truth—and the Bible has it. I'm telling you! You just need to give it a chance!"

I didn't feel attacked or anything, just a little uncomfortable. The idea that the stories in the Bible could unlock the door to a life of happiness seemed too simple. I was already doing all the things I was supposed to. I was on the cusp of finding love and purpose; I just knew it. I was in control of my life, not some invisible puppet master.

"Yes, but hoooooow?" I responded smugly.

I was staring into the nothingness of my new living room.

"All you have to do is go to church and start reading the Bible," he said. Then he added, "And the rest will take care of itself!"

"I don't knooooooow," I whined. "I'm not a church person anymore. I'm *spiritual* but not religious. I was forced to go as a kid. I'd rather be brunching than worshipping on Sundays."

I had never told him about my meeting with Margaret, or about how I'd been praying The Lord's Prayer every day for the last year and a half.

"Listen—you are very smart and wise about life in your own cynical way. But have you ever thought to critically examine the Bible like you critically examined textbooks when we were at Georgetown? You can't really master anything until you're well read in a subject. The Bible is no different."

He made a very logical argument. I wouldn't dare do the same thing to my political science books in grad school. It would be looked down upon as lazy and anti-intellectual.

"All you need to do, Mike, is open your mind and your heart. That's it. Just be open-minded. You have nothing to lose. And read all those books we bought—that's the type of education you need to succeed!"

I trusted him because his was a model life. He wasn't some addict trying to lecture another addict about recovery. He was a happy, fulfilled person trying to save me from myself. All I had to do was let him.

Chapter Fourteen

WASH, RINSE, REPEAT

Adam and I were sitting at a bar in Shaw, the newest and trendiest neighborhood everyone was moving to, southeast of Columbia Heights. A few years ago, no one came to this part of town. Now, it was the most expensive place to live. I didn't understand how something like that could happen so fast. Who were the people in charge of things like this? How did they decide the economic order for the rest of us? I was unsure how to operate in a world controlled by other people.

"Yo, are you on Snapchat yet?" Adam asked.

We were at a cocktail bar, the kind where the bartenders wore fancy clothes and charged fifteen dollars per drink. I was sipping on an Old Fashioned, the type of cocktail a person who respects order and tradition drinks. Each time I brought the glass to my lips, I'd get a whiff of the bourbon and orange zest and feel so satisfied with how cosmopolitan I had become.

"No. What's that?" I said.

"It's a new app for sending dick pics to chicks," he said. "But here's the catch—they disappear *for-ever*, so you don't have to worry about your dick floating around on the internet anymore. *But*, if she wants to save your pic she can take a screenshot, and the app will tell you."

Unexcited, I said, "Wow, sounds interesting."

I was exhausted by all the new *must-have* apps that kept coming out. It was too much to keep up with, and most of them didn't make my life any better. All the apps on my phone felt like a bunch of digital pets that I had to feed, walk, and spend time with. I resented them.

"Don't you understand what this means, man?" he said. "It means there's an easy way to get laid!"

"Nice. Maybe I'll try it out," I said. "Has it worked for you?"

"Not yet. I got two screenshot notifications this week—for, *you know*, some select pics I sent—and I'm currently DMing both chicks. They seem hungry."

"What does DM mean?"

"Jesus Christ, Mike! Do you live under a freakin' rock? It means direct message."

"Oh. That makes sense," I said, and then took the last sip of my drink. "Well, I hope it works out and leads to a meaningful, long-term relationship with the future mother of your children."

"Oh, fuck you. Take the stick out of your ass."

We both laughed and then ordered another round. Adam was always giving me advice about hooking up and dating, though it was more the former because very few people did the latter these days. The smart phone had changed everything. It was rewriting the rules of engagement between men and women, and I was scared I was being left behind. It seemed like I couldn't find love.

"So, like, do any of your hookups every turn into regular relationships?" I asked.

"Yeah, one of them I would call my girlfriend—last spring," he said. "Remember *fire crotch*? That was her. Turns out I liked more than her freckles!"

We both laughed. Adam rarely opened up to me about anything too personal. I was never sure if he was the most success-ful guy out there chasing women or if he was just as lonely and miserable as I was. It seemed like he was always going on dates, and whenever we would go out with a group, he'd usually have some new girl hanging on his arm. I guess he knew what he was doing.

"Isn't it wild to think that our parents were all married by now?" I said. "I've been thinking about that a lot lately. My aunt and uncle had my cousin when they were our age. Can you im-agine being in charge of a kid right now? We wouldn't be able to be *here*, at this bar on a weeknight. In the city!"

"Yeah, man," he said. "But our generation's doing things better. We get to have way more fun and see more things and go more places and sleep with more people. It's the way things should be! I bet they look at us and are *soooooo* jealous."

We both downed our cocktails and decided to order shots next. The bartender, who was wearing a white dress shirt with a black tie, looked at his watch and made a funny face. I wasn't sure if he was telling us he liked our style or if we'd better slow down. I wish he would have just said what he wanted to say without the guessing game.

"Adam, think about it!" I said. "You and I have had more sex—more *orgasms*—than all our dads, uncles, and grandpas—COMBINED! And we're only twenty-four! This can't be natu-ral."

"Natural, smatural," he said. "The difference, Mike, is feminism and The Pill. I was reading about the history of the sexual revolution for my mid-century American politics class, and it wasn't all about the hippies, you know. Feminism and The Pill gave *us* the keys to the kingdom. So why the hell are you complaining about it?"

He made a good point. I guess I'd never thought of it like that. I didn't know how things were supposed to be. It was all so confusing.

"Listen, I just want to find someone to settle down with," I said.

"Are you kidding me?" he said. "Jesus Christ, man."

"No, no," I said. "Well, I mean, sure—not right now. I mean, you know, I want to be married one day." I looked down. "But, yeah—I'm having fun now."

"That's more like it!" he said as he slapped me on the back. "Just keep having all the sex you can. The rest will work itself out."

With that, he slammed his shot glass down, got up, and went to the bathroom. I stared into the amber liquid in my glass and wondered whether I would ever find Her. I needed to find the person who would complete me, who would make me happy. Where was She?

• • •

I was mesmerized by the new world I had just entered, a world that I would be occupying for the next fifty years. I was the newest member of the white-collar, creative class, the professionals whose ideas, intellectual property, and services ran the world yet produced nothing tangible. And, oh, what a world it was!

There was a dress code: business casual in a muted, traditional color palette. There were rules and values to abide by: always show deference to the partners and clients, respond to emails within twenty-four hours, and don't make excuses. And there was a whole lexicon I had to learn: one was supposed to *touch base* and *circle back* and *follow up*, always with a focus on *creating synergy* and *being data-driven* and *looking for opportunities to create efficiencies across silos*. I didn't understand half the stuff that came out of people's mouths, but I dutifully played along and did what they did.

On my third day, I found out that I'd be doing work in support of a Senate re-election campaign. It was exhilarating from the very beginning: the late-night conference calls, the private polling we used to inform our strategy, the campaign staff who always seemed to be yelling, the people I saw on cable news coming to our office for meetings. It was like I'd been invited behind the red curtain to see how our political system *actually* worked. I had made it into the power players' network!

I liked my team a lot. We were small, just five of us, which made us tight-knit. There was me, the rookie; three other twenty-something guys who were the consultants; and our boss, Charles. It was the first time in my life that I felt part of a fraternal group, like I belonged, like we were all in it together. It's like I had brothers and a dad, except we were colleagues and weren't obligated to each other. We shifted with ease between discussing client deliverables and discussing the hottest piece of ass in the office.

Our client, on the other hand, was *not* someone we fantasized about. Her name was Rosemary, a deputy campaign manager, but we internally referred to her as B.R.—The Black Rose. She was a raging bitch, an emotionally volatile, angry woman who thought she had to walk like a man and talk like a man in order to do her job well. The problem was that the type of man in charge she modelled herself after was The Asshole, which, like The Black Rose, no one likes working with—or for.

Each workday began the same way. I would wake up at six fifteen, brush my teeth, drink an energy drink, and open up my work laptop. I always started by searching on Google for media mentions of our client's boss—the senator—and his opponent. I'd scroll through Twitter to see what the latest outrage was about, then I'd go to all the national newspaper websites and scan the headlines. After that, I'd go to the cable news websites and watch any controversial TV segments from the night before. I'd draft an email and type a list of relevant political headlines, link to their original sources, and write one to three bullet points with summary information, no less and no more. Then I'd send the email to my team, and Charles would forward it to our partners. I never knew what my press clippings were used for or why they mattered. All I knew is they were important to our business.

I usually sent the email by seven, and then I'd shower and get dressed and run out the door to catch the Metro. After a hellish Metro transfer at the Gallery Place station, I'd get to our firm's office around eight. But first, I always stopped at the coffee shop on the bottom floor to order a large black coffee for breakfast. Then I'd take the elevator up to the eleventh floor and go to my cubicle. I'd pull my laptop out of my briefcase and log in to read all my unread emails, always filtering for our client's messages first. Then I would write bullet-by-bullet talking points for the first meeting of the day. I had to be prepared.

The Nine AM, as we referred to our daily morning conference call with our client, was brutal. B.R. was a one-woman firing squad who assembled tens of people each morning for her ritual fusillading. There were the other consultants from New York, plus the field staff in the senator's home state of Kentucky. Sometimes, there were senior advisors calling in from the senator's office on Capitol Hill, and we always assumed there were other silent callers from the White House or party leadership on the line, too.

Each meeting would start with our client's chief of staff asking for each functional group's status. When it was almost our team's turn, the core of my stomach and my legs would always tremble. I was scared to death. If you didn't have the right answer, B.R. would publicly execute you. It was a bloody way to start the day.

After The Nine AM was over, we would have our team huddle, which was the best part of the day. This is when we got to breathe a collective sigh of relief and come up with our plan of attack for the day. There was always so much energy and urgency during these meetings. I always walked away ready to conquer my job, ready to prove to my peers and our client and the firm that I was meant to do great things and would become a consultant in no time.

"I really think we ought to be focusing on getting the campaign to procure new digital tools to decrease the feedback loop between canvassers and decision-makers," I said. "Their current method of not communicating across the business units after each direct mail campaign results in bloat and ineffective response to changes in the national media coverage."

I was arguing for something that seemed so obvious to me. But Charles was not having it.

"Listen, kid. You're still green—you've still gotta' cut your teeth in this business before you start callin' the shots. Until then, you can leave the big strategy up to me and the rest of the boys."

Charles was tall, with ruddy cheeks and a round belly that his tie called attention to. He looked like he had a full head of hair from the front, but when he turned around, you could see a bald spot in the back. He only wore white dress shirts, the same ones I now wore, and his leather loafers had tassels.

"But the client has clearly indicated to me—to *us*—that we should explore *all* options, not just traditional solutions."

I would not relent. I *knew* I was right. The data supported it.

"The client is wrong," he shot back. "We are doing quick wins to justify billing $300 an hour—each!"

The rest of the day would be filled with meeting after meeting after meeting. Sometimes I would remember to eat lunch, but most days I just kept working. There simply was no time. Around six each night, we would walk across the street to the corner market and stock up on coffee, energy drinks, potato chips, and candy bars, expensing everything back to the firm. Together, we would sit down at a conference room table and break bread, feasting on these synthetic foodstuffs. It sustained us for our final few hours of work each night.

Around seven-forty-five, I'd make a call to my guy, Hakim, an Ethiopian cab driver I'd befriended one drunken night in Adams Morgan, and schedule a pickup. He'd drive from wherever he was to come get me so I didn't have to wait twenty minutes for the Metro, since trains barely ran after the rush hours. I billed all of these rides to my firm, who in turn billed it all to the client. It was part of capitalism's rules of engagement. At first, it felt dirty. But after a while, I got used to the grime. It was a small perk I couldn't refuse to use.

When I got home, I'd usually eat hummus and pita chips for my final meal, drink some super greens juice for nutrition, take a shower, brush my teeth, and then collapse into bed. All the personal text messages and emails would go unread, my eyes and mind too tired to process and respond. Friends and family were now the exclusive domain of the weekend.

Wash, rinse, repeat.

Wash, rinse, repeat.

Wash, rinse, repeat.

We worked so much. We worked twelve-hour days, five days a week—and usually Sunday nights to prepare for Mondays. This was my new life as a working professional. It wasn't the glamorous work life I'd always imagined. I thought I would be working somewhere else, doing something else, achieving great things and changing the world.

Yet here I was.

Chapter Fifteen

THE GRIND

I was walking south down Eighth Street in Capitol Hill after taking the Metro across town. There weren't very many people outside because of how cold it was, but a couple homeless men came out of nowhere and started following me, asking for money. I obliged because I am a good person.

"Hey, Mike!" Matt said as he waved at me.

It was Sunday morning, and I had agreed to go to church with Matt. As I approached, he came toward me and then wrapped his arms around me. I could feel a loose brick under my right foot, which unsteadied me.

"Hey, man," I said as I leaned into his hug without lifting my arms.

"I'm really glad you came," he said. "I think you'll like what you hear. And if you don't—well, it'll just be ninety minutes of your life that you won't ever have to waste again."

He led me into the church, which wasn't actually a church but an old movie theatre that was being used as a church. The outside of the theatre looked like the old-fashioned kind you'd see on TV shows or at Disneyland, the kind with the ornate awning and giant metal sign with flashing light bulbs. The inside looked just like a movie theatre, too, with rows of red velvet chairs and walls made of curtains. There was a big movie screen that was being used to project not a film but church teachings. In front of the screen, where there was supposed to be empty space, was a rock band and a podium-as-pulpit.

We walked up a ramp that hugged the theatre wall and turned into a row about halfway up. We were greeted by Lauren, Matt's girlfriend for the past seven months.

"Hi, Mike!" she said as she leaned in to hug me.

"Hey, Lauren. How's it going?"

"I'm woooonderful. It's a beautiful day today. I'm so glad to be here with you and Matt."

She was bubbly but not overflowing with gas.

We sat down in our seats, and the chairs reclined just like in a real movie theatre. I looked around and noticed that everyone was youthful and pretty, their skinny jeans and T-shirts communicating that they were *cool with god* as they sipped their lattes. Everyone was white.

The lights dimmed, and the sound of the strums of a single guitar filled the theatre. The anticipation was growing; the show was about to start. As the tempo of the guitar sped up, other instruments layered on top. The sound was getting louder and fuller. The lights went dark, and then a single spotlight shined down. I clasped the ends of the arms of my chair, readying myself for what was about to happen.

A few seconds later, a man entered under the light. He had shoulder-length dark brown hair and a thin beard. He was dressed in black from head to toe, wearing an earpiece like a headliner at a concert and holding a mic. Then he began to pace in a small circle as his head bobbed up and down. He brought the mic to his mouth and said, "Can you feel the Spirit moving within you? Can you feel your soul stirring?" He paused and then added, "Are you ready to send all your worldly problems to the cross of Christ and be renewed, together, as one body?"

I looked at the people on my left, and their faces said *yes*.

They were so ready. I felt uncomfortable and wanted to sneak out, but I knew I couldn't do that to Matt. The music was entering the climax of its crescendo. I could feel the sonic buildup inside of me, just like at a concert. The crowd was waiting with joyful anticipation for the sounds to peak and then release like a flood.

And then, the drop.

The entire band and backup singers and lights burst to life. "Everybody stand up!" he shouted. "Let's rejoice in what we know to be true!"

The crowd leapt to their feet and sang along to the lyrics that were projected on the screen. I put my hands in my pockets and tensed my shoulders. I wanted to disappear, to not be there. I leaned over to Matt and said, "Wow—what an opening!"

I always cracked stupid jokes when I was nervous.

"Isn't it great?!" he said. "Just let go and enjoy it! It'll be awesome, just you wait!"

I stood there without moving my body, too anxious to let go. I scanned all the people around me and saw genuine elation in their faces. I couldn't believe it. They looked just like the faces at all the clubs and concerts I'd been to, except sober. Their eyes were closed as they lifted their arms into the air and reached toward heaven. They were singing along to the music with such emotion painted across their faces, a diorama of feelings that silently communicated their hopes and fears and triumphs and tribulations to all whose eyes were open. I wanted to feel what they were feeling. But how? I was depressed and medicated, unable to feel good things like a normal person.

The music ended and everyone sat down, and then the pastor walked out to the pulpit. I leaned over to Matt and whispered, "Do you actually believe in this stuff?"

"Yeah, I do" he said. "Even if it's all made up, it doesn't matter. It provides a program for life that provides true freedom to its members. Why do you think everyone here is so happy?"

I looked around. He was right—everyone was so freaking happy, just like Matt. They were always smiling and always making eye contact. It was strange yet so human, like the way things should be—the way things used to be. Before TVs and computers and video games and smart phones ruined everything.

The pastor started preaching but I wasn't paying attention. I was too occupied with the realization that there was another parallel way of life that existed and that could possibly be better than my own. *How did I get here? Who are these people? What are they worshipping? And why the hell did I become friends with Matt?*

He just showed up one day! I didn't even want to be his friend at first. Yet here we were, sitting next to each other—at church. It felt like life just happened and put me on a path that I wasn't walking toward on my own.

I couldn't stop thinking about all the angles informing my life's circumstances. I was overwhelmed with realization after realization after realization. What if all the things I thought were true were actually lies? What if moving to the East Coast and going to Georgetown was a mistake? What if I wasn't meant to find love and purpose in D.C.? What if I was in the wrong place? Maybe I was working too much and not sleeping enough. Or maybe it was the pills messing with my mind.

Before I knew it, the service ended. I was in a daze, still sitting in my chair.

"What'd ya think?" Matt said.

He was hovering over me to indicate that I needed to stand up and move. So I stood up and considered the words I was about to speak so as not to offend or condescend.

"I liked it!" I said. It was a lie. "It was…slick. Very well produced. Everyone was so nice."

We exited our row, went down the ramp, and walked through the lobby to the front doors. On our way out, someone handed us each a leaflet.

"What'd ya think about the Gospel message?" he pressed.

We were standing outside on the sidewalk. I didn't really remember what the message had been about. I had been too busy observing the people and thinking about my life. I glanced down at the leaflet. Conveniently, it had a summary of the service's Bible readings, themes, and action items for the week. In big bold letters it read *SWALLOW YOUR PRIDE.*

"I liked how he talked about moving beyond our human pride," I said. "Like, how he emphasized that we are all human and react to things in the same way, you know? That pride handicaps most people from doing what's right."

I couldn't believe those words had come out of my mouth. In reality, I thought it was too contemporary. I was looking for some vague old order, some purer form of worship—and this wasn't it. This church was too much like regular life. It was profane.

"It was very modern—not like my Catholic church growing up," I said with a grin. "Very refreshing," I added.

Matt and Lauren stared at me with such intent, eating up every word I was dishing out. Their heads nodded in agreement with each word I spoke.

"Ain't that the truth, Mike?" Matt said. He wrapped his arm around Lauren's shoulder and pulled her in. "Well, what'd ya say about next week?"

"Too soon."

We started walking together toward the Metro.

"Hey, I did want to ask you something.," I said as I turned toward him. "Do you have any advice, for me, about work? I'm just so tired already, and I haven't even been in my job for a year, you know. And, I guess, I don't really know what to think because it's...not what I thought it would be—work—you know?"

"Just pray about it," he said without having to think about it. "And read the Bible, Mike! And, of course, all your books."

He smiled, and so did Lauren. I smiled back, gave them both a hug, and said goodbye. Then I started walking in the other direction. I pulled out my earbuds, opened my music app, and scrolled to my Life Soundtrack. I tapped shuffle and sound surrounded me, blocking out all the noises of the people and cars and buses that were around me. Then I began my journey home.

• • •

Work got harder as the months went on. There was no respite from the grind. I kept waiting for a break, for a moment to
catch my breath. But it never came. This was the way it was in
America. Not like I thought it would be, not like it was in other
places, not like it should be. It was work all the time. There was
no life to this life.

Charles told us last week that we would be getting a new
team member for a new client project, something that had to do
with connecting voters' social media profiles to the voter registration rolls we already had. He was vague in his language about
why, exactly, we were getting someone new. Something about
needing a jolt to our system and *maximizing our potential* on
capturing future work for the firm.

Today was Monday, and we were waiting for this person to
show up and start creating our work plan together. As the five
of us were walking back to our desks after going to The Nine
AM, I heard a *click-clack* sound ricochet down the hallway. It
was getting louder and louder, the sound of confidence coming
our way.

We all stared in awe at her grand entrance to our stark white
office space. As she crossed the threshold from tile to carpet,
she flipped her hair back and pulled her work bag tight against
her shoulder. Her hair was auburn and shiny, and the office
lights reflected off its strands and radiated outward. Her dress
was sleeveless and short, fitted but not slutty. Her calves were
shapely and slightly flexed because of the green stilettos she
was wearing.

"Hello, gentlemen," she said. "My name is Amanda, and
I'm here to get this project moving."

She was so direct. She was so confident. She was so sexy.

I leaned forward and extended my arm out. "Hi, I'm Mike,"
I said. "It's nice to meet you!"

"And you," she said back without missing a beat as she

shook my hand with a perfectly firm grip. "I look forward to fleshing things out for you and collaborating on solutions for our client."

The other guys exchanged niceties with her, and then Charles leaned forward. He puffed his chest out, grabbed his belt to pull his pants up, put his hands on his hips, and rocked his legs back and forth as if he were finding the perfect position to do a squat. He always did this little physical routine when asserting his dominance.

"Alright, alright, alright, you kids—let's get going—to the conference room, now!" he said as he pointed the way with his arm.

I plunged my hands into my pants pockets to readjust my erect self. I could feel it trying to burst through my zipper. I needed it to go sideways, so I did my best to guide it ninety degrees to the left. The problem with wearing suit pants was that the thin fabric didn't leave much to the imagination.

I was so hard and horny for her. Of all the possible side effects of the pills that I could have experienced—nausea, upset stomach, vomiting, headaches, death—I experienced increased libido around the clock, which wasn't even near the top of the list of the most common side effects on the back of the bottle. It would've been great if I had a girlfriend or an F.W.B.—a friend with benefits. But I didn't; I was alone. Just me, my hand, and my member. And my P.I.E.D. It didn't make any sense. How could I have erectile dysfunction *and* increased libido at the same time?

I rushed ahead of the group to be a gentleman and hold the door open for Amanda.

"Let go of the handle," she said as she walked toward the conference room.

"Wha—what do you mean?" I said.

"I don't need a man to do anything for me. You are being patronizing, and it's actually pretty demeaning, to be honest."

I couldn't believe it. I was just trying to be a nice guy!

Once we were all inside, Charles closed the door and then

turned around to face us.

"OK, we're safe," he said. "Time for real talk."

He walked over to the speakerphone and pressed the call button. The deep hum of the dial tone came on, and then he pressed the button again to hang up. What this little ritual meant was that we were now cleared to talk crap about our clients—without anyone eavesdropping. We were two-faced for a living: kind and agreeable in front of clients but cruel and intractable behind closed doors. You had to act differently depending on your audience, which was one of the key lessons for young professionals in D.C. that I was learning. I had to become a chameleon.

"Amanda is here to provide fresh thinking—*strategic* thinking—for our new project. You jokers can't get it done on your own," he said.

My stomach sank.

"And I'm not risking our year-end bonuses because we can't get our fucking act together!"

He was raising his voice. I knew he was getting fired up because the blood vessels on his temples flared out each time he punctuated his sentences. We usually got bonuses of between $2,000 and $5,000 twice a year if we met our project goals and the firm's annual strategic goals—well, my peers and I did. Charles, since he was a managing consultant, could get up to $30,000. It was a ton of extra money, and it was the only motivating factor for caring at all and working hard and staying late. It made it worth it—or, at least, it made it *feel* like it was worth it when the cash appeared in my checking account for my first bonus (sans forty percent taken out for taxes).

"You guys have been spinning your wheels for three weeks now. We were supposed to provide a plan to John a week ago, and we haven't delivered shit. Amanda's here to whip this team into shape."

John was our client's boss, The Asshole who worked seventy-hour weeks, ran triathlons, and was banging our office manager. She was a kid fresh out of college, and he was married with three kids. John was a mean guy, no doubt formed into a monster because of the insane pressure that comes with running a national-level Senate campaign.

"John knows we're late?" I said.

Charles snapped his head toward me and held a long, uncomfortable glare before opening his mouth. I knew in that moment that I shouldn't have said what I said.

"Yeah, Mike. John fucking knows we're *fuc-king* late because he called me into his office in Farragut last week and reamed me out! Do you guys even understand how much shit I take to protect you? I'm constantly having to answer questions I don't know because we can't get our shit together. And now we're at risk—and the partners know about it!"

His temples were now beet red, and the veins looked like they were about to burst.

"Do you have any other smart-aleck comments for me?"

I didn't say a word. I stared into my lap, wishing I didn't have all my student loans so I wouldn't have to work this stupid job. I just wanted to be happy, to do something meaningful. I wanted to do work that used my talents, but I didn't know how to find it or whether it would pay enough for me to live on. I wanted to be anywhere in the world except in this dingy conference room with florescent lights burning holes into my eyes. I just wanted to be in love already and fulfilling my destiny. I thought I would have both by now. What had gone wrong?

"Listen, guys—I mean, guys and *girls*. I mean, listen team!" he said. He looked at Amanda to acknowledge her presence. "We found the right road, but we took the wrong direction. And now we have to fix it."

My stomach sank again. This was consulting code for *someone's going to get fired*, and now we were all put on notice. *Crap! I can't get fired! I can't afford to get fired! I can't let my family down.* My heart was racing.

"We've figured out that the client's direct mail campaign increased voter registration by seven percent versus the four percent of the digital marketing campaign. But what's the so-what?"

This was more consulting code. It meant that our analysis wasn't good enough, not even good enough for a philandering asshole paying our firm $300 an hour for each of us to figure out how he could get his candidate another six years in office. I hated everything about the situation. This was not what I wanted to spend all my time and energy on. I hated everyone and everything that led me to this place, to this job, to this life.

I stared up at the fluorescent lights, closed my eyes, and zoned out to the orange circles that were moving inside my eyelids. I needed to get the hell out of dodge. But how? I was sending money home every month to my mom, and there was barely any left over for me to spend on stuff everyone else had, like nice clothes or the latest smart phone model. And no one had told me about all the taxes, for godssake! I didn't understand how I could work so much yet have so little at the end of the month after all the deductions for things I never signed up for: disability, Social Security, Medicare, state taxes, federal taxes, and environmental cleanup.

But it didn't matter, anyway. All I could do was keep working to get a promotion to consultant so I'd make more money. Then everything would be OK. I just knew it.

Chapter Sixteen

PANIC ATTACK

There are four types of people I know who don't have student loans: rich kids with college savings accounts or trust funds, racial minority and victim-status kids who got full-ride scholarships, Chinese kids of wealthy Communist party leaders, and Christian kids whose parents adhered to sound financial principles based on teachings in the Bible (or some rough approximation thereof). Adam fell into the first group while Matt fell into the last. I wasn't in any special category. I had so much student loan debt it felt like being shackled to a ball and chain. I had never thought twice about taking out all the loans for college and grad school because I had no other choice—the tuition was just too damn high.

When I started college, I briefly romanticized about being the type of student whose humble middle-class roots would instill in me a drive to pull myself up by my bootstraps. I would work two jobs and go to school full time and do all my readings and turn in all my assignments on time—and never complain. I would stay up late every night, including Saturdays and Sundays, to work toward my degree and only sleep four hours each night. I would subsist on cheap noodles and instant coffee because it would be all I could afford and I just needed to get it done. I would be dignified because of my self-sacrifice.

But the economics didn't work out because I *still* worked two jobs in undergrad and *still* couldn't afford tuition and rent. I *had* to take out student loans. But it never felt real because I never saw the money. I didn't have to work for it, and I didn't feel gratification in getting it. I just borrowed and borrowed and borrowed to get me through my four years of undergrad, and then borrowed and borrowed some more to get me through my two years of grad school. Taking out loans for my bachelor's degree was prudent; taking out loans for my master's degree was indulgent. But I had to! There were no jobs, and I needed to be competitive; a Georgetown master's degree promised certain things.

Nothing ever felt more real in my whole entire life than the day I got my first student loan repayment bill in the mail, exactly six months after I graduated with my master's degree. The letter said it was from the U.S. Department of Education, but when I opened it and unfolded the sheets of paper, it said my repayments would be serviced by some company I'd never heard of. In big bold black characters at the top of the first sheet was a five-figure number: *$97,273.52*.

My stomach sank. This was the total amount of loans I had taken out to finance my six years of school. I scanned down the page until my eyes stopped at another number: *$837.13*.

My chest tightened. This was the minimum monthly payment I would have to make. And the first monthly payment was due in *two weeks*. I shuffled to the second sheet of paper to find another number, this one in small print: *$201,033.07*.

I gasped for air. This was the total amount I would repay over twenty years with all the interest that would be added to the principal. I would end up paying double for my degrees. What a racket! No one had told me it would be like this! Where were the guidance counselors and financial planners and responsible adults when I needed them to explain the system to me? I couldn't believe it. I felt betrayed. I felt trapped.

My breaths shortened, and I started to hyperventilate. My chest felt as if it were burning from the inside out. My stomach sank so low it felt as if it were on the ground. My body warmed, and my skin went flush. My muscles tightened and spasmed. I didn't know what was happening, which scared me and seemed to make it worse. Was I possessed by a demon? Was I dying of a heart attack? Was this the death I had wanted just a few years ago?

I paced back and forth from the living room to the bedroom and back again to try to make it stop. I started shaking my limbs, trying to rid myself of the thing that was possessing my body. I clenched my fists and slammed them against the wall, trying to stop the thing that had overtaken me. My body was convulsing, and I was scared.

It just kept going; it just kept happening. I didn't know what to do! I thought I was suffocating, that my face must be turning blue. But then I felt so hot, like my hair must be on fire. I thought I was burning to death. Is this what hell feels like?

I didn't know what else to do, so I ran into the kitchen, opened the refrigerator, and took a pitcher of water and dumped it over my head. The cold water shocked my system, its chilly liquid meeting my hot skin and creating fusion as it rushed down my body.

I stood there like a pathetic person in the puddle of water that was forming across the kitchen floor. I put my hands on the counter to stabilize myself. I took a long, deep breath and then exhaled slowly. Then another and another and another.

My muscles stopped twitching, and my skin cooled. My chest loosened, and my stomach moved back into my torso where it belonged. I stood there, confused and mortified, in soaked clothes. All I could hear was the *drip-drip-drip* of the water falling from my body onto the wood floor.

I think I had a panic attack. Now, I was full of rage.

I walked into the living room and looked down at the video game console I hadn't touched in years. I had decided long ago

I was too mature to play video games, too important for such child's play. But in that moment, I decided I wanted to blow some strangers' heads off, so I reached down and pressed the power button until the lime green ring glowed to life. I took my favorite game out of its plastic case and dropped the disk in the console's tray. And then, I went to war. I stood in front of the TV, dripping water onto the rug, as my thumbs triggered a rapid-fire stream of bullets into every person that crossed my path.

But it wasn't enough. I needed to clear my head, to sweat out all my anger and stress and rage. I needed to run.

I put on my gym shoes, grabbed my earbuds and P.W.K., and darted out of the apartment. I did some stretches, put my earbuds in, and tapped play on my Life Soundtrack. I started running south, through the neighborhood and down The Exorcist Steps until I reached the Potomac. Then I ran on a path that hugged the river.

I ran hard, my legs pounding the pavement with every beat of the music blasting through my ears. I didn't know what I was running to or running from. I just ran.

I thought about everything that had happened since I had gotten to D.C. I hated that things weren't working out like I thought they would. I hated that I was still single and hadn't found Her yet. I hated that my dreams of becoming a diplomat were dashed. Most of all, I hated that I had tried to kill myself and that I was still taking pills.

I could feel my lungs expanding and contracting fast and heavy and see the sweat dripping off my arms and legs.

And then I stopped.

I had made it to the top of the stairs of the Lincoln Memorial. I looked out at the National Mall, at all the white marble monuments lit up against the dark gray sky, and thought about how I was conditioning myself for the life I was supposed to live. *I am strong, and everyone else is weak. I am the one who will rise above my lot in life and make it.*

Then I raced down the steps, feeling the *tap-tap-tap* of my shoes against the marble stairs. I ran north through Foggy Bottom, past traffic circles with statues of guys on horses, over Rock Creek Park, and into Georgetown. I sprinted across M Street, through red lights and moving cars that didn't see me coming, until I was back at my apartment. Back to where I started from.

I leaned forward and put my hands on my knees to steady myself as I panted. Sweat dripped off my face onto the sidewalk and started to make abstract patterns. I looked up at my bedroom window. All I saw were horizontal lines from the window blinds, the light shining from the inside.

I realized I was living the American Dream.

• • •

I was riding an uptown bus late one night on my way home from a client dinner downtown. I didn't know why, but I was in a reflective mood. I decided I didn't want to take the Metro and be underground, but I also didn't want the speed of a cab to take me door to door. I just wanted to take in the city and its people while thinking about my life. I just wanted to be.

I looked outside the window and saw rows of tents stream by. They were set up by the homeless people who camped out on the sidewalks at night after all the politicians and power players and lobbyists and bigwigs went home to the suburbs or Georgetown or Capitol Hill. As the bus idled at a red light, I looked up and saw a giant hotel building made entirely of glass. Most of the building was dark except for a smattering of rooms that created a lit-up checkerboard pattern. I wondered who decided to turn the lights on in the empty rooms. More than that, I wondered why we didn't let the homeless people sleep in the empty beds in the empty building.

My Life Soundtrack was playing, and I was scrolling through Instagram, first to check on my Instafamily, then to pass the time. The kids in my Instafamily were growing up so fast it was hard to believe. Sara was such a good sister to Silas. Though she could be a little bossy at times, I could always see the joy on her face as she cared for her little brother. She protected him wherever they went, no matter what they were doing.

In one photo, she was holding his hand tight and leading him up a staircase one step at a time. In another, she stood guard to block him from the edge of a swimming pool, keeping him from falling in. And in another, she was holding him as he cried after scraping his knee, consoling him through his pain. I wondered if I would ever have a family like theirs one day.

I swiped back to my main feed and scrolled through all the other photos. At the top were photos from close friends and family, but there were also funny memes and ironic social commentary and musicians and artists and local businesses now in the mix. I also followed amateur athletes and outdoor adventurists and vagabonds and hippies, who all lived counter-cultural lives. Their photos reminded me that I could escape my life at any moment and do something else. Be somewhere else. Be someone else. Have any other life than the one I currently had. All these lives on Instagram were better than mine.

I opened the Google app and searched: *how to improve chances with women*. It gave me almost two billion results. Where to even start? I was overwhelmed by all the answers and not sure which ones were true and which ones were made up. Then I opened Facebook and clicked on the profiles of women who were mutual friends—whatever the algorithm gave me. Maybe She was closer than I thought, someone who knew someone I knew, too. Maybe I needed to try harder and cold message a bunch of cute brunettes on Facebook.

I tapped the button on the top of my phone to turn off the screen. I slid it into my pocket and looked up to stare out the bus window. Deep down, I hated Instagram and Facebook and Twitter and all the social media accounts I had been peer-pressured to create over the years, even though I now spent most of my free time using them. I didn't have cable TV, so my phone was my main screen. But I didn't understand why everyone was spending so much time online in an alternate digital world, instead of offline in the real physical world. I wondered if the apps ruined my chances of finding Her. I wondered if technology was keeping me from finding my destiny.

The bus was getting closer to my stop, so I pressed the button on my earbud string to stop the music and then took them out of my ears, wrapped them around my hand, and put them in my briefcase. It was the public transit version of turning the stereo volume down in your car when you got close to your final destination. I looked around the bus and saw that every single person was hunched over, their faces illuminated by the glowing screens that entranced them. I wondered if they would all be hunchbacked when they got old, their necks and spines permanently fused into a position of digital consumption.

The bus's hydraulics hissed as its right side lowered to the curb and an elderly black man boarded. He took a seat in the handicap section, placed his cane underneath the chair, and then pulled out his phone and cassette player. He put on his headphones, the same kind I used to have as a kid in the 90s, and then fiddled with the player until music started playing.

But he forgot to plug his headphones into the audio jack. He didn't seem to know that everyone could hear his music, that his private moment was now public. My stomach sank for him. I looked around to see if anyone else noticed, but everyone had their own earbuds in or headphones on. Nobody did anything about it. Nobody was paying attention.

I didn't know what I should do. I stared at the strip of blue LED lights that illuminated the row of seats he was sitting in. Should I say something? Would it be weird to just waltz over and let him know? What would I want someone to do if I were him? Why wasn't anyone else doing anything? Why wasn't anyone else paying attention to what was going on right in front of them?

I decided I had to help him. I stood up and grabbed the yellow loops hanging from the stainless steel rails, one by one, until I made my way over to the man.

"Sir," I said. He didn't hear me. "Sir!" I said louder.

His shoulders popped up because I startled him. Then he turned his head toward me, his mouth agape.

"Sir—your headphones are not plugged into your cassette player," I said as I made exaggerated motions with my hands as if he were deaf. "We can hear your music."

He looked down, confused, and then traced his hand against the headphone's main wire until he made it to the end, the metal stereo plug dangling against his leg. He grabbed the plug with his right hand and positioned the player with his left hand until the two made contact, ready to transfer sound directly to his ears.

Then he set the player down on the seat next to him and stretched out both hands toward me. I held out my right hand in return, and then he grabbed my forearm with both his hands and squeezed hard.

"Thank you, son," he said.

Chapter Seventeen

JUST SWIPE RIGHT

It was a Saturday afternoon and spring had finally arrived, the air not quite warm but not quite cool. I knew it was spring because I sneezed uncontrollably all day long, my sinuses no match for the pollen. Adam and I were walking around Eastern Market on Capitol Hill, browsing the fresh produce on the tables that lined the covered outdoor walkway. We didn't intend to buy anything, but it was a thing to do and a place to be.

"Hey, man," I said. "Do you have any advice about, you know, dating? About finding someone who's, you know, worth it?"

"Are you on Tinder yet?" Adam said.

"What's that? Does it have to do with starting a fire?" I said, half-serious.

"No, man! It's a hook-up app disguised as a dating app," he said. "For guys, it's basically like being a kid in a candy shop. The chicks put out on this thing! It's got a higher R.O.I. than Snapchat."

He said it with such glee. We walked past rows of blossoming flowers in sidewalk planters that had little black fences on three sides. I couldn't believe how vivid the flowers were, how just a few weeks ago everything was dreary and gray but now everything was bright and colorful. Plants weren't like this in San Bernardino. Everything looked the same all year round back home: brown.

"Have you been on any dates?"

"Oh, yeah!" he said. "But here's the thing—there's an unspoken, agreed upon rule that if you take the time and energy to show up in person on a first date, you might as well go home together and get off. So once you start chattin' with a chick and she agrees to meet up, you're basically guaranteed to get laid."

"Wow," I said. "That's pretty wild."

I could smell fresh-baked pizza in the air. I craned my neck to try to find the source of the best scent ever, but didn't spot any stalls. Maybe the pizza was inside the market building.

"Yeah, man," he said. "Gay guys have had apps like this for yeeeeears. They don't waste any time before hooking up with each other. Now it's our turn!"

We both laughed. It seemed so ridiculous, and even too good to be true, that you could get sex after only one date. I guess this was equality for my generation. I guess Tinder was a sign of progress.

"This is the future, man. In a couple years, everyone will only be finding each other using apps."

Adam was looking down at his phone, his thumb moving too fast for my eyes to follow. He leaned over and angled the screen toward me, but that caused us to block the flow of people coming in and out of the building. All of D.C. seemed to be outside thawing out from the long, cold winter. After receiving a few passive-aggressive shoulder swipes, we moved to the side.

"See, it's super easy," he said. "Just a few photos and a couple sentences and you're done."

"Nice!" I said. "Do you have any advice for setting up my profile?"

I didn't *want* to find women using an app, but if this was

going to be the only way to meet my future wife, to meet Her, then what choice did I have? The world was moving so fast it was hard to keep up. Sometimes I wished it were the 1950s when things were simpler and men and women all operated off the same script and set of rules.

"Just swipe right," he said. "It'll guarantee success."

Later that night I downloaded Tinder and set up my profile. I was apprehensive—an app! for dating!—but knew that I had to hop on the bandwagon lest I be left behind. The thought of continuing to be alone and miserable and sexless terrified me. Why couldn't boys and girls just get along? Why did we have to resort to using our phones to meet each other? I was baffled by postmodernity.

The app was pretty simple. All it asked for were my name, age, job, and a description. I typed onto the screen: *Mike. 25. Analyst.*

But then I decided I needed to sound more important, so I changed it to: *Mike. 25. Consultant.*

But what to put for my description? I didn't want to sound desperate, but I had to write something that made it seem like I cared. I also couldn't put anything that made me seem creepy— the Millennial woman's *creep-o-meter* was a well calibrated tool. I needed to sound authentic, like an honest guy just trying to meet an honest gal.

I typed: *Looking to meet fun, outgoing ladies.*

Hmm, I thought. *Is that enough? Does it effectively show my personality? Does it include enough sexual innuendo? What would my future wife respond best to?* I decided it was fine but then added: *Don't take yourself so seriously.*

Satisfied with myself, I tapped *Next* to upload photos. I tapped another button to open my phone's photo album and scrolled through hundreds of pictures. It was an endless visual stream, a timeline of my life and the things I had done and the places I had gone. But there weren't any good ones of me, nothing that was yearbook worthy. I ended up choosing a photo of me posing with my mom and sister in front of our Christmas tree three years ago, the last time I was home. The other photo I added was me in my winter running gear, posing in front of the Lincoln Memorial—the first and only selfie I had ever taken.

Perfect! These photos will communicate to Her that I am a family man and that I am fit. I tapped *Done*, and the app burst to life with a pile of faces stacked on top of each other like a deck of cards. I heard Adam's voice in my head: *just swipe right*.

So I did. I took my thumb and flicked the digital cards to the right. I didn't even look long enough to read the names or ages or jobs or descriptions—until I swiped right on an ugly one. *Crap! I'm going too fast.* Since there was no undo option, I slowed down to at least consider how hot each one was based on the single picture that advertised her body.

As I was swiping, I noticed that it showed how far away the cards were. *How voyeuristic*, I thought. But what about privacy? Couldn't I just walk down the street with my phone and match her profile picture to someone walking by? I would know her name, her age—her job! Is this even legal? Is this predatory? What has the world become?

Nervous, I pressed the button on the top of my phone and the screen went dark. They were all gone in an instant. The stack of faces, the pile of single ladies, the deck of potential sex. Vanished!

But the very next day, I had a bunch of unread messages waiting for me.

· · ·

It was too easy. I had more sex in the span of two weeks than I had had in two years. And all I had to do was *just swipe right*.

First, there was Chloe. It took afternoon coffee plus two more dates until she got on her knees and gave me the second-best blowjob of my life.

While we were getting drunk on our third date, I placed my hand on her lower back. She giggled and leaned into me and then slowly crossed and uncrossed her legs. I took this as a sign that I was going to get lucky. I moved my eyes downward to peer at her inner thighs, as far as the light would let me see, and she giggled again. We split the check and walked outside.

We hailed a cab back to my place, and when we stumbled into my bedroom, she got on her knees. I didn't even say anything. We didn't even kiss! She just picked a spot in the middle of the floor and kneeled down.

"I'm ready," she said.

Her tone was casual, her jaw was relaxed, and her eyes were closed. Her hands laid on her knees like a schoolgirl during story time.

"Umm, OK?" I said, confused at how clinical the situation had become. "So, you just…uh…want me to stick it in?"

"Ahhhhhhhh," she hummed.

With her eyes still closed, she opened her mouth as if she were in the dentist's office getting her tonsils examined. I unzipped my pants, opened the fly to my boxer briefs, and walked over to her. I lowered my hips to align my crotch with her mouth. Then I took my penis and dropped it on her tongue.

She closed her lips, and her warm, slippery mouth worked its way up and down my shaft, which was growing bigger and bigger and bigger.

"Oh, yeah, just like that," I said. "Keep doing that, just like that."

My head rolled back and I closed my eyes to enjoy what was happening.

"Mm-hmm!" she said. "Mm-hmm! Mm-hmm! Mm-hmm!"

I looked down. She was saying *mm-hmm* every time I hit the back of her throat. But it wasn't a regular *mm-hmm*. It was a weird, mouse-like *mm-hmm*, like she was some specimen in a Pavlovian experiment. It was weird. Now I wanted it to be over.

"You ready for it?" I said.

The staccato *mm-hmms* wouldn't stop until the trigger stopped. So I finished in her mouth and never heard from her again.

Next, there was Jen. I thought there was real potential, like we were actually going to date for a while and ease into sex, like it used to be back in the halcyon pre-app days. We hit it off from the get-go, and I made her laugh—well, she laughed at my jokes, which made me think she was into me. Plus, she let me pay for our first date, which was a rarity in this town.

I grabbed her hand while we were walking around Logan Circle after meeting for drinks on our second date. She smiled and leaned in, like it was the next thing she was supposed to do to complete our scene out of a rom-com. The scent of her perfume was intoxicating, pulling me in for more.

"This feels good, doesn't it?" I said.

"Yeah. I think I like this," she said. "This is cute."

Cute? Cute! What the hell does that even mean?

"Soooooo do you think we're ready for the next step?" I asked.

"I mean, if you mean—like, I guess if you think that would be good?" she said and then looked down. "Sure, yeah—yeah, yeah, yeah."

She was searching for words that she never found.

"Yeah, I think so," I said, confident and in control. "Wanna hang out at your place and take it easy? We can take it slow, see how the night goes, you know?"

"OK," she said as her head moved sideways. "Yeah, OK."

When we got to her apartment, her body language was guarded. Her shoulders were slumped forward, and she was holding her limp left arm with her right hand. She led me into her bedroom, and I looked up and was taken aback by all the plants. There were potted plants on the window sills, plants hanging in macramé baskets from the ceiling, and vines overflowing from the dresser and tabletops. There was a framed print on the wall next to the bed that said *EVERYTHING HAPPENS FOR A REASON*.

"Nice garden," I said with a smirk. "I bet you breathe easy in here."

She didn't say anything. She was undressing herself because

there we were. We had already made the effort to get in a cab and travel to her place, already agreed through innuendo on our date and romantic walk that we would get each other off. And that's exactly what we did.

She laid on her back and I got on top. Her eyes never made contact with mine the entire time. Soon enough I pulled out and finished on her chest.

Then I turned onto my back and we laid there side by side, staring at the ceiling and the hanging plants in silence. It was so awkward; not the silence, but how long it stretched on for. I rolled my head to the right and looked at her, which she noticed in her peripheral vision. Then she began to cry.

"I just...I just...I just *hate* men so much," she said, her voice disappearing into her hands as she cupped them over her face. "I just want to be loooooooooved!"

I didn't know what to say. What could I say? I barely knew her. And I knew that talking would just make it worse. Why would she sleep with me if she hated me? It made no sense. I got up and grabbed a blanket and tucked her into bed like she was a child. Then I put on my clothes, closed the door behind me, and took a cab home. I never saw her again.

And then there was Stephanie. I couldn't tell what Stephanie looked like before I met her the first time because every single picture in her profile was of a group of girls. And they all looked like a variation on the same person: blonde hair with brown roots and elbows out while squatting. They were telling the world: We are fun and peppy! But we also like to have sex because we are empowered.

And boy did Stephanie deliver. After having just one drink each on our first date at a bar on Fourteenth Street, she leaned into me and whispered, "I'm soooooooo horny right nowwww," her vocal fry emphasizing just how much she wanted to bang.

"Alright," I said. "I'll give you what you want. Let's get out of here—my place or yours?"

"Mine."

And then, for the first time in my life, I was the one who got fucked. She rushed me into her bedroom and ripped off my clothes. She shoved her fists into my stomach so hard that I fell backward onto the bed. Then she took her panties off, climbed on top of me, and sat on my face.

"Eat me out, bitch!" she yelled.

Yes, ma'am! She had pubic hair, which I didn't expect. It tickled against my nose. I'd never been with someone who didn't wax or shave down there. In fact, I don't know if I'd ever *seen* any pubic hair in a single porno my entire life. But I didn't care because I was so horny. She smelled and tasted amazing, and was so wet.

The both of us were into it, me grunting like a wild boar and her screaming like a feral cat. I was so hard, a twenty-something living out a real-life fantasy straight out of a teenage wet dream or a 70s porno. *God, I love this app!* I stared at the arm that she was using to steady herself against the headboard and saw the words *just breathe.* tattooed in script. I didn't get it.

Before I knew it, she was backing away to lower herself onto me. After sitting all the way down, she slapped her hands down on my chest and began riding me, up and down and up and down and up and down. I turned my neck and looked at the wall of glass that was on the other side of the bedroom. There were no curtains, and I could see people and cars a few stories down, moving by on the street and sidewalk. I guess we were both exhibitionists now.

"Ohhhhh, yeaaaah," she said in between moans. "I loooove your diiiiiick."

"I love your…everything. I love this, yes!" I said.

Her two small dogs were yapping along to our moaning and panting. It felt like we were being watched by four-legged voyeurs. But I didn't care because we were animals, too.

I pushed her off and got on top. I bent her backward so her legs reached all the way back, past her head and against the headboard. Then I lifted up her butt, pushed down on the back of her thighs, and entered her. I started jackhammering her just like I saw the guys do to the women in the pornos. They always loved it—to be dominated and brought to the edge. I closed my eyes and imagined all the women's faces I had watched in the thousands of pornos I'd seen. I imagined them biting their lips and making faces and moaning out in ecstasy. I was rock hard.

Then I heard a scream.

"Ouch!" she yelped.

"Crap! I'm so sorry!" I said.

"It's fine," she said. "Just…I dunno…get back on your back."

I rolled onto my back and adjusted my head on the pillow. I put my hands behind my head, and then looked up and stared at her body. I could feel myself going soft, which embarrassed me. She got into a squat position, but I had trouble sticking it in. Eventually, she wedged it in and rode me fast and hard. I wasn't even sure if I was still hard, but it didn't seem to matter to her.

"Take me!" she yelled. "Take me, you little bitch!"

I closed my eyes and imagined someone else. I guess the real thing was never as good as what was on the screen. But it didn't matter, because she kept going, up and down and in circles, like there was no tomorrow. It's almost as if I wasn't even there. I was just being used.

I had already finished minutes ago. I often finished inside women without mentioning it. It was 2013, and it was *their* responsibility to be on The Pill if they were going to live like men. If there was an accident, it was their problem to fix—I didn't want to have anything to do with it, and I didn't have money to pay for it anyway. It's what everyone said was the right thing to do.

I was feeling proud because of my newfound winning streak. But all this easy sex made me feel empty inside. Women were becoming too disposable these days. But at least it made me feel something—anything! It was a good sign that I was on the up and up. Each time I slept with a chick from the app, I walked away feeling more like a man, like I had conquered something.

Stephanie and I became F.W.B. for a couple months until I

found out that she had also found Adam on Tinder and was riding him, too. Alas, none of these chicks were keepers. They were just more stops along the long road to true love. I decided I would just keep having fun and have as much sex as possible until I found Her in real life. Plus, this was the best cure to my P.I.E.D.—better than those white pills.

Chapter Eighteen

PANDERING PURPOSE

I opened my messages app and typed *M* into the search bar. Matt's name came up, and I tapped on it. Our chat history came to life, the log of our yearslong texts in a reverse chronological thread that didn't seem to have a beginning. It's like our conversations—our friendship—never left me. It was there in the background, saved to the servers that stored all my phone's data across the globe, ready for me to revive at the tap of my thumb. It was creepy.

> Come over to my place for
> dinner tonight. We're having
> some people over. Pizza and
> beer

I got Matt's text while I was on the Metro on my way home from work. I couldn't say no to free pizza.

> Sure. What can I bring?

> Just yourself

When I got to his place, I texted him to come let me in. There was a doorbell, but I wasn't certain it worked. His apartment was in an old building that had seen better days, and things were not like the amenities in the new buildings that were cropping up all over the city—the Millennial Dorm Rooms. Those meta-modern buildings made entirely of glass had twenty-four-hour concierge and security, stalls to wash your dog, pool and foosball tables, movie screening rooms, rooftop pools and gardens, lounge spaces, and a price tag so high you ended up paying the majority of your net monthly income on rent. If you had the money, you could live like you were in college well into your twenties and thirties. You could be an adolescent forever. As a *lifestyle*. I couldn't believe it.

Here

Coming

A minute later he appeared to open the building door, and then we walked down a long center hallway lined with apartment doors. The floors were so squeaky—and so slanted. It was kind of like walking through a funhouse at the carnival. I think it's what they called *character*.

We walked across the threshold, and his two roommates greeted me.

"Hey, Mike," one of them said. "It's so good to see you!"

"Yo, Mikeeeeey!" said the other. "Glad you could make it, brother."

Both of these guys also went to Matt's church. They were nice. A little *too* nice, just like Matt. And happy—so *very* happy.

Matt led me into the kitchen where he opened the fridge and leaned down to grab two beers. Then he took a bottle opener and cracked open each one. *Fsssk, fsssk.* I always liked to hear the sound of the pressure being released. It was so satisfying. He handed me a bottle and then clinked the neck of his bottle against mine.

"Cheers," he said. We both tilted our heads back to take a

sip. "And welcome to small group."

My eyes widened as I swallowed my beer. He had tricked me!

"I'm sorry, small group?" I said. "You invited me over for pizza and beer. I did *not* consent to Bible study."

I could feel the anger swelling inside me. But I also didn't want to be a jerk about it, lest I be accused of being an ignoramus or bigot or—worse—*anti-religious*. I knew he cared about my well-being and just wanted me to be happy. But what he had done was a *bona fide* bait-and-switch. And it pissed me off. I did not consent!

"Oh, it's for your own good," he said. "You're so alone and so isolated. It's not normal. You need to live in community. It'll be fun!"

I pursed my lips in defiance. *Great*, I thought. *Now I have to make small talk with a bunch of Christians and pretend like I'm not some sad, miserable loser. Small group* was just code for *Bible group*. The non-religious branding makes it seem so innocuous, like it's some local club where neighbors get together to play cards and eat casserole. But it's not. It's a Christians-only club, and once you become a member you become obligated to the rest of the group and they try to hold you accountable and you're not allowed to be selfish. It's so incompatible with the sovereignty of the modern-day individual. I was already getting stressed out just thinking about it.

"Just keep an open mind and have fun—there's no pressure," he said.

Matt led me back into the living room where there was a group of people sitting around. There were two married couples, which was weird because I didn't hang out with married people. I wondered how old they were because they looked too young to be wed. People in the city didn't marry until their thirties. There were also three women without rings on their fingers, who were all wearing infinity scarves like it was some Christian girl uniform. One of the women had such large breasts the scarf seemed to float around her head like a donut, its fabric walls perpendicular to the floor. There was also another guy, who had a beard and small glasses that made him look literary. Then there were Matt's two roommates and Lauren, who was now his fiancée. Their engagement reminded me that I was still single and unloved.

"Hey, everyone. For those who haven't met him yet, this is my friend Mike," Matt said. "He's the guy I've talked about before. This is his first time coming to small group—so don't freak him out!"

Everyone let out a forced chuckle. But I didn't laugh. I was feeling angrier about the whole situation. He talked to them about *me*? He told these complete strangers things about *my* life? I felt betrayed.

"Before the pizza gets cold, let's do a quick prayer," he said.

Everyone stood up and shuffled into formation, which was a rough approximation of a circle, and joined hands. Then everyone bowed their heads and closed their eyes.

"Lord, thank You. Thank You for the food tonight and thank You for the gift of life. Thank You for this group, this community of people committed to knowing You and to knowing each other. Thank You for lifting us up and giving us strength as we lead these busy, stressful lives in the city."

I glanced up to see if everyone had their eyes shut. One of the women on the other side of the circle had one eyelid open and caught me looking around. I quickly clenched my eyes shut and lowered my head in shame.

"And we pray that, together, we will deepen our intimacy with You and with each other tonight. Allow us to be vulnerable with each other so that we can share in the burdens of life. In Jesus's name we pray, amen."

"Amen," everyone said.

The guy holding my left hand gently squeezed it before he let go. Was this some signal? Was I in trouble? Maybe he knew! Maybe he knew that I was depressed and lonely and unable to find the love and purpose I had moved across the country to get.

Christians: they're so sketchy.

The Bible study ended up having nothing to do with the Bible. The whole night was spent filling up on pizza and getting buzzed on beer and talking about work and politics and pop culture. It was not what I had expected. My beer tasted like crap, but I kept drinking it anyway. My pizza, on the other hand, was the kind that had a thick, doughy interior—the type that strategically fills you up *and* sops up the alcohol. It was just what I needed.

Then there was Peter, the guy who squeezed my hand. We had been talking about *Star Wars* and how its stories paralleled those in the Bible.

" 'May the force be with you' is the secular version of 'May the Lord be with you,' " he said. "And the franchise's great battles between good and evil, between light and darkness, between virtue and vice, are all lifted from the stories of the Bible."

"Hmm," I said. "I hadn't considered that before. Maybe this just means that there are only so many stories under the sun. Or maybe…maybe there are only so many ways humans can pass on lessons to each other, you know?"

"Yes, exactly!" he said, excited that I seemed to be open to his argument.

I was feeling something, too. I'm not sure if it was excitement, though. It felt more like breakthrough, like I had finally been challenged out of my default mode or life routine or something. It's like I was getting a firmware update to my operating system. I just didn't yet know which new features the upgrade would come with. Or maybe it was the pills.

Peter then switched topics—drastically.

"How's your inner life?" he said.

Oh, great, I thought. *Another bait-and-switch! What is it with these Christians?* Not even my psychiatrist asked me that type of question. All she cared about was whether or not I was on the verge of killing myself and how many little white pills she needed to prescribe me to keep me numb to the realities of

165

my life. And, how things were going with my counselor.

"What do you mean, *inner life*?" I said.

I knew I had to contain my rage, to stay open-minded and engaged, lest I be labeled intolerant. I could feel my blood pressure increasing, the anger building inside me.

"Oh, you know—the stuff on the inside, the stuff you feel and think but no one else can see," he said.

He paused and waited for me to say something, but words would not form.

"Think of it this way," he said. "There's an external life and an internal life, a public life and a private life. And in this country at this moment in time, we are only taught to focus on the external public life—the worldly things, like jobs, money, and material stuff and social status. However, that's only a small fraction of what makes us human, Mike."

I didn't know how to respond. I felt so put on the spot and so ashamed that maybe what I thought I had been working so hard to hide was visible to other people after all.

Our Father, who art in heaven.
Our Father, who art in heaven.
Out Father, who art in heaven.

I said it over and over and over again inside my head to calm myself from the nervous anxiety I was feeling. I felt as if I were being put on trial, as if all my darkest secrets and greatest shames were about to be printed on the front page of the newspaper.

"Well," I said as my voice cracked. "I...I...I think a lot. I am tortured. I can't get out of my head. You know what I mean?"

He kept staring at me and then nodded. It was a signal to continue.

"And, I'm just so disappointed about life. It's...it's not what I thought it would be."

He nodded again and then looked down.

"And...and...I just feel like, like life has *ruined* me. And now I'm clinically depressed and I hate my job and I can't find a girlfriend!"

I couldn't believe I was saying these things out loud to someone who two hours ago was a complete stranger. My body was trembling.

"And…and…I'm scared that I'm broken forever, that this is what my life will be like forever."

He looked up again and stared into my eyes like he was connecting to the feelings inside that were now coming out.

"And…I feel…I feel such shame! I feel like I'm letting down my mom and sister. I want to be freed from my pain! And now I'm on these pills…"

He leaned toward me, grabbed my forearm, squeezed it, and said, "You will soon be set free."

"But how?"

"Through Christ alone."

• • •

A knot was forming in the pit of my stomach.

"Listen, kid—you're great at your job and you're quick to learn, but to this company, you're nothing special. You are a tool to make money. And there are a lot of other tools in the toolbox."

Charles and I were sitting in a conference room at our firm's office. The conference table was black and so was the giant speaker phone that sat in the middle and all the chairs that surrounded it. The walls and ceilings were stark white like a hospital operating room.

"But I don't understand," I said. "I have *met* or *exceeded* all the criteria for promotion to the consultant level. I spent two weeks writing my self-appraisal and listing every single thing I accomplished in the last performance cycle—and they all mapped to the requirements for promotion!"

He didn't say anything. He was looking down at the table, avoiding having to answer for the firm. I was staring into the giant flat-screen TV mounted to the wall across from me and seeing myself reflected back.

"Charles—I have worked my ass off, and you know it! I've helped grow business on our account because the clients trust me. I regularly stay late, work on weekends, and produce the work of two—even three—consultants! And I'm an analyst!"

"That may be," he said. He slowly lifted his head and his eyes met mine. And then, in a calm, clinical voice, he said, "But you have not been in your current position long enough to be eligible for promotion to the next level."

"That's bullshit!" I shouted as I leaned forward and slapped my hands on the table.

"Watch your mouth!" he shot back.

I was furious. I couldn't believe how unfair the situation was. I knew I needed to be careful, to not come off as entitled. They always said Millennials were entitled, and I was diligent to not be that stereotype at work. But I couldn't understand why I wasn't being rewarded. Why wasn't the system based on merit like they said it was? Why wasn't I being recognized for all my hard work? Was the system corrupt? Were the people running the system corrupt? Most of my colleagues were completely mediocre, the ones with family connections and fancy degrees, and yet they all seemed to be moving up the corporate ladder.

"Mike, you know I think the world of you," he said. He lowered his voice and softened his tone. "I depend on you, and I turn to you to help me figure out some of our biggest client problems. I also speak highly of you to the partners—they are on board with investing in you and your career here. They know you outperform most of your colleagues."

He leaned forward, his forearms on the table and his hands clasped. He was trying to make me feel better, to make me feel like a human in this dehumanizing situation.

"But I need you to understand," he said. "There are *rules* in place. An employee has to be in his or her current position for at least two years in order to be eligible for promotion to the next level. Unfortunately, you have only been in your current position for twenty-two months. I'm sorry the timing didn't work out in your favor."

I went silent. I was staring at the ceiling, my arms crossed across my chest in defiance. I was thinking of all my peers who had gotten promotions. What made them so deserving? Sure, most of them did good work and were dependable. But some of them were liabilities to the firm and to the clients—the ones I had to follow to clean up their trail of imperfections. I had to overcompensate for their lack of performance in order to deliver to the clients, and yet they still got promoted. What about me?

"Charles!" I yelled. "I *deserve* a promotion, and you know it. So does everyone! What is two months in the grand scheme of things? It's just some technicality, you know. Other than those two months, I'm golden. I am a *gift* to this firm."

"Stop right there, Mike. *No one* is a gift to this firm," he said as he pressed his index finger into the table. "This is a business. We are here to do work and make money—that's it! No one asked you to be a martyr for the rest of us, Mike!"

My throat tightened and my face got hot. I didn't know how to respond. I started to panic about money. Jess had turned eighteen and was living off her college loans. I didn't want her to be in all the debt that I was in. I *had* to come through for her and my mom. I needed this promotion to make enough money to support them, to provide for them. I thought it was going to work out.

"And…and…and, external *pressures* and *forces* are also at play," he said. He paused, reading the dissatisfaction on my face. "Sometimes these things aren't as simple as they should be. And for that, I am sorry."

"But what about Cynthia?" I said. "She's *terrible*. And you know it. She is a handicap to the firm. She's so mediocre. Yet she got a promotion. Why?"

I was being flippant on purpose because I had a point to prove. My anger was creating a standoff with Charles—and with the firm.

"Mike," he said, exasperated that he had to answer for the sins of the firm. "There are external *pressures* to make things more *equitable*. Do you understand?"

He maintained strong eye contact with me as his right hand sliced through the air to underscore the words he was emphasizing. Silence hung heavy in the room as our standoff continued. And then it hit me: she was only promoted because she's a woman, for godssake!

I was livid. I straightened up in my chair, and he let out a long sigh. Then I pursed my lips and stared at the speaker phone. She didn't deserve it. She was a charlatan, a fraud who was faking it till she made it—except she would never make it because she'd never be any good at her job. She was the type of person whose resume positioned her as some savant and gift to the corporate world when, in reality, she was just another Washington swamp creature, a leech on the system and everyone who was good. She was the type of person whose online profiles said she was an *accomplished professional* and *dynamic leader* whose *record of creating innovative solutions led to award-winning industry recognition*. But she was none of those things. I resented her because we all had to accommodate her—and all because she was a *she*. And she was only twenty-seven!

"Wow," I responded nonchalantly. "Sounds like *gendered* affirmative action to me—like some *quota system*. Un-real."

Charles said nothing. He was too smart to confirm something like this on the record. He was in the business of drawing lines and forcing the rest of us to read between them. It was corporate doublespeak, a way to avoid accountability at all levels of the firm. We all had to learn to live by the rules of this game whether we liked it or not.

"Listen, Mike," he said. "You'll definitely get the promotion next cycle. We—*the firm*—are committed to growing your career. I'm sorry, it's just the way it is."

"But what about Sam? He started when I did and we're the same age, but he came in as a consultant. Why did I start as an analyst?"

"Because, Mike. His uncle is on our board of directors. It's just the way it works, OK?"

Another McSpecial, for godssake! I wasn't satisfied by any

of his answers. What became crystal clear to me in that moment was that if you don't like the game, then your only option is to stop playing it. I just didn't know if there was another game out there worth playing. I didn't think my first job would be like this. I had thought by now I would be working a job that fate had led me to. What I now knew for sure was consulting wasn't it. That, and purpose doesn't pay.

Chapter Nineteen

THE ONE

There was a new app everyone was talking about where you could hail a cab from your phone, except they weren't cabs— they were regular cars driven by regular people. It was origi- nally made for rich people so they could book black cars with tinted windows to and from all the important places rich people came and went to. But then they made a version for regular peo- ple, a cheaper version with non-black cars. It was called Uber.

I wanted to try it out, this Uber thing, so I turned on my phone to download the app. All it asked for were my name and credit card information. Then the screen turned into a map with little cartoon cars moving around like ants at work.

I thought for a moment where I should take my first Uber ride to. It was a Saturday afternoon in the middle of winter, frigid and gray out, and I had nowhere to be. I didn't have any- where to go either. *The National Mall? No, too cold. A coffee shop? No, too boring. The Library of Congress? No, too much security.*

I looked down at the screen, and all the little cars that were there just a couple of minutes ago had thinned out. *Crap!* I needed to book a car *now*. There were just two cars left waiting to be summoned.

Where to? the app beckoned. I was caught off guard with having to know my final destination. There was no room for spontaneity, no time to just take a ride to a place yet unknown. It was efficiency for the sake of productivity. I randomly typed a word, *n-a-t-i-o-n*, and then it did the rest for me, and the first address that magically appeared was the National Gallery of Art. *Hmm*, I thought. *Why not?* I tapped *Request UberX*. It said the car was three minutes away. I grabbed my P.W.K. and my earbuds, put my jacket on, and ran out the door.

Crap! I forgot to put my pickup address in. I pulled my phone out of my pocket and tapped open the app. But then I realized it already knew where I was—it knew *exactly* where I was. I was a little blue dot, moving side-to-side in tandem with my pacing up and down the sidewalk, nervous at the prospect of getting into a complete stranger's car. I wondered if I should cancel the ride and run away.

But before I knew it, the app dinged, and a silver sedan pulled up to the curb. I was tense as I approached. I put my hand up, like a Boy Scout taking a pledge, to signal to the driver that I was not about to walk up to a stranger's car and open it. He was a middle-aged black man wearing a brown flat cap.

He rolled down the window and said, "Are you Michael?"

"Yep," I said.

"Alright, alright—I'm Curtis." He paused because I didn't move. "Get in!" he said and then laughed.

I walked forward to open the door and got into the back seat. It was a regular car, a normal, no-frills vehicle with fabric seats and cup holders and a green air freshener in the shape of a tree hanging from the rearview mirror. There was no plexiglass separating me from the driver like in a real cab, and there was no ashtray for cigarettes or a slot to slide cash through. It was the type of car your mom or dad would drive, except there were no crumpled-up fast food bags littering the floor.

It felt odd. He was a complete stranger, for godssake! And

now I was in his car, my life in his hands. Was this even legal? I sat in silence as he drove south toward the National Mall. I was focused on the cars and buses and people zooming by, one long blur of moving, living things that created a kaleidoscope of color. My left leg shook nervously, anxious about the new and unknown experience I was having. I didn't like not knowing.

"This is the future," he said.

"Mmm-hmm," I said.

I didn't want to talk. I was on edge. As he turned onto Constitution Avenue, he stopped in the middle of the right lane and put his hazard lights on. The cars behind us piled up, and horns began to honk. I felt like it was my fault—I needed to get out fast. I reached into my pocket to pull out my wallet.

"No, no," he said. "You're all done. The app pays me."

"Oh, right," I said. "But what about a tip?"

"It's included in the price. Don't worry about it."

There was no exchange of cash, no swiping of credit cards, and no tip. I opened the door and got out. It felt like I had just robbed a store, like I took a giant package of toilet paper and walked out. It felt wrong. *I* felt wrong.

I waited for the crosswalk light to turn green with the outline of a person and start its countdown clock, and then I walked across the street. I entered through the museum's heavy bronze doors, stood in a vestibule that was blasting hot air, and was inspected by a security guard. By now I knew the D.C. routine: I spread my legs and put my hands behind my head, and a security guard took a metal detector wand and traced my body to check for guns.

After I was cleared to proceed, I pulled my earbuds out of my jacket pocket, untangled the wires, and plugged the end of the cord into my phone's audio jack. I opened my music app and scrolled to my Life Soundtrack. I tapped the shuffle icon and sound enveloped me. And then I walked upstairs and wandered from gallery to gallery, from French Impressionism to Dutch Baroque, as each song led into the next.

Listening to music while looking at art made me feel new things. I don't know why I'd never thought to do it before, why I'd only now discovered such a brilliant combination. I guess this is what it feels like to be spontaneous. What I was hearing and what I was seeing created new feelings inside me. It was the sensation of discovery, of wonder and awe. I realized that I hadn't felt this good in years. It's like I was alive again, brought back from the dead. I wondered if the pills had stopped working.

I turned a corner and entered the Italian and Romanesque gallery. They were everywhere—Jesus, Joseph, and Mary; the congregation of saints; the choir of angels—all the Christian figures. I walked slowly from painting to painting and stared closely at their faces. I held my arms behind my back like I was some sophisticate who *knew* art. I examined their faces and saw agony but also joy. There was suffering, but there was also happiness. Their faces expressed the range of human emotions, the feelings that I have felt—the feelings that I have *lived*.

I looked to my right and saw a teenaged white girl making faces in front of a painting of the Virgin Mary while her friend took pictures on a phone. First, she stuck out her tongue and clenched her eyes shut. Then she sucked in her waist and stuck her butt out with her palms on each cheek. Then she crouched down and made some sort of hand signal near her crotch, like it was a gang sign.

"Yeah, get it, girl," her friend said. "You little slut!"

She ran over to look through all the photos her friend had taken. She was swiping so fast with her finger it was hard to know whether she was seeing anything at all.

"Which one do you think will get the most likes?" she said.

"This one with your tits and ass hanging out."

"OK, let's post it!"

I couldn't believe it. Where were their parents? What a bunch of Junior McSpecials!

I wandered into the next room through a narrow doorway linking the two rooms. I turned and saw light flash off a small painting near an archway that led to the main hallway. I walked toward it like a moth to a flame, and a new song began to play. I could feel the faint vibrations of the heels of my shoes hitting the wood floors and moving up through my legs. I pulled my arms forward and put them in my pants pockets.

As I got closer to the painting, I realized it was Jesus crucified on the cross. But it wasn't a dark, gory painting. It was bright and full of light. His blood was bright orange, still brilliant hundreds of years after the artist first put paint to canvas. It was unexpected, incongruous with the way I expected His death to be portrayed. I don't know why, but it stirred something inside of me. I began to cry.

I felt embarrassed so I backed up and shuffled around to find a place to hide, but there was nowhere to go. I lowered my head to conceal my tears from the other people in the room, but I knew a few had already noticed. Ashamed, I rushed out of the gallery and escaped into the men's restroom off the lobby so I could hide.

I found an empty toilet stall and slammed the door shut. I nervously fiddled with the lock until I finally got it to slide into place. The sound of the metal latch scraping against its slot made me feel safe. Then I unlocked my phone to check in on my Instafamily. I scrolled through their feed, gazing at all the new pictures of the kids and the places they had gone and the things they had done since I had last seen them. I wanted to reach out and touch them so badly. Their life looked so perfect, so ideal, so Platonic. They were everything I wanted.

And yet?

And yet.

• • •

I was sitting on the couch, looking across the room into the unlit kitchen and staring at the flame that was heating a kettle. I had come home from work and immediately turned off my phone, didn't put any music on, and kept the TV screen dark.

There were no air conditioners or heaters humming in my apartment building because we were in between seasons, the weather outside still and mild. It was silent except for the hiss of the flame below the kettle and the simmering water inside. My mind was distracted by the very lack of distractions.

This was turning out to be the best year of my life. In the back of my mind, I wondered: *Why me? Why now? What does it all mean?*

Maybe things were improving because Matt had forced God back into my life. Maybe things were finally falling into place because I had done my time and paid my dues. Maybe my manifest purpose in life would soon appear but not look the way I had thought it would.

Or maybe not. Maybe I was getting more confident because Adam had told me what to do to increase my success with women. Maybe all the sex was supposed to prepare me for even better sex with Her. Maybe I was preparing myself for the day when my one true love would appear.

Or maybe not. Maybe things in my life were unfolding the way all lives do, with their ups and downs and their explicable and inexplicable circumstances. Maybe my trials were no different than my neighbor's, the human condition more universal than I'd like to admit. Or maybe it was the pills.

The world was full of so much noise, it was hard to find the signals. People talked so much yet said so little. I consumed so much yet digested so little. My eyes were tired at the end of every day after hours of staring into computer and phone screens. My mind was exhausted at all the buzzing and dinging I got at all hours of the day, an endless drip of emails and texts and notifications. It was hard to know what was real versus what was artificial, what *was* versus what I wanted *to be*. I felt paralyzed by the tsunami of information that crashed over me every day.

This, I came to realize, was my central dilemma: finding truth amidst the disorder. What is truth? And who is God, anyway?

I had long resented the notion of a god, the idea that some foreign agent was in charge of my life. That there was some intelligent being out there who had put into motion the laws of the universe and the rules for life on earth and then walked away like some sociopath. I chose to ignore the possibility of a god-head, a deity who I knew didn't care about *me*, one person on this planet of billions. I would live my life and do what I wanted, on my own, because I was the most dependable person I knew. God became forgotten to me.

But then something happened inside me, and I found Him again, like two old friends serendipitously running into each other on the street corner.

"Hello, old friend."

"Hello, old friend."

"Where have you been all this time?" I would say.

"I never left," he would say back.

"But you abandoned me when I needed you most!" I would shout.

"I did not!" he would shout back.

"You never answered my prayers when I needed you to!" I would retort.

"I did!" he would retort back.

"No, you didn't!" I would cry.

"Yes, I did. I always do!" he would cry back.

"Why do you tease me like this?" I would demand.

"Why do you deny me?" he would demand back.

"You are so cruel to me," I would say.

"I am who I am," he would say back.

"You are so far away from me," I would declare. "You are not where I need you when I need you."

"I am a God who is near," he would declare back. "I am also a God who is far away."

"Who are you?"

"I am the way, and the truth, and the life."

And now my greatest fear is that *I* would abandon God—

again. Maybe it would happen when I'd have another major de-pressive episode. Maybe it would happen when I started watch-ing porn again. Maybe it would happen when I didn't get what I wanted. Or maybe it would happen when someone I loved was taken from me.

I knew I would search for God again when I found myself in the pits of despair, looking up for something to illuminate the darkness. I would blame God when things didn't go my way, when people disappointed me, when life failed me. I would only thank God when I got what I wanted, when people exceeded my expectations, when life surprised me.

The sound of bubbling water was rising, and the kettle was whistling. I looked across the room and into the flame. It flick-ered, and I thought to myself: *why must it be so?*

Chapter Twenty

DESPERATE LOVE

It was the message I'd been waiting to get my whole life.

> Hello. As I was browsing
> through some of the profiles,
> the description you'd written
> about yourself sounds like
> an especially intriguing
> match for an incredibly close
> friend of mine and I'd like to
> know if you're still
> interested in pursuing a new
> relationship at the moment.
> Since I've just recently
> signed up and I'm not sure
> how often most of the users
> tend to login or if their
> relationship status has
> changed much from first
> joining the app, if you'd like

to consider one more option,
please get back to me.

My heart started racing in excitement as I read the message in the Tinder app. It came from someone with a profile that had a single picture and no text in the biographical section. *Maybe this is it! Maybe this is the thing that people say happens when you finally find The One.* That it comes out of nowhere when you least expect it. That it comes from some shared social connection who plays matchmaker. That it comes just as you decide to give up on love.

Hi. Yes! If you think we'd
be a good match, please put
me in touch with her.

I hesitated to tap the *Send* button. It seemed too good to be true.

And yet?

And yet!

What if I missed out on finally meeting the love of my life, the soul mate who would complete me? I sent another message.

I'm not like most other guys.
I'm looking for a deep
connection.

She didn't respond back for hours, which made me anxious. Waiting around for her message felt like trying to go to sleep the night before Christmas as a kid. It was excitement mixed with nervousness mixed with skepticism, the last so you wouldn't be too disappointed if you didn't get all that you wanted. When my phone did eventually buzz and the screen came to life with a new notification, my heart sped up again.

Her name is Desiree and her
email is
mellifluousmelody@fshmail
.com Good luck…I wish you

> much success and happiness
> on your sacred journey of
> love!

What transpired was three weeks of intense emails, back and forth and back and forth at all hours of the day and night. She was everything I imagined my one true love would be: smart, humble, funny, ambitious, interesting, passionate, literary…and the list goes on and on. Put simply, she was amazing. We bared our souls to each other over email.

> I have always yearned for a love that is
> quietly confident, a love that is kind. For so
> long, I thought there was something wrong
> with me because I could never connect with
> a man in the ways I so desired. It made me
> wonder whether I am to perhaps live this life
> alone, in solitude, but in peace in knowing
> that it must be so. But now, I have met you.

Her words penetrated me and reverberated inside my core. She said all the things I wanted to hear. Each day I woke up to read another email from her was another day of real serenity. She made me feel hope again that there was someone out there with whom I was compatible, someone out there who thought like I did and dreamed like I did and wanted the world to be the way I did. Someone out there who could end my misery and finally make me feel happiness again.

> Desiree, you make me feel. I, too, have
> longed for a love that is unconventional, a
> love that is assured, a love that is pure. My
> life's experiences have slowly but surely
> chipped away at that ideal love I so
> desperately want. As the days and months
> and years go on, I wonder whether I have
> become too damaged to ever love like I want
> to love. But with you, I feel again.

Sometimes our messages to each other were just a sentence or two, something light and funny to help each other get through the day. But other times our messages were like novellas, paragraphs and paragraphs of our innermost thoughts and feelings. I emailed her, a total stranger, things I'd never told anyone else in my life.

We were so excited to find true love in each other that we decided to take our relationship to the next level. We decided to talk for the first time ever by phone one Sunday evening.

I waited in anticipation all day until the sun went down and the clock struck seven thirty, which is when we'd agreed I'd call her. I was edgy as the hours slowly ticked by, finding excuses to go places and do things to distract myself from the moment when I would hear her voice for the first time. I knew it was going to be amazing and that I would soon forget all my pain and sorrow and unrealized love interests after hearing her talk for the first time, her voice a balm for my agony.

In the middle of the day, I fantasized about what she would look like. She was probably petite with dark brown hair. She probably had a small waist with big boobs and an even bigger butt. I masturbated to the thought of having sex with her, with my dream woman. I didn't even need porn; I just needed my imagination. I stood in the bathroom, my left hand stroking myself over the sink, as I imagined her bent over and moaning in ecstasy as we made love. After I finished, I looked into the sink and thought, *Soon this will all be a thing of the past.*

I sat on the couch at seven twenty-five and watched the hands of the clock on the wall move closer to the time when my life would finally start. The staccato *tick-tocks* of each second passing sounded like time in slow motion.

And then, the clock struck seven thirty. I took a deep breath and exhaled slowly. Then again and again and again. Thoughts of failure raced through my mind. What would I say? Would I be funny enough? How could I stop myself from offending her? What if she didn't like the way my voice sounded?

Now it was seven thirty-three. *Crap! Don't be a pussy—it's now or never.* I grabbed my phone and opened up her last email, which had her phone number in it. I lowered my right thumb over the number and then hesitated. My thumb hovered, shaking, over those ten digits while my mind continued to race through all the *what ifs*.

I tapped my thumb against the screen, and a notification popped up. It gave me two options: *Cancel* or *Call*.

I tapped *Call*. I heard the dial tone, and my heart started beating faster. Then the dial tone disappeared, and I heard the sound of a phone being lifted from a receiver. I was so excited, so ready to finally talk to Her.

But there was no voice on the other end.

"Is that you, Desiree?"

There was silence, and then static noise.

"Desiree, it's Michael. It's me—it's really me!"

There was more silence and then a response.

"Hel-lo," she said.

But it wasn't a she—it was a robot voice, and it was a man!

"Flee from sex-u-al im-mor-al-i-ty. All o-ther sins a per-son com-mits are out-side the bo-dy, but who-e-ver sins sex-u-al-ly sins a-gainst their own bo-dy."

"What? Desiree? Desiree!"

"Re-pent, re-pent, re-pent, re-pent, re-pent, re-pent, re-pent, re-pent…"

I lowered the phone and tapped the red button to end the call. Not a minute later, my phone lit up with a notification from Tinder and I opened the app to read it. It was from the person who had connected me with Desiree. Maybe *she* was Desiree? I was so confused.

> Will your wife be interested
> in your hobbies???? Repent
> now!!! Turn to Christ!! He is
> the only way to true
> happiness. You can be
> saved—start today, start now

Fuck. You.

I was livid. What type of person takes the time to mess with someone's life like this? Why would someone mess around with another person's *feelings* like this? I was so disappointed and so angry. I threw my phone against the wall, and then I clenched my fist, ran toward the wall, and punched a hole through the plaster. I hated my life.

• • •

"Dude, you got catfished!" Adam said, laughing.

We were walking down H Street after leaving our second bar of the evening. It was a damp, gray Friday—the type of weather that so perfectly matched my mood.

"What does that mean?" I said.

"You don't know?" he said in an already exasperated tone because he would have to explain it to me. "It means some fat forty-year-old virgin who lives in his mom's basement baited you like a fish, reeled you in, had his fun, and tossed you back in the pond."

"Oh," I said. "How literal."

Adam was already tuning me out. He tended to do that, to stop being present midway through our conversations. My tolerance for this particular idiosyncrasy of his was beginning to wane. Now that I was a working professional, it took real effort and energy to make time to hang out with people. His lack of respect toward this fact was becoming more and more offensive to me. It's like he was still living his student lifestyle, except we were both twenty-six now.

"Well, whatever it's called, it's messed up," I said. "It's sadistic!"

I was trying to play it cool in front of him, but inside I was a wreck. I felt like every time I made a stride toward becoming more vulnerable, toward opening myself up to finding love, it would always backfire and I would end up right back where I started from. Worse, every time it happened it was like another small piece of my heart died a little death, permanently ossifying itself and turning to stone. What made me feel so uneasy about it all was the realization that if it kept happening I might have no heart capable of loving. I would just be left with a stone cold *something*.

"Dude, you're overthinking all this," Adam said as he was tapping his phone. "It's just someone having a little fun. What's wrong with that?"

I was incensed that he was so flippant about the pain Desiree—or *whoever* the hell she was—had caused me. Had he ever stopped to consider that I'm not like him and that I've lived a different life than his?

"No, I don't think I am," I said. I could feel myself growing defensive, my chest inflating and my voice growing louder. "I'm just trying to find a girlfriend, and instead, some jackass decides to mess with me—to mess with my emotions! That's not OK, you know!"

He was chuckling, but I wasn't sure if it was about what I had said or if it was about what he was looking at on his phone. Either way, it made me mad.

"And, and it's not like I did anything to deserve this, you know. I signed up for the dumb app because *apparently* that's the only way to date these days. Everyone's on these dumb apps instead of talking to each other in real life. It's so goddamned stupid!"

I could feel my chest tighten as my blood pressure increased with each proclamation. I felt angry. I felt convicted. I felt righteous.

"Hey, man, look!" he said. He held up his phone to show me someone's profile on Tinder. "See this chick? She's sitting across the room to your right—but don't look!"

"Let me get this straight," I said. "You're checking on Tinder to see if any of the real people in this bar are single?"

"Yeah, man. That's how we do it in 2014!"

"That makes no sense!" I said. "Just look at her left hand to see if there's a ring, and then go up and talk to her, you know.

Right? Am I crazy?"

"Dude, these apps are the best thing to happen to us. It's like a gift to all men from feminism," he said. "You need to appreciate all the pussy you can get now. Because once you find your supposed *one true love*," he emphasized with air quotes, "then you'll marry her and then you're stuck with one vagina for the rest of your life. Just live it up now while you can!"

"But why is that a good thing?" I retorted in defiance. "Why do we have to have all these hookups and meaningless sex until we find someone worth it?"

"Jesus Christ! Because it feels good, duh," he shot back. "And I don't know about you, but I love making a bitch moan. That's why!"

I wasn't satisfied with his answers. It's true that I was horny all the time and thought about sex at all hours of every single day. But I also knew that things were not as they should be, that this wasn't how men and women were supposed to exist. I felt bad about myself more than ever before. Not just because I got duped into baring my soul over email to a four-hundred-pound man, but because I always felt bad about myself after hanging out with Adam. His advice never seemed to work out for me.

"Yo, Mikey boy, my Uber's here—catch you for drinks another night next week?" he said as he got into a burgundy minivan.

He didn't even tell me he was ordering a ride home, or wherever he was going.

"By the way, you can pay me back for drinks on Venmo," he said as he leaned out to grab the door handle.

"What the heck is *Venmo*?"

"A new app to pay me, sucker."

I just stared at him.

"One more thing, man," he said. "Have you ever considered whether you're batting out of your league?"

Then he slammed the door, and the car drove away.

Chapter Twenty-One

HER

I was riding an Uber back to my apartment from Matt's. We had spent the evening sitting on his couch arguing about abortion and gay marriage. After three beers and two losing arguments, I was ready to leave and booked a car home while Matt finished telling me about the lack of social-anthropological grounding for same-sex marriage.

I was ignoring the driver and all the things happening outside because I was on my phone catching up with all that had happened over the past few hours. Every time I turned my phone on, I felt a pang of anxiety. I think it was because of all the little dots. The red dots had a number inside to indicate how many unread emails and texts and notifications I had. The blue dots had no number inside, just a vague signal of a new feature that had been loaded into the app overnight—like magic. Both colors did the same thing to me: they controlled me. They forced me to do something to make them go away. I resented those dots.

The overwhelming number of apps on my phone stressed me out. I decided I needed to one day purge myself of all the

PAUL BENSON

games and useless utilities, like a digital ruler, that cluttered my phone. I'd grown up, I decided. I no longer had time to do mindless things on my phone. I just needed it for the core stuff: Google, email, texting, maps, banking, camera and photos, and the internet. And talking on the phone, too (sometimes, but rarely). And Instagram and Facebook and YouTube and Twitter and Uber and all my news apps that gave me the information I needed to affirm what I already believed to be true.

But first, I had to download Venmo. I already had my banking app, plus two other payment apps. And now you could also transfer money over text message with the latest software update, so I didn't understand why I needed *another* option. But when a friend like Adam sets a social directive, you either follow it or you become ostracized. *What's wrong with you?* he would say. *Who doesn't have Venmo?* he would decry. I *had* to get the app.

After it finished downloading, it prompted me to connect it to my bank account. I opened my banking app and copied my routing number. Then it uploaded all my contacts from my phone, and all I had to do was type an *A* in the search box and Adam's name came up. After a few taps, I transferred forty-five dollars to him for the beers, plus a tip, and it returned me to a home screen that showed a feed of all my contacts' payment activity.

I looked closer and saw my payment to Adam. Written in tiny little letters at the bottom was the word *public*. *What the hell! I didn't choose to make that public for the whole world to see!* I felt exploited. I felt bamboozled. I did not consent!

I tapped the settings menu to figure out how to change the default setting. I tried to find a privacy menu that would have an option to make my transactions private so people couldn't creep on who or what my money was going to, but there was no such setting. There was no way to control my privacy, to control my information. *Another app and another data mine*, I thought. I was so disappointed at the feeling of helplessness this stupid app was making me feel. Was I in control of anything? Or was it all a farce?

I looked out the window and saw people hunched over their phones on the street corner, waiting to cross the street but oblivious to everything happening around them. Angry and helpless, I decided right then and there to go on an app deletion spree—from the backseat of some stranger's car. I held my index finger down on one of the apps until they all started jiggling with little *X*s in their upper right corners. Then I took my finger and tapped as many *X*s as I possibly could until I was left with only two screens of apps. I felt instant relief.

Then I looked up because the car had stopped. The driver was staring at me through the rearview mirror. The look on his face was pretty clear: *get out*.

As I walked up the stairs to my building, I got a notification that Adam had *liked* my payment with a little heart. *Ugh!* I did not need—or *want*—a response to something so dull.

I opened the building door to find stacks and stacks of boxes, at least twelve brown boxes with various logos and colored tapes affixed to their sides. This was the new normal on Sunday nights for urbanites. All the boxes were full of a week's worth of groceries and meal kits packed up in little baggies and wrapped up in insulation with a bunch of dry ice to make sure the food didn't spoil. I found it insane to spend so much money on so little food with so much packaging when there were multiple grocery stores within walking distance. It seemed a little *too* convenient, like these companies had to convince the McSpecials that they had a grocery shopping problem in order to sell them their solution.

As I unlocked my mailbox, one of my neighbors walked down the hallway toward me. I turned and said, "Hi." He didn't say anything back. His eyes were shifty, darting from side to side to avoid making eye contact with me. In a previous time, we would have considered this behavior to be suspicious and possibly criminal. But today it was the status quo in a city where everyone was conditioned to peer into the soulless screens of their phones and avoid interacting with the real-life humans around them. What was the world coming to? I just wanted to know my neighbors.

When I got into my apartment, I put my P.W.K. on the coffee table and then went to the kitchen. I opened the fridge, grabbed a beer, twisted the metal cap off, and took a long swig. I needed to keep the buzz going. I was feeling good after deleting all those apps. I had taken control.

My phone vibrated. It was a text from an old friend from high school.

> Yo Mikey. Chris m died.
> Heroin overdose. Check out
> facebook

Wow, I thought. *We're only twenty-six and people from high school are dying already?* I didn't think it would happen this soon. I didn't know Chris that well, but I was curious to see what was going on, so I swiped over to the Facebook app and tapped to open it. I typed *c-h-r* into the search bar and his name came up. I tapped on his picture, and his profile came to life.

His profile had become a living memorial with hundreds of comments posted in the days since he died. But there was also everything else—a public history of all his interactions and the thousands of comments, likes, and pictures from his life that were all timestamped and logged. I wondered what would become of this digital record of his life. *How does a dead person consent to keeping all his data on Facebook's servers? Do his family members inherit all his data?* The whole thing weirded me out and made me want to delete my Facebook account right then and there.

> Chris was the most amaaaaazing person.
>
> i'll miss chris and all the love he gave to the world
>
> I can't believe such an amazing human being has been taken away from me!!!!

> My best friend went to heaven and I'm a
> fucking reck...someone help plz

I couldn't believe all the comments. None of the nice things people had said were true. Chris was a *terrible* person in high school and a drug addict as an adult. And on top of that, people were using his death as an excuse to talk about themselves. The narcissism! Not even death was sacred anymore.

I needed it to stop. I couldn't take it anymore! I held down the button on the top of my phone for five seconds to power the operating system off—*completely off*—and then put it in a kitchen drawer and slammed the drawer shut. Then I walked away, unsure of what to do next, unsure of how to exist without my phone.

• • •

When I stopped searching, I finally found Her. It was Sunday morning, and my phone, which now slept with me in bed, kept buzzing with notifications. I reached over, eyes still closed, and patted the mattress until my hand hit its cold metal back. I grabbed it, turned it over, and pressed the home button. The bright light from the screen hit my groggy eyes like a freight train, so I slid it under the blanket to bring darkness back.

I lay in bed for a few more minutes, mentally preparing myself for my last day of rest until I would have to return to work the next day. Then I got out of bed and walked over to the window to open the blinds to let the light in. I squinted and then slowly let go so I could acclimate to another day. I walked back to my bed to grab my phone and pressed the home button.

> MIKE: wake up!
>
> I found someone you have to meet. She is perfect for you!
>
> Wake up, wake up, wake up!!!

Mike this could be it. This
could be the love you've
been searching for

You've gotta meet her. Text
me back ASAP!

They were all from Matt.

                                                        Hey

My phone started ringing.

"Good morning, Matt," I said.

I put him on speakerphone so I wouldn't have to use the
muscles in my upper arm to hold the phone up to my ear. It was
too much work sometimes, talking on the phone.

"Mike!" he said with excitement. "Lauren and I were at a
wedding yesterday, and we met all sorts of people at the reception. But there's a young lady that we really hit it off with, and
I think you need to meet her. She's perfect for you!"

"Uh, huh," I said. "Sure."

"No, Mike—I'm serious. This is how this stuff happens.
You just gotta keep an open mind and take a chance and see
what happens."

"OKaaaaaay. So how am I supposed to meet this supposedly
perfect woman?"

"I'm glad you asked. Lauren and I already invited her to
lunch today, and you are coming. Meet us at noon at Dan's
Digest in Capitol Hill."

I didn't say anything back. I was thinking about whether I
wanted to waste my afternoon meeting some stranger who probably wasn't going to be Her. I couldn't help it; I had become so
skeptical about love, so cynical about life. Ever since I got catfished, I was too scared to even try again.

"Uh, hello? Mike, are you still there?"

"Yeah, yeah," I said. "OK. See you there. Text me the
address."

"OK, bye!"

I brushed my teeth, took a shower, and got dressed. I went through at least five combinations of shirts and pants before I felt confident enough to leave my apartment. I wanted it to look like I had tried, but not like I had tried too hard. I couldn't seem desperate.

Then I summoned an Uber to take me to the restaurant. I said The Lord's Prayer in my head for the entire fifteen-minute ride, over and over and over again. It helped to calm my nerves. I also thought it couldn't hurt to get God on my side before meeting Her. Who knows? Maybe prayer does work. Maybe God does exist. Maybe He's going to deliver this time.

When I got out of the car I texted Matt.

Here

So are we. Where are you?

Outside

Well, come inside! We're in
the waiting area

This is it, I thought. I took a deep breath and then exhaled slowly. *Just be cool*, I thought. *Just be cool. It's no big deal*, I thought. *It's no big deal. You've got nothing to lose*, I thought. *You've got nothing to lose.*

I walked in, and Lauren waved at me to come over to where they were standing. I walked forward, past a window bench with waiting customers and a bar with feasting patrons, until I reached them.

"Hey, Mike! It's so good to see you!" Lauren said as she leaned in to hug me.

"Hey," Matt said as he leaned in to hug me, too.

I looked at both their left hands to admire their wedding rings. They were tangible reminders of how single and alone I still was.

"Mike, this is Michelle. Michelle, this is Mike."

"Hi, it's nice to meet you," I said.

I extended my arm out to shake her hand. She leaned in to hug me, too.

"And you!" she said. "Matt and Lauren told me all sorts of things about you last night."

"Oh, did they?" I said coyly.

"Oh, yes indeed," she said. "Things you wouldn't want you grandmother to hear!"

We all laughed. What a perfect introduction! I liked her already. She was so pretty in a nerdy way. She was short, maybe five feet and a couple inches, and thin, perhaps a hundred and fifteen pounds. Her hair was light brown and her teeth were off-white and she had no makeup on, which was alluring. She was wearing a sand-colored sweater over a baby blue collared shirt with dark blue jeans and leopard print ballet flats.

"Hey, the table's ready," Matt said. "Let's go!"

We followed the waitress into a different room and sat in a booth, Matt and Lauren on one side and Michelle and I on the other. The restaurant was designed to look like it was a hundred years old even though it had been open less than a year. The ceilings were made of embossed tin, and the floors were made of little white hexagonal tiles. The tops of the dark wood booths had glass panels with metal wires inside that were crisscrossed in diamond shapes. Everything was picture-perfect, made for all the diners who were holding their phones to take pictures of their food—and of themselves. We were living in a new era, that's for sure.

"So, Michelle, did you tear up the dance floor last night?" I said.

I wanted to demonstrate to her that I had a good sense of humor, that I didn't take myself too seriously.

"Hah," she said. "I wouldn't put it quite like that. I danced with both the groom and bride, which was such fun, and also the groom's father. He was such a treat! But to be perfectly honest with you, my feet were killing me by the time all the dancing started. I had been wearing heels all day—and I wasn't smart enough to bring flats for later. Stilettos are such an injustice to all of womankind!"

We all laughed. She was such a confident conversationalist. The way she talked had periods instead of question marks at the end of each sentence. It was so attractive. I was so hot for her. I couldn't believe it was actually happening, that I was feeling *something* for *someone*. Maybe I was single for so long because I wasn't ready for love. Maybe I had to become the man I was meant to be before I could find love. Maybe it was all going to work out, just a few years later than I had planned it would.

I texted Matt on my way home.

> How do you think I did?

You barely talked. You just
stared at her! Lol. But
there's hope

> Damn. OK. I hope you're
> right.

She goes to our church!
Different time, but same
place! You'll need to come
back now!!

I didn't respond. I just wanted Her—and nothing else.

Chapter Twenty-Two

ANOINTING THE SICK

I don't know why, but one Sunday I felt compelled to go to church. Back to *the* church. Back to the Roman Catholic Church. I didn't like Matt's church. It felt too much like everything else, too much like an extension of everything I hated about normal life. I don't know if my single visit to his church-cum-movie theatre last year did anything for me, but it did make me start to question whether I was doing it all wrong. Doing *life* all wrong.

I took the bus across town, back to Georgetown where I had barely gone ever since grad school ended, and walked down Thirty-Sixth Street following the blue dot on my phone. As I got closer to the church, I looked up and saw a neoclassical building, the height of its four white columns large and imposing. I looked upward to the triangular pediment that capped the columns and saw three big gold letters across its front: *IHS*. Rays of sunlight danced off the edges of the letters. I didn't know what it stood for, but I had seen it in some churches when I was a kid. It felt familiar.

I turned around and was surprised to realize that the church was on the same block as the row house where I had met Margaret all those years ago to confess, in shame, that I had tried to kill myself. In fact, I realized I had never noticed this church all the times I had walked down this street during the two years I was a grad student. It's like a homing device was now inside of me, calibrated to draw me to things that have always existed but that I have never had the eyes to see. What was moving within me? I wondered if it was the pills.

I turned back to the church and walked up the gray granite steps to the front doors. I looked up at the colonnade and felt a sense of awe at its height. A shiver ran down my spine. Then I walked through the doors and an usher greeted me.

"Good morning. We're so glad you're here," she said.

She maintained her smile and eye contact with me while she reached across and handed me a bulletin. I turned to my right and shuffled sideways inside a small pew against the wall on the far right. It was in the very back where I wouldn't be noticed.

I sat down and scanned across the rows of walnut wood pews whose ends were capped in white. The church was large—impressively so. The walls and the Corinthian columns lining them were a light gray. I looked up and gazed at the coffered ceiling and moldings outlining the windows, all painted white. The floors and altar were tiled in white marble. The monotone palette was punctured only by the jewel-toned colors of the stained glass windows. The church was a sanctuary of aesthetic purity.

The sound of an organ filled the air, and everyone stood up. A slow procession down the center aisle began as the choir and congregation started singing the opening hymn. First in the procession was an altar girl. Her outstretched arms swung a gold chain connected to a canister of burning incense; smoke swirled out and around her. Next was an altar boy holding a crucified Jesus Christ on a wooden cross that was at least ten feet tall; he stared up at it like he was afraid he couldn't carry it all the way. Then there were two more altar boys each holding a large white candle whose flames danced down the aisle. A woman holding a big red Bible in the air, her eyes closed, followed. And then there was the priest, the head. He was wearing a green vestment, and his palms were pressed together as if he were praying.

As the music faded out and the altar servers took their seats, the priest walked to the center of the altar, behind a grand marble table, and stretched out his arms wide and high.

"May the Lord be with you," he declared.

It all came rushing back to me.

"And also with you," I responded without thinking. But the rest of the congregation responded differently: "And with your spirit."

Crap! I guess some things have changed, I thought. But everything else was just as I remembered. The Mass had the same order, the same hymns, the same cadence as it always had. I felt at ease, knowing what to expect. There was stability in the familiarity, comfort in the tradition.

A lector, an older white woman who was wearing a maroon dress, walked up to the podium on the altar, leaned into the microphone, and said, "A reading from the Letter of Saint Paul to the Colossians." She paused, looked down, and then started reading the passage.

"Brothers and sisters: Let us give thanks to the Father, who has made you fit to share in the inheritance of the holy ones in light. He delivered us from the power of darkness and transferred us to the kingdom of his beloved Son, in whom we have redemption, the forgiveness of sins. He is the image of the invisible God, the firstborn of all creation. For in him were created all things in heaven and on earth, the visible and the invisible, whether thrones or dominions or principalities or powers; all things were created through him and for him. He is before all things, and in him all things hold together. He is the head of the body, the church. He is the beginning, the firstborn from the dead, that in all things he himself might be preeminent. For in him all the fullness was pleased to dwell, and through him to reconcile all things for him, making peace by the blood of his cross through him, whether those on earth or those in heaven."

The front of my throat tingled.

"The Word of the Lord," she said.

"Thanks be to God!" we all said back.

She stepped down from the podium, turned toward the cross on the back wall, and bowed. Then the priest stood up, walked to the center of the altar, bowed toward the same cross, and walked to the podium.

"A reading from the Holy Gospel according to Luke," he said as he held up the big red Bible.

"Glory to you, Lord," replied the congregation.

Together with everyone else, I made a small sign of the cross on my forehead, then on my mouth, and then on my chest. It all felt like riding a bike, going through the motions and responses without really thinking about it. You never forget it; it never leaves you.

The priest opened the Bible and started reading.

"The rulers sneered at Jesus and said, 'He saved others, let him save himself if he is the chosen one, the Christ of God.' Even the soldiers jeered at him. As they approached to offer him wine they called out, 'If you are King of the Jews, save yourself.' Above him there was an inscription that read, 'This is the King of the Jews.' Now one of the criminals hanging there reviled Jesus, saying, 'Are you not the Christ? Save yourself and us.' The other, however, rebuking him, said in reply, 'Have you no fear of God, for you are subject to the same condemnation? And indeed, we have been condemned justly, for the sentence we received corresponds to our crimes, but this man has done nothing criminal.' Then he said, 'Jesus, remember me when you come into your kingdom.' He replied to him, 'Amen, I say to you, today you will be with me in Paradise.' "

The priest finished the reading and began his homily, which I tuned out. I was instead occupied with sorting through all the thoughts racing through me. *Why am I here? What's led me to this place? How has my life turned out the way it did? Am I going crazy?* Maybe it was the pills.

My eyes wandered along with my mind. I tilted my head back and looked up at the ceiling. There were brass chandeliers hanging down, their light casting a warm glow that brought to life the Stations of the Cross on the walls. The light gave depth to the fourteen white bas-relief tableaux of Jesus's suffering that lined each side of the sanctuary. I stared into Station 7, where Jesus was hunched over carrying a cross.

The tingly feeling at the front of my throat returned, which just as soon turned to tightness at the back. It's the same physical reaction you get when you're overwhelmed by meeting someone new and it feels like you've known them forever. An energy rushes through you, activating dormant chemicals that give you the high of consciousness. And I felt it now, again—the energy, the chemicals, the joy. I felt a kinship with Christ's suffering, like His story was just like mine. *Could it be? Could my life be like His?* I couldn't say for sure.

A loud thump echoed through the church, and I snapped out of it. I looked up and saw the altar servers shuffling around. I looked down at my watch. It was already twelve forty-five, but we hadn't even taken communion yet. I wondered why Mass was running long. It should have been over by now. Catholics don't have the attention span for anything longer than an hour.

"Today is a very special Sunday," the priest said. He was standing near the front, below the altar, on our level. "We will be anointing the sick before we take Communion. All who seek physical or spiritual healing may reach out as we come near you."

And with that, the cadre of altar servers accompanied the priest as he made his way through the sanctuary, stopping to pray over the sick. He would take his thumb, dip it in oil, and draw the sign of the cross on the person's forehead. Then he'd close his eyes and say a prayer, leaning into the person's ear.

The choir punctuated the ritual by chanting the same chorus over and over and over again, with no verses to interrupt the flow. Their waves of harmonies created ripples of weeping through the congregation. I could hear people sobbing and sniffling as the sick were receiving something sacred.

"Shepherd me, oh God, beyond my wants, beyond my fears, from death into life."

Then their vocals would fade out, and it would only be the organ filling the air until the choir began again. This went on and on and on.

As the priest came toward my section, I saw a middle-aged black woman on crutches stand up and bow her head to receive an anointing. The back of my throat tightened again, and my eyes started watering. I clenched my jaw in an attempt to compose myself, but it didn't work. I lost control. I began to weep.

"Shepherd me, oh God, beyond my wants, beyond my fears, from death into life."

Chills cascaded across my skin each time the choir reached the peak of the music's crescendo—*God.* I was spellbound. *I am sick, too!* I wanted to shout it to the congregation, to finally make my suffering known to all. I just wanted to be set free.

But I didn't because my sickness wasn't physical. I had nothing to show, no evidence of my suffering to display to the congregation. Mine was a sickness within, hidden from the world, a mental illness that was invisible. Yet I yearned to be blessed with the same oil the priest was anointing the sick with. I just wanted to be whole again. I just wanted to be happy, for godssake!

• • •

One day I woke up and felt like a new person. It was like someone had wiped down a dirty car windshield and I could see clearly for the first time in a long time, finally able to drive in the direction I wanted to go. But I felt embarrassed. What if people found out that I had to be put on medication, that I couldn't handle life on my own?

I decided I didn't want to be on the pills anymore. But I also knew that I couldn't just walk in to Dr. Bailey's office and tell her I was going to stop taking them. I had to be tactical in order to get what I wanted. And what I wanted was to no longer have synthetic chemicals coursing through my veins. I wanted again to feel a life that was purely my own.

It was a Thursday morning in December, and I was missing my morning work meetings to instead go to the hospital. I had been seeing Dr. Bailey every two months for the past three years just to get sixty-day refills for my prescription. Most of my sessions with her lasted less than ten minutes. It was all so transactional.

The past three times I had seen her, I made sure I answered the questionnaires about my happiness, sadness, anxiety, and depression *very* strategically. The trend I created and reported over the last three appointments was that I was getting progressively happier and that I wasn't depressed or anxious anymore.

Of course, I didn't really know if I was cured, if I had actually become happier because of the pills. To be honest, I figured that I'd never be cured of my depression, the black dog that would likely be a permanent part of my life. I was moving toward acceptance. Nonetheless, the pills had to go. I needed to get my life back. I needed to be in control.

"Hello, Michael. How are your counseling sessions going?" she said as I walked into her office and sat down.

"Oh, very good," I said. "I like getting things off my chest— to get stuff out that's all bottled up."

"Very nice," she said.

It was a lie. I never went to any counseling sessions. Well, I tried to find a counselor after I saw Dr. Bailey the very first time, when she told me I'd need to supplement the pills with therapy. But I had called every counselor in D.C. that was in network with my health insurance plan, and not a single one was accepting new patients—and I couldn't afford to pay out-of-pocket for someone out of network. So I said, *Screw it! I'll just take the pills and be my own counselor.* Every time she'd ask me how my counseling sessions were going, I'd just make it up.

"Michael, in reading through my notes and your self-reported questionnaires, it seems like you have made great progress over the past thirty-six months. Do you feel different than when you began the course of treatment?"

"Oh, yes," I said. "I really do feel so much better. The medication has truly impacted me positively. I don't even know if I need it anymore. I mean, of course, that's for you to decide—whatever you think is best, you know. But I feel so much better, truly."

I wriggled around nervously in my seat. Was I being too patronizing? Could she tell I was lying?

"I am medically discharging you from my care."

I guess not.

"Do you know what that means, Michael?"

"No."

"It means that we—my office and this hospital—are relinquishing legal responsibility over your care. On paper, you are officially well again. You are no longer showing symptoms of depression and anxiety…or *suicide*."

She delivered her words in a tone that matched the florescent lights casting their cold glow on us. But it was her last word that hung in the air like an omen. Was that what this was actually about? Was I even human in this situation, or was I just a statistic waiting to happen?

"What about the pornography?" she said.

I raised my eyebrows and opened my mouth. But I didn't know what to say.

"Michael?" she said. She stared at me over the rim of her glasses.

"So much better, Doctor," I said. "I tried hard to, you know, reset things…*down there*. I feel normal again. Thanks for diagnosing me with that!"

"OK," she said. "Very nice. Keep up the good work."

That was the last thing she ever said to me. I got up, checked out at the front desk, and began my journey home.

I spent three years on those pills. Those pills opened the floodgates to emotions deep inside me I never knew existed. Those pills made me learn to know what happiness felt like.

Those pills made me relive all that had happened in my life to understand that I was sad for most of it. I was so sad until I took those pills.

But those pills were no panacea. Those pills made me feel like I was being controlled by a foreign agent. Those pills made me feel like a zombie some days, like the life that was happening to me was just a blur. Those pills made me feel shame for having to take them.

But those pills may have saved my life. Of course, one can't know for sure whether those little pills, those white caplets that I took once in the morning and once in the evening every day for three years, ever did a damn thing for me.

But those pills. Oh, those pills! Those pills made me realize something true: darkness was my closest friend.

Chapter Twenty-Three

DANCING IN FRANCE

Michelle was so good for me. On our third date, which was at a restaurant and not a bar, I asked her to be my girlfriend—to give it *a label*—and she said yes. She introduced me to new things like kale and yoga and public radio, had strong opinions on most things yet always stayed agreeable, and listened to everything I had to say. She became a part of my daily routine and made everything in my life better. She was making me whole again.

Before I knew it, she had convinced me that we should go on a trip together across the Atlantic Ocean to Europe. Why we couldn't just go to Baltimore for the weekend I couldn't say. But because Michelle was now my everything, the missing thing in my life that made me feel complete, I couldn't risk losing her. I had to be perfect. So I said yes.

We agreed to each pay our own way, split right down the middle like the modern couple we were. I put everything on my credit card while she used her vacation fund, something I'd never heard of before. She was just like Adam and Matt: from a loving, stable, intact family with money. I wondered why I'd missed out, why my family was broken and poor. I pitied myself.

We were in Paris for the first leg of our trip, which was just as I had expected: charming, romantic, idyllic. But it was not surprising. I had seen so many pictures and videos of Paris my entire life—in TV shows and movies and travel books and blog posts and Google searches—of the Eiffel tower and Notre Dame and the Arc de Triomphe and the Moulin Rouge, that I felt no sense of discovery in touring the city. What I *did* fully enjoy was consuming an ungodly amount of coffee, cigarettes, cheese, and crepes—or, as I liked to call them, The French Four. But none of these things hit the spot like pizza did. I knew we should've gone to Italy instead.

We avoided going to the Louvre because the internet said that the line of people just to see the Mona Lisa was hours long. We went to the Left Bank instead but then decided to leave because it was overrun with Chinese brides and grooms taking wedding pictures. So now we were traversing up the winding cobblestone paths in Montmartre, in the eighteenth arrondissement. It looked like a village out of a children's fairytale book, a little *too* perfect and saccharine. It was *allegedly* a place once inhabited by local artists and writers, but that was hard to imagine given all the souvenir shops that lined the streets.

I turned and yelled, "Come on, Michelle!"

Either she was always falling behind, or I was always rushing ahead. It was hard to tell.

"I'm coming!" she yelled back. "Just go ahead without me. I'll meet you at the top."

I got to the top of the hill and was rewarded with a stunning view of Paris. Then I scanned the plaza and noticed that no one was paying attention to each other. Everyone was holding their phones in the air to take pictures. Couples and families were holding selfie sticks, their phones attached to the end of the telescoping poles, so they could take pictures of themselves. Back when I was a kid, my mom made me go up to a stranger, ask if he could take our picture for us, and hand over our camera. I guess the times have changed.

I flinched at the touch of a hand on my shoulder.

"Hi, babe," said Michelle. "This is just so lovely. I can't imagine anything more picturesque! Isn't it stunning, Mike?"

"Yeah," I said. "It's alright."

"Oh, you're no fun!" she said. "Have you ever considered letting yourself just *be*? It's OK to show excitement on the outside. You have my permission, Mike. I just want to see the real you."

I smiled and then turned around to face the giant Sacré-Cœur Basilica. It had an all-white exterior with small domes and medium-sized domes and one very large dome. It was different, not like a typical European Gothic church.

"C'mon!" I said as I grabbed her hand. "Let's get in and then get out!"

We walked up its front steps and entered through the center doorway where an inscription was painted above: *Sacratissimo Cordi Jesu*. I looked out at the church and saw tourists taking pictures and speaking in all sorts of languages. Children were running around while parents argued. Old ladies were kneeling to pray while people lined up to light votive candles and deposit coins in the metal donation boxes.

It didn't feel sacred. It felt profane. It made me wonder if people had ever even worshipped here, if the past had a history. It was hard to imagine this place being anything other than a tourist's landmark, a building built as a spectacle for the spectator. But where was God?

"What should we see here?" Michelle said.

She was scanning a brochure and tracing a map of the church with her finger.

"I dunno," I said. "Whatever you wanna see."

She looked up and smirked. I wasn't sure if I should be totally in control, like I was at work, or whether I should let her call all the shots. I didn't know how a relationship was supposed to work—at least, not without being accused of being a sexist for acting like a man. I was a little paranoid about it.

I leaned in and whispered in her ear, "Let's just go up to the altar and look around. Then we can sneak away and make out somewhere."

She giggled and then pulled away.

We walked down the center aisle, and as we got closer to the altar, the underside of the large dome began to reveal itself. Glints of gold turned to bands of light that bounced off the curved surface. I grabbed Michelle's hand, and we tiptoed our way to the front, our necks craned back and eyes fixated on the mosaic portrayal above. Jesus was dressed in white with his arms outstretched and his heart, which was gilded in gold just like the rays of light bursting behind him, on the outside of his body.

I was mesmerized. I let go of Michelle's hand and walked toward the altar. I kneeled down on one of the stools that lined the perimeter, lowered my head, and clasped my hands. I needed to do what Margaret and Matt had told me to do—to pray. I needed to worship something! So I closed my eyes and said The Lord's Prayer.

Our Father, who art in heaven,
hallowed be thy name;
thy kingdom come,
thy will be done
on earth as it is in heaven.
Give us this day our daily bread,
and forgive us our trespasses,
as we forgive those who trespass against us;
and lead us not into temptation,
but deliver us from evil.
Amen.

All the echoes of noise inside the church faded into the background. I opened my eyes and looked up at Jesus. A shiver ran down my spine. He seemed to be floating in midair, drawing closer to me. I stared at him, deep into his eyes. I kept waiting for him to blink, to communicate something back—anything! But his eyes didn't move. He was still.

I got up from the stool and turned around to find Michelle

staring at me. She made a face that I'd never seen before, which made me feel insecure. I wondered if she thought I was weird for kneeling down to pray. I wondered what her inner life was like. Did she ever think she was going crazy for talking to an invisible guy in the sky? Did she ever have racing thoughts and dreams unrealized going on inside her head all the time like I did?

"Alright, let's get out of here," I said.

As we made our way down the hill past all the cafés and the accordion players and caricaturists, I stopped in a gift shop to buy something I saw in the window. It was a plastic ashtray with Mona Lisa's face printed on the bottom. I bought it, not because I planned to smoke cigarettes when I got back to D.C., but because it seemed to so perfectly capture the cheapness of being a tourist in Paris.

"You know, Mike," Michelle said, "Catholics are pagan worshippers of Mary and the Saints. I hope you aren't actually messing around with their messed-up Christianity when you're inside one of their churches. There's a reason the Protestant Reformation happened."

My eyes grew wide in disbelief at her comment. I had nothing to say back.

When we got to the bottom of the hill, Michelle hailed a cab. We ducked into the back seat, and the driver, who was wearing a tweed sports coat and matching flat cap, said, "*Bonjour!*" At that point during our trip, it was clear that the French really did a great job of fulfilling American expectations.

"From where are you?" said the cab driver.

"The United States," I said. "Washington, D.C., the capital, to be specific."

"Ahh, Americans!" he said. "The global terrorists!"

"I'm sorry, what?" I said. "I don't understand."

"Afghanistan!" he said. "*Putain de merde!*"

I didn't know how to respond, so I didn't say anything at all. I hadn't thought about the War in Afghanistan in years. I didn't even know why our soldiers were still there. Is it even considered a war when there's no reason to fight?

I stared out my window to avoid conversation, watching Paris blur into long streaks of light, as we made our way back to the hotel. As the car slowed to make a right turn, I saw a car burning on the sidewalk. There was a group of protesters who looked very angry. A few of them were holding a big white banner that said: *UBER: TERRORISME ÉCONOMIQUE!*

Our driver looked at us through the rearview mirror, made a face of disgust, and said, "*Putain* Uber!"

We didn't say anything. Michelle was staring out the other window, taking it all in. I turned my head to the left, my head and cheek flat against the seat back, and looked toward her. Then I reached over and grabbed her hand. Startled at my touch, she swiftly turned to her right and then slowed herself to meet me where I was. We locked eyes.

"Hi," I whispered.

"Hi," she whispered back.

"What's up?"

"I'm fine."

. . .

We were standing on the Metro platform as we waited for the train. White lamps in the shape of globes hung low over the tracks, reflecting off the tiled walls to light the way for the train to find its passengers. The tunnel ceilings were short and the station intimate, not like the vaulted concrete ceilings and soaring empty spaces of Washington's Metro stations. Why was everything beautiful in Europe but ugly in America? Something must have gone wrong in the United States.

The train arrived, and we boarded. Michelle took a seat, and I stood facing her to protect her, holding onto a horizontal bar. Streaks of light flashed by the train's windows as we moved through the tunnel, which seemed to slow down time. For a moment, I was transported back to my first Metro ride during my first week in D.C., so alive with all that life had in store for me.

I wondered about all the time that had passed and all the life that had happened. What did I have to show for it?

We arrived at the tenth arrondissement and got off the train. Michelle took out her phone, and we followed the blue dot out of the station. I looked around and saw lots of young lovers and French hipsters and Parisians in skinny jeans who pretended not to care. Empty bottles of wine and spirits littered the curbs and benches that lined a canal whose water was a mossy green. Drunken lovers were canoodling in the unlit shadows created by the streetlamps and trees, the scenes reflecting off the static surface of the water. It looked like a still life painting but in motion.

"Where is this place?" I said.

"We're almost there," she said, her faced glued to her phone. "Just a couple more blocks, and then we take a right."

"What's so great about this neighborhood anyway?" I said.

"Oh, I don't know," she said. "I just Googled hip places, and Canal Saint-Martin was at the top of the list."

"Oh," I said. "Cool."

"OK, we're here!" she said.

I looked up and saw *Le Comptoir Général* written in giant neon letters across the building. We walked through the front doors, and then I grabbed Michelle's hand and led her through the crowds. There were black-and-white checkered floors and lamps with fringe like the ones that old ladies have in their homes. Vines were hanging down from the ceiling, and old furniture was haphazardly placed in every nook and cranny. We turned a corner and were greeted by a pirate ship-turned-bar. It was all so strange, all so curated, and all so French.

We walked toward the bar to order drinks. I scanned the room and felt like a foreigner because of all the French women staring at me—at *us*. I wondered if they could tell we were Americans. The French women I was eyeing either wore no makeup or just some red lipstick. It was so seductive because it was so classy. I wished American women didn't wear so much makeup. Some of them looked like clowns.

"This place is so rad!" she said. "I just *love* the aesthetic. It's so, I don't know, *chic* and unpretentious. How fabulous!"

"Yeah, it's pretty cool," I said.

I had a series of mini moments of panic every time I saw a cute little brunette with a bob eye me from across the room. *Maybe Adam was right*, I thought. *Maybe I'm not done having my fun. Maybe I need to keep exploring what's out there and experiencing the variety of women.* The thought of taking home a Frenchie was titillating!

I ordered two shots and a beer for myself, plus a glass of wine for Michelle. I downed both shots while Michelle wasn't paying attention. A sting hit the back of my throat, and I felt an instant rush.

"Here you go—cheers!" I said.

We clanked our drinks and took our sips. Then I put my hand on Michelle's waist and pulled her in.

"I love…being here with you," I said.

She gave me a serious stare and then pulled away.

"Well, I love being in France!" she said. "I just love the French way. The food, the fashion, the *passion*. What a wonderful way to live! I love everything about this country except for the cigarettes. Pee-yew!"

I looked around and saw small groups of people dancing in different areas. There was no designated dance floor, and it wasn't pitch black like the clubs back home. It was so strange to be so free to just *be*. I didn't understand why the Parisians were so confident and unashamed and not insecure—in public! All the boys were courting the girls, but they weren't humping each other on the dance floor like they did in America. It made me yearn for an imagined life back home that was better, a little more French. Why couldn't boys and girls get along like this is America?

I extended my right arm out toward Michelle.

"Let's *danse* like we're in France, *bébé*!"

She chuckled and then gave me her adorable I-want-to-but-I-don't-want-to-give-in-so-easily look.

"It'll be fun," I said. "We can shake our hips like all these French hipsters are doing—and leave some room for the Holy Spirit."

She laughed and then capitulated.

"Alright," she said. "Dance with me, *bébé*."

And dance we did. We shuffled back and forth like it was 1955. I kept looking at what the French were doing so I could mimic their moves. We danced so much I forgot about where we were. I forgot about my money problems, I forgot about the stresses of my job, and I forgot about all my unfinished business back home. I stared into Michelle's eyes and saw life staring back at me. I wanted to hold onto this feeling forever.

I grabbed her hand and led her to a wall of windows. In the middle was a glass door that opened into a courtyard. I pushed open the door, and the cool air hit my hot, sweaty skin like a shot of Novocain. Everyone was standing around smoking, so I walked up to a random guy, made motions with my hands, and he pulled a cigarette out of his shirt pocket.

"*Merci*!" I said.

He held a lighter to it, and I sucked in air to get it going.

"*Merci, merci beaucoup*!" I said.

I stood there drunk and sweaty and tired, smoking my cigarette and wondering how I had gotten there. I looked up at the sky for the first time in a long time. I saw stars through the haze of the city's lights and felt so human. I didn't understand why I never stopped to look up at the sky in D.C., why I never slowed down to pay attention to anything around me.

"You smoke?" Michelle said.

"I do when I'm in Europe!" I said.

"You're so happy," she said. She leaned into me, kicked one of her legs back, and squeezed my hand tight as she nuzzled her head on my chest and looked up at me. "I've never seen you like this. It's like you're a different—a *better*—person."

"Does this mean…" I said with a cheeky grin.

"No way!" she said. "Just because you're so happy doesn't mean I'm going to give away my virginity!"

I looked at her. There were no words to match the moment. She was right: I *was* happy and not ashamed of it. I loved that she helped me self-actualize. Ours was everything I had always thought a relationship should be. She would help me become a better person so I could finally get the love and purpose I deserved.

Chapter Twenty-Four

GLOBAL GENERICA

Things weren't as I expected while traveling abroad, not like they were six years ago. All the things I had had to do when I studied abroad in the U.K., all those international student and expat and tourist things, I didn't have to do anymore. I could use my phone, I could use my credit card, and I didn't have to even try to speak the country's native language when I traveled from country to country. The world seemed to be getting so much smaller with everyone now using the same smart phones and apps and dual lingua franca of English and emojis. I felt sad at the homogeneity of it all. It hardly felt like an international trip.

After five days in Paris, Michelle and I took a train to Amsterdam for the second part of our trip. While we were in Paris, we stayed in a hotel room with two beds, and she didn't invite me once into her bed. I asked her to come into my bed multiple times each night to take our relationship to the next level, but she refused. I hoped that Amsterdam would be different, that all this time together would change her mind. I needed to be intimate with her. I have needs, for godssake! I am a man.

"Come on, Mike, we're almost there!" she said.

We were walking from the train station to some place Michelle had researched we go for lunch. I was falling behind because our luggage wheels kept getting stuck in the tram tracks. I would stop every few blocks to yank a wheel out of the track while she would stop to admire the buildings.

"Do you think an American-sized couch would fit through that window?" she said. "I think you'd have to hoist it up from the beam and pulley. See that? At the roof's peak?"

I didn't care.

"Oh, yeah," I said, without looking. "It probably would."

"Oh, I just love it!" Michelle exclaimed. "And look at those vines and daffodils in the flower boxes! I. Love. This. City. Can we please get jobs at some global corporation and move here?"

I laughed and then leaned in to kiss her.

"No," I said. "The novelty would wear off in a month."

"Oh, you're no fun."

We crossed a walking bridge that went over a canal, stopped to admire the houseboats, and took pictures of the row houses with our phones. I looked around and wondered where the Red Light District was, the place where you could legally smoke weed and pay for sex. Of course, I'd never pay for sex. I was too virtuous for that. But I wanted to see it with my own eyes, a place that was one-hundred percent devoted to pleasure— without guilt or consequence.

"We're here," she said as she outstretched her arms. "Welcome to the *foodhallen!*"

I looked up and saw façades made of red brick with two giant stone arches punched through. Michelle led us through one of them and down a long corridor. Light was streaming in from one side with dust particles floating in the air.

"We're almost there!" she said. "Oh, what fun! It looks just like the pictures I saw online."

We turned and entered a cavernous hall that had food stalls lining the perimeter. It had a pitched roof made of glass and metal that was painted white. It looked just like Union Market, the food hall in D.C. where McSpecials spent their weekends. The fact that Amsterdam had a food hall that looked just like the one back home, with the same trendy fusion food, made me feel sad. Then what made the cities different? It was Global Generica.

"I know exactly what I want," I said. "Those fried balls…what are they called?"

"*Bitterballen!*" Michelle said. "That's all you want? For your meal?"

"Yeah," I said. "My friend at work told me I had to get them, you know?"

We split up to get our food and then met back at a table tucked away in a corner. I bought two orders of *bitterballen*, excited to taste what all the fuss was about. They had a crispy exterior with ground mystery meat inside and were served with a ramekin of spicy mustard that was a darker yellow than the stuff back home.

After sitting down at a table, I grabbed a ball, dipped it in the sauce, put it in my mouth, bit down—and shrieked.

"Fuck!" I said. "Fuck, fuck, fuck—it's so fucking hoooooooot!"

I spit it out, and Michelle jumped to her feet.

"Babe, are you OK?" she said. Just as soon as she put her hand on my back I flinched my shoulder to swat her away. "Mike? Mike!"

"Yeah, I'm fine," I said. "I'm fine. Just sit down. Eat your food, and then we can get out of here."

It was worth the pain. Those *bitterballen* were like crack cocaine.

After we finished eating, we left the *foodhallen* and walked a few blocks toward the sun. We found a corner café to hang out in while we passed the time. I inspected the shop while we waited for the coffees we had ordered. I couldn't believe what I saw—it looked just like the coffee shops back in D.C. and the same ones I'd been to in Brooklyn and the same ones I'd been to in L.A. There were exposed brick walls and Edison lightbulbs hanging down from the ceiling. The tables and chairs were made of reclaimed wood, and there were potted succulents on the tables and window sills and counters. The locals were even eating toast with smashed avocado on top, just like we ate in the U.S. I was so disappointed. Global Generica was real.

We grabbed our coffees and *stroopwafels* from the bar and walked outside to the patio. We sat down at a table that had a prime spot to people-watch.

"It's just so beautiful," Michelle said. "Mike, don't you just love being in this city? Just imagine how quaint it would be to live here full time. I could have a small garden in the front of our row house, and we'd ride bikes everywhere."

"Yeah, it's alright," he said. "Nothing special…"

I tuned her out. I was too busy staring at all the people walking by, my eyes concealed behind my sunglasses, wondering why the world now felt so small. I looked around and noticed the way everyone was dressed. Some of the clothes people were wearing seemed fashionable, but the same athletic leisure clothing everyone wore back home dominated. It was the same five brands, the same five pairs of shoes, and the same five zip up jackets. Fathers, mothers, and children; students and teachers; tourists and prostitutes—they all wore the same damn thing. The ubiquity of athleisure clothing was the spiral notebook of global fashion: basic, utilitarian, and forgettable. They all wore the Global Uniform. I hated it.

Seeing the Dutch dressed just like Americans across an ocean made me reminisce about all those years ago when I studied abroad in the U.K., when I was so young and carefree and didn't have student loans or a retirement account to worry about. I couldn't believe life moved so fast, that I had already gone from high school student to college student who studied abroad to grad student in D.C. to working professional. There was no time to catch my breath, no time to take an inventory of why I was doing all the things I was doing. It was like I had lost control of my life but not in a reckless way. It felt like I'd been sucked into the vortex of life, becoming part of its rhythms and cycles and laws of physics, straining to keep above the torrents and trying to assert myself as an active participant. I felt out of control.

"Mike…Mike…Mike!"

My body jerked upward.

"What's wrong with you?" Michelle said. "You're not acting like yourself."

"Sorry," I said. "I guess I was daydreaming."

"Well, we've got to go," she said. "We told our Airbnb host we'd meet her there at five thirty to check in."

"OK," I said.

"I looked up the place on my phone. It's only a few blocks away," she said. "We'll check in, and then we can nap if you'd like. Or we could catch the last hour at an art museum!"

"A nap sounds good," I said.

We stood up, gathered our empty mugs, and brought them inside. Then we grabbed our luggage and walked west for about ten minutes. It was late afternoon, and the sun was low and large in the sky. Its amber light beamed through the narrow streets and created all sorts of interesting shadows.

We got to the outside of the apartment building, and Michelle texted our host that we had arrived. There was a person standing a few feet away leaning against the building. She lifted her phone, glanced down, and then walked toward us.

"*Hallo*," she said. "Are you Michelle?"

"Yes, indeed!" Michelle said.

She gave us the key and some instructions on how to get in and other things to know. Then she unchained a bike from a tree and rode off into the sunset.

We walked up three flights of stairs, unlocked the front door, and rolled in our luggage.

"Oh, my gosh, Mike!" Michelle squealed. "It's a Millennial pink chair. It's gorgeous! I love it. I want it!"

I glanced down at a chair that looked like someone had spilled stomachache medicine all over it. The chair back looked like someone had taken a bunch of loaves of bread and stitched them together.

"I hate it," I said. "It's too trendy."

"Ugh!" Michelle said. "You're being *so* negative! Stop it!"

The whole Airbnb thing was just so weird. Instead of booking a hotel room or a hostel, like normal people would do, we were staying in someone else's place. I felt like a voyeur, like I had been teleported into someone else's *life*. Their framed family photos sat on the console table, and their makeup and grooming supplies sat half-used in the medicine cabinet; sticky notes with personal reminders littered the insides of the nightstands. It felt wrong.

I walked into the bedroom and saw the same bedframe, side tables, and dresser found in every twenty-something's apartment back in the U.S. It was all made out of Swedish sawdust. The tyranny of IKEA was incensing. It's like you couldn't escape it. Was it democratic or homogenous? Was there even a difference?

Michelle walked in and looked around.

"Oh, it's just so charming," she said. "What a cute bedroom! Shall I sleep in this one?"

"Yeah, it's quaint," I said. "But so generic."

Global Generica.

• • •

"Does this dress make me look fat?" Michelle asked.

She arched her back and put her hands against her waist. She was so cute when she acted insecure. The truth was she looked good in everything. She was fit, beautiful, and confident. I didn't understand why she constantly needed me to affirm that she looked OK.

"Do a little spin for me," I said.

She giggled and then obliged. I loved how tight the dress was around her waist and butt.

"Good enough," I said with a smile. "In fact, better than good—fantastic! You look like a million bucks. Wanna be my hot date tonight?"

"Oh, dahling, I thought you'd never ask!" she said.

Then she walked toward me, leaned forward, and gave me a long, wet kiss.

"Mmm," I said. "I like that. I want more of that. Maybe later tonight?"

"Don't even think about it, Mike! You know the rules."

"But rules are meant to be broken."

"Not these ones!" she said. "Besides, isn't this fun? You chasing me, you pursuing me, you wanting me, you waiting for me. It's the way it was meant to be."

"Not really," I said. "I like to enjoy the spoils of my hunt, you know?"

"Oh, stop it!" she said. "You're no predator. You're just a boy looking for someone who will make you a man."

I didn't understand what she was trying to say, but it stopped me in my tracks. I was already a man. I had already conquered women. Did she really think I was some child? I grabbed the bottle of beer I was drinking and finished it. I was already six beers in, and Michelle was still working on her first glass of red wine.

"Are you ready to go?" I said.

"Yeah," she said. "After I use the bathroom. And I need to put on lipstick! Oh, and I think I need to double-check my hair."

Tonight, we decided we'd go to the club. I was looking forward to getting hot and steamy with her—just like I used to when I went out to bars and clubs all the time, back when I was a student.

We left the apartment building and walked to a side alley to unlock a bike that the owner said we could use.

"Shall I?" she said.

Michelle sat on the seat, and I sat on the rack atop the back wheel, holding onto the rack's metal bars. She peddled while I held on for dear life. The two of us, me drunk and her merry, rode across town to our final destination.

"This is awesome!" I said. "I feel like I might die at any

moment! Yeeeee-hawwww, motherfucker!"

"Watch your language, please!"

Michelle laughed and then picked up the speed. We rode through Vondelpark and weaved through runners and moms with strollers. Then we crossed over tram tracks and rode over a few more bridges. The lights reflecting off the surface of the canals made the city look like an impressionist painting. I closed my eyes and smiled, my mouth in a fixed state of happiness. I felt so alive.

Michelle slammed on the bike brakes, and I stumbled sideways off the bike, almost hitting a lamppost.

"Ooooops!" she said. "Are you OK, babe?"

We laughed some more. Now we were in Leidseplein Square. I looked up and saw something familiar, something I'd seen on Instagram: a FEBO shop. The place where you could get food from a wall!

"I'm starving," I said. "Let's get some grub."

I walked toward the storefront and anchored each leg into the ground so I wouldn't fall over. I scanned the wall, up and down and left and right, trying to figure out which door I would choose. I spotted burgers, hotdogs, sandwiches, and chicken legs. *Hmm*, I thought. *Wasn't there anything better?* All I really wanted was a slice a pizza, the thing that would instantly satisfy me. But I didn't see any cheesy triangles of goodness through any of the windows.

Then I saw something encrusted in a crispy outer layer, and knew I had hit gold. I walked forward and put two Euro coins into the slot, unsure about their denomination but confident because they were the big ones in my pocket. I opened the clear plastic door and pulled out a deep-fried log of *something*. I tore open the packaging and bit into it, and something savory immediately hit my taste buds. I wasn't sure if it was meat or not, but I didn't care—I was drunk and hungry and happy.

"I love it so much!" I shouted.

I turned around, but Michelle wasn't there. I stumbled out of the shop and onto the sidewalk, where I found her sitting on a bench.

"Hey," she said. "Doin' alright, cowboy?"

"Hell yeah!" I said.

"The club's just across the square," she said. "Are you ready?"

I gobbled up the rest of my food, tossed my trash in a garbage bin, and then nodded my head. I followed Michelle, who was leading the way with her phone, across the square, and then we joined a crowd of people outside.

"Welcome to Paradiso!" Michelle said.

We were standing in front of a grand building made of red brick. It had tall arched windows and a big clock at the top. The bouncers called us forward, we showed our passports and gave them a bunch of Euro bills, and then we walked in.

"This place is awesome!" I shouted. "Let's just have fun and let go tonight, babe. I just want you."

She looked away and didn't say anything back.

A wave of electronic dance music hit us after we passed through the lobby. There was a main dance floor that was packed with people and lights and lasers and smoke. I looked up and saw two levels of balconies with white banisters and railings that surrounded three sides of the dance floor. I looked across and saw a DJ who was on a pulpit in front of a stained glass window of a cross. The club was a church.

I grabbed Michelle's hand and pushed our way through the crowd until we found a spot on the main floor. Michelle started to dance, holding one arm up in the air while moving her other arm around like she was waxing a car. I moved behind her and started dancing, moving closer and closer until my crotch was rubbing up against her butt.

"What's that?" she said as she turned around.

"Uh, a flashlight?" I said.

She looked like she was tolerating me, like she was tolerating the entire situation. But I didn't care. I just wanted to enjoy being drunk and being in Amsterdam and being with her and just letting go. I wanted to seduce her on the dance floor, to get her to open up for me. I wanted to rip her clothes off then and there and make love to her at last.

"Let's keep a healthy distance between us, Mike," she yelled. "We can still have fun. I like you so much! I love being here with you on this trip. Let's keep it special."

The bass dropped, and we put our hands in the air, reaching higher and higher and higher, trying to touch the sound, trying to grasp the light. The crowd jumped up and down to the beat, necks loose and swinging backward to rejoice in the moment. I could feel my heart thumping to the beat of the music, the alcohol pulsing through my veins. I was one with the music.

And then the bass disappeared, and the sound turned ambient, floating through the smoke that hovered above the crowd. I looked up at the DJ, who was wearing a hoodie. He was swaying back and forth, teasing the crowd with the sounds he was creating. It was now pitch black except for one faint lamp behind him, which created a halo around his head.

I leaned into Michelle so I could feel her warm body. The music began to build, the notes getting shorter as the volume increased. The crowd was silent with expectation of what was to come. Heads bobbed up and down while shoulders moved left and right. I grabbed Michelle's hand, squeezed hard, and closed my eyes. I wanted to feel the moment in all its vivid glory. The layers of sound were climbing, the crescendo about to peak.

Our Father, who art in heaven.
Our Father, who art in heaven.
Out Father, who art in heaven.

I kept saying it in my head, not out of anxiety but out of exultation. Just say it. Just say it. Just say it.

The bass dropped, and I raised my left arm into the air, stretching it as high as it would go. I clenched my eyes and moved my head up and down while the palm of my hand opened and closed to the beat. As the music continued to pick up speed, I felt my mind wander to a place I hadn't known, a place of complete bliss. I felt still.

Another drop and the crowd went wild. I opened my eyes and saw three pillars of light behind the DJ shooting up from the pulpit and meeting each other at their apex. I craned my head back and traced their edges up to the circular stained glass window that was now illuminated. In giant letters on the plaster arch around the window were three words: *Soli Deo Gloria*.

Chapter Twenty-Five

NEW SOLUTIONS, OLD HABITS

I finally hopped on the bandwagon and signed up for a stream-ing music subscription from a new app called Spotify. I had avoided it for so long because I *liked* that I owned my music, that I had a library that I was building over time, something I could share with my future children and pass down. But the world was changing so fast and now songs were free and dis-posable and the entire concept of an album, a holistic work of art, was becoming extinct. Giving in to the nouveau status quo felt like rolling over and letting the tech bullies and capitalists beat the crap out of me. They were making us *lease* every-thing—including music, for godssake! But I did it anyway. I had no choice.

It felt wrong to have the world's entire music collection available in my pocket—in an instant—for ten dollars a month. Yet here I was, streaming music and beaming the sounds through the air to my new Bluetooth speaker while I worked to manipulate its fancy algorithms to trick it into knowing what it thought my music tastes were. I wondered if this would be the end of my Life Soundtrack, or if I'd be able to rebuild my playlist on Spotify.

I was sitting on the couch with my laptop. I had about thirty tabs open in my browser window, which served as my to-read list. I noticed that I used my laptop less and less these days. It was like a trigger, an indication that I'd have to do work if I turned it on, so I avoided it. I guess staring at a computer screen at work for twelve hours every day does that to a person.

A message from Adam appeared on the screen. *That's weird*, I thought. *I didn't know a text message could come through on a laptop. It must be a new feature as part of a software update.* I had to click my trackpad to open the notification and read it.

        dude what is up

                      Not much. Just hanging at
                            home. You?

        i'm bar hoppin with some
        buddies in shaw. wanna
        come out?

                      No…Michelle's going to
                          come over soon.

It was a lie. She wasn't coming over because she had already texted that she was too tired to travel from the Hill, where she lived, to Columbia Heights, where I lived. Such were city relationships: three miles as the crow flies but forty minutes as the human commutes. It was hard to see each other every day, especially on weeknights after a long day at work.

        dude why you tryin to settle
        down so soon?? you should
        still be sowing your wild
        oats all over this town!!!

Adam was a digital aesthete. He lower-cased all his letters because it was *cool*. As for me, I appreciated proper grammar and punctuation.

> I like Michelle. A lot. She's
> a good person. And I don't
> care about sowing my oats. I
> just want stability and love.

> you sound like my dad

It stung. Now I was feeling insecure—not in my relationship with Michelle, but in my state of life. Was I really too young to be in a committed, monogamous relationship? Maybe I was doing it all wrong.

I ignored the rest of Adam's texts and instead scrolled through Twitter, which gave me the information I wanted but not the information I needed. I always felt stupider after scrolling through my feed.

An advertisement for a new kind of boxer brief kept showing up every twenty or so tweets. It promised to *Guarantee to Improve Your Chances With Women.* Curious, I tapped on it and learned that its novelty was that it had a pouch for your scrotum, separate from your penis, to make your bulge look bigger. Maybe this was what I needed for Michelle to finally want me. I had to have it! I clicked a couple buttons, my browser automatically uploaded my credit card information and my mailing address, and then my phone dinged with an email confirmation. It would be here in two days.

I clicked back to my main feed. The week before, the Supreme Court had ruled that same-sex marriage was legal—and everyone had an opinion about it. I searched for President Obama's account to see what he had to say about it. His latest tweet was pinned to the top of his feed.

> Today is a big step in our march toward
> equality. Gay and lesbian couples now have
> the right to marry, just like anyone else.
> #LoveWins

I scrolled through images of the White House lit up in rainbow colors with a crowd of people packed outside. It was surreal that this was happening just a few miles from where I lived—and that I was experiencing it virtually through a computer screen. Then I scanned the tens of thousands of reactions.

> *@POTUS Imagine no religion. There's no God. Loving one another unconditionally is what matters. WTG USA! #LoveWins #Humanism*

> *@POTUS You sir, shall stand 1 day before Jesus Christ the LORD & give account for the sins into which you have led our nation (Acts 16:31)!*

I didn't know what to think—or *feel*. Nobody talked about it back in San Bernardino. I didn't even know anyone who was gay back home. The idea of two men or two women marrying each other seemed *weird*. Plus, it's not like they could make babies. And all those hashtags—how cheap! What did they even mean? What purpose did they serve? Where were the historians and philosophers and public intellectuals and anthropologists and clergymen in the debate to help make sense of it all? I felt unconfident about the meaning of the moment. No one important asked me what I thought about it before they decided what was to be. What a racket!

I decided to ditch Twitter, so I opened a new tab. I typed in the name of my student loan servicer, and the browser's memory autofilled the rest. All I had to do was hit enter. After the page loaded, I moved the cursor arrow to the top right corner to sign in. I waited anxiously for my account dashboard to load. The little spinning circle kept spinning and spinning, taunting me with the power it held over me and my life. My right leg was shaking.

Then the numbers appeared.

$99,202.33

For godssake! The principal balance went up! Not down!

How could it be? What criminal scheme had I been roped into?

$25,129.13

That's how much I had paid over two and a half years. I couldn't believe it. It was immoral. Car loans weren't like this! You took out money, agreed to pay it all back plus interest so the bank made some money, and then you paid it off in five years. But student loans were some perverted loan, some Frankenstein financial product that made no sense. What grifters had created this system to enrich themselves?

The reality of my financial slavery made me want to run away, to quit my job and book a plane ticket back to the U.K., where nobody had any debt and I could just be happy. In Europe, you were born into a class, and you knew from a young age what you'd be able to do for the rest of your life. There was certainty in the Old World. Here, in the New World, I was trapped by the false promises of social mobility.

Now I felt like crap. In less than fifteen minutes, I had gone from feeling good about life to feeling like everything was going wrong. I was so stressed out and everything felt like it was bottled up—just like before the pills. I wondered if it was because Michelle wouldn't let me have sex with her. What was I supposed to do for a release? Maybe I needed the pills again.

I clicked the browser's menu and scrolled down and then clicked to open a new incognito window. A fresh browser window opened and the cursor summoned me to type in the fix I was looking to get. I felt a rush, like a cocaine addict who starts salivating at the sound of a little plastic baggie rustling. I typed in the URL to my favorite porn site and then hit *command+T* in quick succession and typed in five more URLs to other porn sites I used to frequent. I was so hard even before the first site had loaded. Like a dog, it was conditioned to know what treats were in store.

My screen filled up with big lips and big boobs and big butts. I scrolled to the list of most viewed videos and clicked on the first one. I slid down and rested my head on the couch arm so I was lying horizontally. I pulled my pants down and put the laptop on my chest. My right hand was on the trackpad while my left hand was on my crotch. I clicked *Play* on the first video and began to stroke myself.

But it wasn't enough.

I right-clicked all the most viewed videos so they'd start to load in new tabs. Then I tabbed between each one, going from a teen with a dad to a woman getting it in the backdoor to a threesome of Asian women, all doing their part so I could get my fix. Hearing all the women scream in ecstasy put me over the edge. I kept stroking and stroking and stroking, doing the thing I knew how to do that would make me feel better.

Then I exploded.

I let out a huge sigh of relief. It was the hit I needed. I lay there, my mess all over my stomach and the back of my laptop, in shame.

And then I fell asleep.

• • •

"Why won't you have sex with me?"

"Excuse me?"

Michelle and I were lying on the couch on a Thursday night streaming Netflix. We had just finished the second hour-long episode of a new TV series everyone was talking about, and now the screen was dark while it automatically queued up the next episode. I didn't care to watch the show, but I did care about participating in watercooler talk about it at work, so here I was using the limited hours in my day to see what the hubbub was about.

"I took a vow of purity," she said as she reached over for the remote and pressed the pause button. "And I am committed to that vow."

I was on my back and stretched out across the length of the couch, my head against the pillows and armrest. She was nestled on her back between my legs, her head resting on my lower chest. All I could see was her shiny hair and the neat part on the right side. I could smell the scent of whatever shampoo she used, which was absolutely intoxicating.

"I'm feeling really small right now, in this moment, you know," I said. "Please elaborate."

I was trying to keep the conversation light to show her I was open to whatever she needed to tell me.

"It's part of my faith as a Christian to not have sex before marriage. The Bible is really clear about it, Mike," she said.

Then she shot up and adjusted herself so she was properly sitting on the couch—well, sitting on my legs, which were lying limp on the couch. I knew this meant the conversation was about to escalate, so I pulled my legs out from under her and adjusted myself so I was sitting properly on the couch, too. Now we were on opposite ends of the couch, facing each other.

"You pressure me too much. You need to understand that the price I put on my body is the price I put on myself. I'm not giving in to today's culture. Sex before marriage is a sin."

"But I have needs, Michelle!" I said. "Do you know what it's like being a man? It's terrible! We're horny all the time and need regular release in order to function. We're men! It's how we are hardwired! Do you want me to apologize for being a man? For being born this way?"

She didn't say anything. She just looked at me with contempt. Michelle had made me wait three months before she even allowed me—allowed *us*—to start making out and cuddling on the couch. Nary a blowjob was offered, and now I was at my wit's end. I figured that after a while she'd change her mind, that I'd negotiate my way to spreading her legs. But it wasn't happening!

"Listen, Michelle. I have worked...I have *struggled* for many years. Remember when I told you about being diagnosed with depression?"

"Yeah, I remember," she said.

"Well, that wasn't all...there's more..."

I felt so ashamed. I never wanted anyone to know. But I knew I needed to tell her.

"What is it, babe?" she said. "You can tell me."

I didn't want to speak the words out loud, so I just sat there in silence.

"I know you've grown so much as a person," she continued. "You've done a great job. Matt and Lauren have told me all about your progress, about your salvation."

Nice, I thought. *She's starting a tough conversation by giving me a compliment.* It's exactly what they taught us to do in leadership training at work when you have to give constructive feedback to low-performing employees.

I cleared my throat and said, "It's not *just* that I'm not a virgin."

I looked up at her to see her reaction, to see if it was safe to keep talking. She looked tense, like she didn't want to hear what I was about to say next.

"I was also addicted to…to *pornography*. It was really bad. But I thought it was normal! I thought all guys my age watched porn every day! It's how I learned about the birds and the bees."

I waited for her to hug me or to start crying or to fall deeper in love with me. But none of those things happened. She just stayed silent.

I raised my hands, gestured toward my chest, and said, "I can tell you're holding back. Just say what you need to say!" I paused, waiting for her to respond. "Let's go, come on! Just get it out. I can handle it."

I wasn't getting angry. I was getting insecure. Any criticism about my manhood would be an assault on my masculinity. I hoped she would tread carefully so I wouldn't go silent on her and spiral into another cycle of self-pity and shame.

"Who are you, Mike?" she said with disappointment on her face. "I've thought so many times—I've felt so many times— that you only see me as some object…like some replacement for all those dirty women who gave themselves up to you. Sometimes you make me feel like you only want me for what you can get out of me. And now this? Porn?"

Then she started crying. "You've led such a life of sin!" she shouted.

I didn't say anything back. My phone buzzed and lit up with a news notification, so I reached over and grabbed it off the coffee table.

> *Shooting in San Bernardino, Calif. Kills at*
> *Least 14; Two Suspects Are Dead*

"Oh, my God, Michelle!" I said. "There was another mass shooting—this time in San Bernardino. That's where my family lives!"

I opened my phone app and tapped open my favorites list to call my mom. The dial tone kept ringing and ringing.

No answer.

I tried again, but she still didn't answer.

I tapped my dad's name next.

No answer.

"You don't think...?" Michelle said as she reached over to hold my hand.

"No. There's no reason my mom wouldn't be at home right now," I said. "I mean, my dad...who knows. He's probably at the casino or with some whore."

She raised her eyebrows. I hadn't told her very much about my family, and definitely nothing about my low-life dad. I was ashamed that I came from a broken family—and a broke one, too.

"I don't know, you know?" I said. "Nothing's like it should be, you know. My mom and dad, they're divorced. I'll tell you about it later."

She looked down and then wrapped her arm around me. I pulled away and slammed my fist on the couch arm. I was angry that neither of them had answered their phones. I opened my messages app to text Jess. She never answered her phone; she only texted.

> Heard about the shooting...
> hope everything's OK.
> Where's mom? Call me.
> Love you both

There was a maelstrom of emotions swirling inside me. I felt insecure and attacked by my girlfriend and anxious and scared about my family. And now I was getting angry at the whole situation. Not mad at Michelle, but mad at my phone and all the ways it interrupted my life.

Why couldn't my phone know when I was having a serious conversation with my girlfriend or when I was in a bad mood and not interrupt me—not taunt me—with its never-ending notifications? A human wouldn't just walk up and interrupt me and Michelle. He or she would know, based on our body language, that what we were talking about was serious. It pissed me off.

"And…one more thing," she said as she wiped away tears from her face. "And then I'm going home."

I looked at her, my eyes relaxed to communicate my submission to the moment.

"Don't ever, under any circumstances, text me the eggplant emoji—ever again."

"What?" I said. "I thought chicks liked it. It's such a tease!"

"You thought wrong. It's dirty…and it's sinful!"

I was already over our conversation. I wondered if this was a sign of friction in our relationship, or if this type of thing was normal. Who could say for sure? I didn't feel like processing it because my mind was dominated by the thought of my parents and sister being gunned down. I needed to know that they were OK before I could start to take an inventory of my sexual sins and work on redeeming myself. I didn't know why Michelle couldn't understand my needs. But what I knew for sure was that porn had messed me up—and now I was suffering the consequences.

Chapter Twenty-Six

FEMALE FAILURE

The most transformative thing to happen to me at work was realizing that I could work less—and no one would notice. I could
work fewer hours, accomplish fewer things, and lower the quality of my client deliverables—and no one would notice. They'd
just assume I was working at the same frenetic pace with the
same volume of quality deliverables as I always had—because
they never paid much attention to me, or to anything really, in
the first place. And did it matter? No, because I didn't even produce anything tangible. Work—my *labor*—was just a bunch of
abstract solutions to made-up problems that we packaged and
sold to our clients as *services*. I couldn't even show my mom
what I did for work because there was nothing to show!

This year was do or die for me. I *had* to get a big promotion
and a fat raise so I could finally start paying off my credit cards
and saving some money. I just wanted to get ahead like Matt
and Adam and all the other people who were my age but had
fancier titles, apartments, and vacations than me. The money I
was sending home every month was enough for my mom to get
by on but not enough to live without worry. I needed to pull

through for her and Jess—and I knew I would because I'd been working my ass off since the day I got to D.C.

> I don't know. You should probably check in with James.

> James is out of the office. We should talk to Martha, who is on his team.

> +Martha

> I'm not sure everyone understands the problem. We are trying to figure out why there are missing metrics for Q2 for the bellwether county direct mail campaigns in the purple states, **not all of the Midwest**. There's a big difference.

> Thanks, Charles. That's great clarity for the team. Martha, do you happen to have any insight into these missing numbers?

> Hi, Mike. Have you checked in with Amanda?

> Ooops, forgot to Cc her. +Amanda

> Thanks, Martha. I'll take it from here.

It was the email chain from hell. And now there was an email from Amanda, who had removed all the clients from the Cc line and just left our team.

> Why don't you boys calm down and let me do my job. The missing metrics were due to an error in the way the report was autogenerated. I've already requested the data team manually write a script to pull the numbers for the report. Once that's done, then we can all sit down together and fill in

the missing numbers. Sound good?
Mmmkay, good.

I was incensed. Why would she take the time to write such a nasty email to her own teammates? It hurt my feelings. And the way she was talking, the way she was trying to emasculate us, was condescending. Imagine if the tables were turned and I called her *little girl* and publicly called her out in front of her colleagues! Just imagine the wrath.

I couldn't stand the hypocrisy. I couldn't stand the current relations between the sexes. I stood up from my desk chair and looked around for Charles. We had just moved into a newly renovated section of our office building that they called an *open concept*, which meant we were now all roving nomads who worked in different spots every day. Everyone lost their offices with walls and doors, and even the cubicles were a thing of the past—now, we worked at long tables. And they weren't even assigned tables; it was first come, first served—every day! It was horrible, but it was a cheap way to house the revolving door of consultants and clients who surged in and out each election cycle. But it was so loud and distracting. It made me feel like cattle.

I spotted Charles and walked over to where he was sitting in a corner on the other side of the room. He had his earbuds in, but I knew he wasn't on a call or listening to music because he had a yellow sticky note on the side of his table. It was our internal team system of communicating statuses to each other, like being on a call or being heads down doing work or being free to talk. It was all part of the new game—you had to wear earbuds at all times to pretend like you were on a business call so people would stop bothering and interrupting you. It's what we had to do to get work done in the new *open concept* office.

I tapped him on the shoulder. He turned around and pulled out his earbuds.

"Hey, Mike," he said.

"Hi. Did you see the email from Amanda?"

"No. What's up? Is this something important I need to

read?"

"Yes," I said. "Well, not *super* important, but it's about our team—about our ability to be one unit, to have each other's backs, you know?"

He gave me a knowing look. He was able to read between the lines I had just spoken. He turned around, scanned his inbox, and read through the email chain, which his screen said had forty-three threads. I waited until he finished.

"Want to grab a bite to eat with me?" he said.

This was his way of bringing levity to the situation.

"Sure," I said.

We grabbed our jackets and walked outside. We always went to the same five places for lunch, and they were all the same variation on a theme: foodstuff in a bowl. We called it The D.C. Bowl: salad in a bowl, Mediterranean in a bowl, Mexican in a bowl, Indian in a bowl, or burger in a bowl. It was all the same thing—vegetables and lettuce and grains with meat, plus sauce, in a bowl. No matter what you got, it seemed to all taste the same and always cost twelve dollars.

"Alright, lemme hear it," he said as we sat down with our bowls.

"I just don't understand why she's so mean to us. We were such a tight-knit team until *she* came along," I said. "Work used to be fun, and then she joined the team and ruined it, you know?"

"I hear you, Mike. But she's doing a great job," he said. "I think she's trying to prove herself—and that's not a bad thing. She's very motivated."

"I know that—I recognize that, you know. But I don't like that she's always making a thing out of the rest of us being men. It's like she always has to point out that she's the only woman. It's like she's playing some kind of victim!"

"Whoa, there," he said, "careful with your language. I think you need to shift your perspective here. Why don't you look at our team structure as an *opportunity* to challenge yourself with having to work with a diversity of colleagues?"

Ugh! More corporate speak. I hated that everything was framed as an *opportunity*, like every single thing at work is supposed to be designed for your personal growth and gratification. Nobody ever acknowledged a shitty situation for what it was: a pile of steaming crap. Instead, they tried to turn it into a golden nugget when in reality it was still just a pile of crap.

"OK," I said. But I wasn't satisfied with his answer. I was just too tired to fight back because I knew it would be futile. I was giving up, which meant Amanda was winning. "I understand what you're trying to tell me. But know that I still think it's bullshit. She's weaponizing her status as a woman—as some sort of *victim*—in the workplace!"

"Listen to me, Mike!" he said. "The world doesn't revolve around you! You are *one* person on this team, and this team is *one* team out of many from our office. And our office is *one* office out of many across this country. And *we* are all here to serve the firm—that's it. There are thousands of us scattered all across this country. It's not just about you! Have you ever stopped to think about that? Have you?"

My face became flush, and I felt extreme embarrassment. I don't think anyone, not a single person ever in my entire life, had ever dressed me down like that.

"Sure," I said. "Thanks for your perspective."

"But do you understand?" he said, his tone stern.

"Yeah, sure," I said.

"OK, then," he said. "Enough with these outbursts. They make you look like a child. And you're not, Mike. You're an adult."

I felt such shame. I wanted to quit on the spot.

• • •

They say catastrophes come in threes. My whole life I've always wondered who *they* were. Were *they* the puppet masters pulling our strings? Were *they* the journalists and scientists and professors and attorneys and doctors and politicians and priests and filmmakers and TV producers so esteemed in society that *they* got to determine what the collective consensus was on all matters of life? I didn't know who *they* were, but *they* were right. Bad things come not as a one-off or as a pair. Bad things come in a triad of tragedy.

"Michelle, is there something about myself that I don't know? Like, do I have a major character flaw that everyone in my life has been keeping secret from me?"

I was in the kitchen cutting garlic to throw into the pan on the stove where the onions were sautéing. Michelle had come over after work around eight, and we had decided to make beef Bolognese and spaghetti squash for dinner. She was on the couch in the living room, looking down at the floor.

"Michelle?" I said with more urgency and volume in my voice.

"I'm thinking, Mike!"

She gave me a knowing stare. I liked her so much because she was so thoughtful. I knew I needed to give her space to collect her thoughts and gather her words. She was always so careful with what she said out loud, which all the people in her life appreciated and respected her for. Words mattered, and hearing them could either deflate my sense of self in an instant or fill me up with unbounded happiness. I listened to every word she spoke.

"Listen, Mike. You are definitely special. You are complex. Your emotions float in a deep chasm inside of you, and they are unordered," she said. "Your feelings are unordered…"

She was so confident in what she was saying. She had such conviction in her voice. In that moment, I felt as if life was giving me a very important lesson. When these moments happen, time seems to slow down.

She finished with, "You excite me. Your layers excite me."

"Thanks!" I said with a smile. "No one's ever put it that way before."

Michelle was so good for me. She was a shock to my system. It's like my hardened exterior softened and my pessimistic outlook became optimistic all because she had come into my life. She made me want to become a better version of myself. I didn't expect to be so transformed. Could one person really have such an outsize effect on another person?

Of course, getting off the pills could have helped, too. I felt more human than ever, like I could feel all the parts of my body and mind working in unison to help me get through each day. There was nothing to numb the thoughts racing in my head and nothing to retard the feelings moving within me. I was experiencing life as it was meant to be felt. And it currently felt good.

"But that's not all," she said.

She paused, so I stopped stirring and leaned into the living room. I started picking at the cuticles around my nails, which is what I did when I was feeling anxious and the person I was talking to wasn't saying anything back.

"But—listen, I think…your problem, *the* problem is that you're kind of self-absorbed. I think it's because you lived so many years without feeling anything. And I think…I think you…"

She paused again as tears began to pool in the wells of her eyes. Then, a single tear streamed down her left cheek, racing toward the corner of her mouth, where it disappeared into her quivering lips. I knew I was about to hear something I didn't want to hear.

"I think you've been hurt so many times in your life, and so many people have disappointed you, that you could never form healthy relationships. You've spent your whole life architecting how to be perfect. It's like you punish yourself to overcompensate or something. But I think you've had a part to play, too. Your expectations—your expectations of people and of life—aren't aligned with reality. They just aren't!"

While she was talking, I was switching back and forth between pursing my lips and opening my mouth to say something—but nothing would come out.

"And…and…I think—listen, God has a plan for everyone—even you!" she said. "But I think you're still too focused on yourself and not focused enough on other people. Other people have needs, Mike. It's not all about you! You have to learn how to exist with other people, not just yourself."

I turned back to the stove and took a pasta spoon and scooped up two servings of spaghetti squash, placing one scoop in her bowl and one in mine. Then I walked over to the drawer with the flatware and pulled it open, scanning for the large serving spoon I needed next. I turned back around and scooped up two servings of the beef Bolognese, placing one spoonful over her noodles and one over mine. And then I grabbed both bowls, one in each hand like a waiter, and walked over to the table. I stopped and stood motionless.

"Your silence is scaring me," she said.

I looked at her intensely. Then she started shaking her head back and forth.

"No, no, no…Mike, you need to talk to me. This isn't normal. Say something, Mike!"

I leaned forward and gently placed one bowl on the table in front of her. Then I walked to the other side and gently placed the other bowl on the table in front of my chair. I pulled my chair out, the rubber pads underneath the legs making a faint scuffing sound, and sat down. I took my fork and pierced the mound of food in my bowl, turning the handle to twist the sauce and noodles around the tines. I placed my index finger along the handle and brought the tines to my mouth. I chewed my food slowly while staring straight ahead into her eyes.

"Talk, Mike!" she yelled. "Say something!"

I didn't.

I wouldn't.

Chapter Twenty-Seven

TERMINUS

The end of the week came, and the workday dragged on because half our clients now *worked from home* on Fridays and didn't respond to emails in real time like they did Monday through Thursday. After I got home around six o'clock, I decided I would be unavailable for the night. No to going out for drinks. No to hanging out with Michelle. No to answering texts. No to Adam and Matt. No to people and the world.

I needed to zone out from the latest, greatest grief that had entered my life. So I turned on the TV, scrolled to Netflix, and binged on six hours of a documentary series about food. The docuseries taught me that our reptilian selves craved real, whole food. That food was nourishment, not just fuel. That we were to become one with what was on our plate. That it was our responsibility to take pleasure in the culinary orgasm that exploded in our mouths.

Whatever.

Halfway through my Netflix binge, I decided to go for my classic food binge: a whole pizza all to myself, half pepperoni and half cheese. Sometimes I just didn't want to commit. I pulled my phone out of my pocket, unlocked it, tapped the browser app, and typed in the URL of my favorite pizza place. This pizzeria had the type of pepperonis that curl up into little, crunchy bowls of salty and savory goodness—my absolute favorite. I tapped around until I had added the little pizza icon from my favorites section to the virtual shopping cart and submitted my order. A few seconds later, my phone dinged with a text confirmation message. It said the delivery guy would arrive in twenty minutes.

I put my phone down and looked up at the TV screen. Netflix had a question for me: *Are You Still Watching?* I was perturbed that I had to move from my comfy position on the couch, which was satisfyingly ideal. *Let me be, Netflix!* I fumbled around to find the remote control. I pressed the right arrow button and selected *Continue Watching*.

I had already finished a six-pack of beer, and now I was moving on to a bottle of vodka that was left over from some party Jud and I had hosted ages ago. Then I opened my laptop and started surfing the web. At first, I read the news headlines and some stories, but everything was so negative it just made me feel worse. Then I opened Facebook to see what was going on, but the only things in my feed were political opinions from my uninformed second-cousins. I typed *instagram.com* into the address bar to check on my Instafamily but realized the web version was too terrible to enjoy using.

I felt so overwhelmed with everything going on in the world that I couldn't take it anymore. I closed all the tabs I had opened and stared at the blinking cursor in the address bar. I didn't know what I wanted or needed anymore. I took a few swigs of the vodka and looked up at the TV. A chef was flambéing bananas, and the flames from the TV were reflecting off my living room windows.

I looked back down at my laptop and opened a new incognito window. Then I typed in all my favorite URLs, the ones I thought I had given up years ago—for good. But they hadn't gone anywhere; they were waiting for me to come back.

As soon as the first video loaded, a window popped up in the lower right-hand corner of the browser. It was flashing off and on with animated sex icons that teased me with neon shades of pink, blue, and purple. Then words started to appear.

> Are you feeling lonely
> tonight?

It must have been a new feature.

> Come into my private chat
> room to see me on camera. It
> will be fun!

I didn't hesitate. I clicked the *Go* button. Before I knew it, a young woman took over my browser window. She looked like a little girl. And she wasn't wearing anything.

> Hey, stud. I'm here to give
> you everything you want. I
> always say yes…

I wasn't sure if she was real. I wondered if a robot was sending the chats. I leaned forward and put my hands on the keyboard.

> Hi. Are you real?

> Yes. I'm here for your
> pleasure. Tell me to do
> something and I will…

I thought about exactly what I wanted.

> Lower the camera and show
> yourself ;)

And she did! I yanked my pants and boxer briefs down and threw them across the room. Then I started fondling myself. I turned my camera on and tilted the screen at my crotch.

Ohhh, yes. Your SO big! I
want you in me!!

                    Yeah? You wanna take this?
                    You want my big cock you
                                  little slut?

Yes, give it to me!

Then she bent over and spread her legs. I rubbed myself faster and faster and faster.

                    I wanna hear you moan. I
                    wanna hear you take me!

It will cost you $4.99 for
audio. Just put your credit
card info in the box and then
you can hear me!

I got up and rushed across the room to get my wallet. But then my phone started vibrating, so I ran back to the couch to pick it up.

"Uh, hello?" I said.

"Hi, pizza delivery. I'm at your building door."

"Oh, crap! Umm, sorry—just leave it on the stoop. Sorry—I can't come out right now. Thanks!"

I hung up and went back to the couch.

I spiraled down into the darkness that was so familiar to me. Down, down, down.

Into the familiar place where I'd been so many times before. Down, down, down.

Only this time, there was a real-life human being on the other end. And she was all mine, no strings attached.

• • •

It was a frigid Saturday morning in February, and I was on my way to meet Matt and Lauren. There was snow on the ground, which was unusual for D.C. When it did snow, it was usually melted by the next day. But this time we had had a big storm roll in the last week, and the temperature had stayed below freezing, and now there was snow and ice all over the city. It helped hide the grime.

I got out of my Uber and texted Matt.

Here. Where are you guys?

My phone started vibrating. I slid my finger across the screen to answer Matt's call.

"Hey," I said.

"Hey!" he said. "We're not at the address I gave you. We're a few blocks away. I'll send you the coordinates."

A new text appeared on the screen. I tapped it, and a picture of a map appeared. I tapped the image, and then my maps app zoomed to life. I lowered my head and followed the blinking blue dot, first down a one-way street and then across a two-lane intersection and finally down a back alley.

Now I was on a regular residential street with row houses, but the other side had dilapidated industrial buildings made of yellow brick with concrete smokestacks that pierced the gray sky. I looked out and saw a small crowd. I walked closer and spotted a hand waving at me. It was Matt.

"Hey, Mike!"

"Hi."

Matt and Lauren leaned in to hug me.

"How are you?" she said. "It's been toooooo long. I saw Michelle recently at a women's Bible study, and she told me all about your trip to Europe last spring. It sounds like it was wonderful!"

"Yeah, we had a great time," I said.

"Come on, this way!" Matt said.

He gestured for us to follow him, and we started walking down the street. I didn't know where I was. All I saw were groups of people bundled in their coats, scarves, and beanies. A car pulled up to the curb, and a swarm of people rushed to crowd around like paparazzi waiting to see a celebrity. Then we turned a corner and I saw the picket signs.

> *My Botched Abortion is now a Freshman at Howard University*
>
> *You shall not kill; and whoever kills will be liable to judgment. -Matt. 5:21*
>
> *We are the PRO-LIFE generation! We are the REAL FEMINISTS!*
>
> *The Unborn Have A Right To Life, Liberty, And The Pursuit Of Happiness From Their Creator*

I grew angry and clenched my fists. I turned to Matt and Lauren, my eyes full of rage, and stared them down.

"You told me we were going to some charity event!" I yelled. "And then to brunch!!"

"Well, this *is* a charity event. We're being charitable Christians so we can save the unborn children," he said. "Think about the babies, Mike! It's murder!"

I finally spotted the signage for the abortion clinic on the building in small letters under a green awning. Then I watched as two black women walked through the screaming crowd to get to the front door. Their faces were awash in sheer terror. They were so young that they looked like children.

"What they're doing…what you're doing…what *we're* doing is harassment!" I said. "Look at their faces! This is not how Christians are supposed to act. This is wrong."

"Whoa, whoa, whoa," he said. "We are *good Christians*. We are *good people*. Don't be so judgmental. We're fighting for the unborn while you're at home…watching porn!"

A knot formed in my stomach, and my throat tightened. I couldn't believe he had said that out loud. I had told him my shameful secret—in confidence—the day after I had told Michelle.

"Listen, Mike," Lauren said. "We thought you were one of

us. We thought you were on our side. You've been dating Michelle for over a year now. We thought she had brought you fully into the circle of Christ."

"I'm sorry," I said. "I'm not that person you just described." I was shaking my head side to side, confused and mad at the same time. "No. No, no, no, no,"

Another car pulled up. I looked over, and a tall, thin white woman stepped out of a red cab. She was wearing a mahogany baseball cap and tortoiseshell sunglasses. I instantly recognized her. She was someone who worked for my firm! The crowd swarmed her, and she covered her head with her arm as she walked to the entrance. I couldn't believe it.

"I'm sorry…I'm sorry…I have to go. Good to see you both," I said.

They leaned in to hug me, and I let them. Then I turned around and walked away as fast as I could. I felt my pocket vibrating, so I reached in and pulled out my phone. I tapped the green icon to answer the call and plugged in my earbuds.

"Hi, Mom," I said.

"Hi, sweetie!" she said. "What're you doing?"

"Oh, nothing. I'm on my way home now. I had a thing to go to this morning but I, uh, left early to, umm, take care of some things for work before Monday. It's really cold here."

"That's nice, Michael. But why're you working on the weekends? I don't think that's necessary. Are they paying you enough to do that, to work on Saturdays and Sundays? Michael, you seem different. I don't think I like what that city's done to you. You're not as engaging as you used to be when you lived here in California when you were my little boy."

"Yeah, Mom, well—it's just the way things are here, you know. I have to work really hard to keep moving up and show that I'm capable of, you know, making it. It's really competitive here. Everyone works all the time, just like me. I have to be like them if I want to stay competitive, you know?"

She didn't say anything back. I looked up at the crosswalk sign, and a green outline of a person lit up. A loud ticking sound started, and a robotic voice commanded, "Walk now." I started to cross the street, and then sirens came blaring around the corner.

"Mom? Mom! Are you there?" I shouted.

I clasped my ears with my hands and ran onto the median. I watched as all the cars peeled off to the left and right to let two ambulances speed through the middle.

"Michael, yes. Michael, I am here. This is your mother! I am here, Michael!" she said.

"OK, sorry about that," I said. "Anyway, what were we talking about?"

"I miss you. Jessica misses you, too. Even your third-grade teacher is wondering about you. I ran into her at the grocery store last week. Remember her, Ms. Anderson? Her kids are grown now, just like you. The girl became a teacher like her mother, and the boy works with his hands—something to do with air conditioning or machines. They're such a nice family."

"Cool, yeah, I remember. That's nice about her kids."

I kept walking west through a neighborhood I'd never been to before. I didn't know where I was going.

"When do you think you'll be coming home...for good?" she said.

"I, uh...you know, things are going really well for me in D.C. And, you know, I'm so close to getting that promotion at work. After the promotion, I'll get more money, you know. California is becoming too expensive, anyway. I can't afford to go home."

"That's so nice, sweetie. I know you've worked very hard...so very, very hard."

My face felt hot, like I was sitting on the witness stand in a court room. I wasn't sure if I even believed anymore that it was all going to work out, that my plan would finally come to fruition.

"Yeah, mom," I said as water began to well in my eyes. "I've worked so, so hard."

"Michael, you can come home at any time. I don't care why

or when…I just want to have you back. I want to be with my son again."

"How's your job going? Is minimum wage even enough?"

"Oh, I'm fine, sweetie. I love the car wash! I meet the most interesting people there. It's amazing how much dirt some of these vehicles have. Where in the world are they driving those things to? I've become pretty good at upselling the customers on car fresheners when they check out, I'll have you know."

"That's good," I said, my voice cracking. I could feel the hot tears hit the cold air and evaporate. "What about Social Security? When can you get that?"

"In two years, sweetie. The government lets you apply early if you need to, when you're sixty-two, but I guess they don't give you as much. I'll be fine, Michael. Stop worrying so much about me! Your sister is doing fine, too. She has all her student loans to get her through college."

"OK."

"I love you," she said.

"Love you, too," I said

I couldn't tell her the truth, because it would hurt too much. I just wasn't sure who it would hurt more: her or me.

Chapter Twenty-Eight

AWOL ADULTS

"I don't know what you're talking about, Michelle! There has never ever been anything to indicate that this relationship wouldn't work out. I thought we were going to marry each other!"

I was yelling at her. I was yelling at my girlfriend because five minutes ago we were lying on the couch talking about our lives and my dreams to keep searching for my destiny, and now she was fuming and looking for all her stuff. I didn't know what I had said to instigate this madness.

"Mike, you sure are *special*. But *not* in the way you think you are!"

Her words penetrated me and reverberated in my core. What was she saying? Didn't she understand me?

"You're just so…so self-absorbed!"

"Oh, for godssake, Michelle! That's the best you've got?"

I could feel my temperature rising and my heart beating faster.

She pursed her lips. "But what if it's true? What if you don't know how to make yourself available to *me*, for *my* emotions.

My emotions, Mike! My feelings! I have feelings, Mike, and they're real and I'm in touch with them. But you are not. And that's the problem. This is a one-way relationship!"

I stopped myself from reacting. I tried to understand her position, but I wasn't thinking clearly. I was mad. I was mad this was happening and mad that I had worked so hard to get her. I was mad that I had worked so hard to find someone to start my life with, only to see it randomly blow up. Why was this happening? I was so confused.

"Where's my sweater? Mike. Mike. Mike. Have you seen my sweater?"

Now she was acting calm and collected. I could tell she wanted to go home. I could tell from the way her arms were guarding her body and all the directions her eyes were moving to avoid me, to avoid my eyes. It didn't matter that we had had so many amazing experiences together over the last year, that she had lain vulnerable in my arms so many times, that I had told her things I'd never told anyone before. None of it mattered now. And now—now!—she was acting as if I were a complete and total stranger. She was acting as if she didn't know me—as if she didn't know how much I'd had to overcome. Why would she do this to me?

"Michelle, I don't think you're thinking clearly. Why don't we just sit back down and talk about this? Everything will be better after we talk."

"No. I can't do this anymore. I've given you so much of my heart, but I've received so little of yours."

I didn't respond. I couldn't comprehend that this was her perception of our relationship, of our love. All the love I had given her took work. It took so much work to open up my heart, to make myself vulnerable, to trust another human with my humanity. I had given her *so* much of my heart. How could she think that I didn't share my heart with her? I was so confused.

"Michelle, you are the *only* person I have ever given my heart to. And now you're telling me it's not enough! What *is* enough, Michelle? Huh? How much of my heart do you need to be satisfied in this relationship?"

She was ignoring me. She wouldn't make eye contact with me. At some point during the last few minutes, she had found her sweater because she was wearing it, and now she was wrapping her scarf around her neck.

Then she rushed back across the living room to look for her shoes.

"Michelle…Michelle…Michelle!" I snapped.

I took my hands and squeezed her arms, and she seized up— stiff and lifeless.

"Why are you doing this to me? Why?"

"I'm sorry, Mike. You did it to yourself."

Her words cut me. She said it with such iciness. This wasn't the warm, loving Michelle I knew. This was someone else, some cold and judgmental bitch. I loosened my grip, and then I started rubbing her arms up and down to try to make it better. To try to make it all go away.

"Michelle, we can work through this. I can do better. I can *be* better. I can give you more of my heart. I'll need your help…I'll need you to help me love more. But I know I can do it. I will do it. I will do it for *you*. Help me!"

She stepped backward, and my arms dropped to my side. She turned around, walked toward the door, and grabbed her coat off the hook. After she put her arms inside the sleeves, she turned around and looked me straight in the eyes. She just stood there and stared at me. Tears formed in her eyes and trickled down her face. I could see the ceiling lights reflecting off their narrow trails, glistening as the tears raced down her cheeks and then around her jaw and chin, disappearing into the scarf around her neck.

She kept staring at me, and she kept crying. She reached down to find her coat zipper. I could hear her inserting the zipper chain into the pull tab. Then her elbow rose up as she pulled the tab up, all the way to the top, until there was no more zipper left to zip.

With her body cocooned inside her coat and me standing

there in a T-shirt and sweat pants, she leaned in to hug me. The sound of her coat crumpling and the feel of its abrasive exterior made my skin turn to goosebumps. She squeezed me, and I squeezed back. We stood there holding each other tight. I could feel her heart beating rapidly and hear her sniffling through the tears.

"Michelle, why is this happening?" I said.

I began to cry because I was overwhelmed by the moment.

"Because, Mike, life is hard. We are all broken. We are all sinners."

"Why does this keep happening to me? Why can't I find love? Why can't I just be happy?"

She didn't say anything. We stood there in silence, crying and holding each other.

"I don't feel in control," I said.

She let go and stepped back. I could see her forming words in her head. I reached across to wipe away her tears with my thumbs. Startled by my touch, she turned around to face the door. I heard the sound of the lockbolt sliding into an unlocked position. Then the spring in the handle went *click* as she turned the door knob and opened the door. I held my breath.

With her body standing over the threshold, she turned around and held the door half open with her left arm. She took one last look at me before responding to my question.

"Because, Mike, you're a narcissist. You only know how to exist in a world that revolves around you. Everything always is and always has been about you—and only you."

My crying turned to weeping.

"When you stop living for yourself," she said, "then you'll be capable of love."

The door slammed shut, and I never saw her again.

• • •

I felt beaten by life. I was ready for the year to be over. I just wanted to escape the tragedies—the ordinary tragedies—of my life and start over. I wanted to run away from my failed East

Coast quest to find love and purpose. But I also knew that was unrealistic. I was an adult now, and being an adult meant doing things you didn't want to do. In fact, that was *the* definition of being an adult.

I thought a lot about all that had happened to me, both recently and in the past five years—the time since I had finished college in San Bernardino and tried to start my real life in Washington, D.C. What had happened to my dreams? What had happened to my drive? What had happened to all my grand plans for love and purpose?

By now I had expected to be married and on my way to a happy life with a house and a dog and two kids. I would spend my Saturdays washing the car and mowing the lawn and chopping wood while waving at the neighbors passing by with their dogs and children. Satisfied with my work, I would come inside to wash up and find my wife taking fresh-baked cookies out of the oven (a weekend treat) and the kids lounging around the den reading books. We would be happy together as a family.

By now I had expected to be an ambassador to a country in the Global South, running my own diplomatic team and executing my brilliant vision for a better world. I would wake up every morning with purpose and work all day with laser precision because there would be no time to waste. I would create new geopolitical partnerships that made the world a better place and inspire a new generation of citizens to work together for a brighter future. I would sell American ideals abroad and deliver economic opportunity back home. I would change the world as fate required of me.

Of course, none of these things happened—and that's the problem. Instead, I am twenty-seven, I am alone, I hate my job, and I am drowning in debt. I'll probably never be able to buy a house because those are now only for rich people and married people with two incomes. It feels as if there's no way up.

What did I do wrong? I thought I did everything right. I did everything they told me to do! The world—my parents, my friends, my teachers, my country—had failed me. What happened to all the adults? They were nowhere to be found. What a bunch of phonies! Even Adam and Matt, my best friends in D.C. and the ones who always tried to help me, had failed me. Adam was too loose, and Matt was too strict. Adam's vision for my life was too libertine, and Matt's vision for my life was too legalistic. How was I supposed to exist in the middle?

All that has happened has happened because I am who I am. I don't know why it has happened, but it has happened. I don't know if life is a continuous timeline of connected events or a chart of disconnected occurrences. But what I know for sure is that the passing of time is the most painful reality of life.

When I was a kid, I dreaded the long days that felt like they would never end. Each day felt like a marathon. It was the same ritual of waking up, walking to the bus stop, eating breakfast in the cafeteria, sitting still during lessons, waiting in anticipation for morning recess, coming back for more lessons, being released for lunch and recess, more lessons, the saving grace of afternoon recess, the final stretch of lessons, and then—*ring!*—the bell that signaled the end of the school day. But then the second half of the marathon would start, another grueling 13.1 miles of homework, dinner, cartoons, playing, chores, and waiting to fall asleep and end another day.

As an adult, time speeds up so fast it leaves you breathless. In the blink of an eye, I came home from studying abroad, finished and graduated from college, moved to D.C., went to grad school and got my master's degree, and started working as a professional. A whole bunch of stuff happened in between, and all the new apps and technologies changed how life happened, but it all still felt like such a blur. Even yesterday feels like a distant memory from yesteryear. I have seen and done so much. I have met so many people. I have lived so much. And all by the age of twenty-seven, for godssake! I was exhausted by life. All I wanted was respite.

I walked into my bedroom and jumped onto the bed. With

my phone in hand, I held down the home button and commanded the music streaming app to come to life. I scrolled to the album I had been playing nonstop for months and tapped *Play*. I closed my eyes as the song burst into its Auto-Tuned vocals.

And then I began to weep.

My thumb pushed against the screen of my phone, back and forth, just like I used to do on the back of Michelle's hand, back and forth. How could she think I only cared about myself? I had moved across the country for my mom and sister in order to be the man our family has always needed. It made no sense.

I got dumped by my girlfriend, my best friends and everyone else had let me down, and I had failed to accomplish what I had come to D.C. to do. The only thing I had left was my longest-lasting, most successful partnership. The being that knew all my intimate secrets, the history of my life, my trials and tribulations, my triumphs, my reckonings, my addictions, my secrets, my everything. I held tight onto the thing I've been in a relationship with for more than five years, the thing that has never let me down and has always said yes.

My phone.

I continued to weep as I held its cold glass against my heart and then fell asleep.

Chapter Twenty-Nine

THE BEGINNING

I needed to get out of my apartment to clear my head. I liked to escape to a café or library or bar or museum, any public place where I could people-watch. It's what I taught myself to do when I felt like garbage, to avoid being cooped up inside my apartment without end. I grabbed my coat and P.W.K., closed and locked my apartment door, and walked out of my building to be greeted by the brisk December air. It was a seven-minute walk to where I was going.

Sinners and Saints Pub was the name of the bar. It was on Eleventh Street in Columbia Heights, and it was my favorite place in D.C. because of the way it made me feel. Only the locals haunted it, the bartender knew me by name, and the inside felt safe. It was womb-like with its low ceilings and dim amber lighting. It's where I could metaphorically curl up into the fetal position and be nursed by the sweet buzz of alcohol. It was my place.

I walked in and was greeted by a small L-shaped bar made of walnut-colored wood. The bartender waved at me, and the lone patron sitting on a stool lowered his head. I turned right and took a seat in my favorite booth in the far corner, which was perpendicular to one of the street-facing windows. It was the perfect spot to think, drink, and watch. There was a green garland outlining the tops and sides of the window, along with colored C-9 Christmas lightbulbs.

The bar wasn't crowded because it was a Thursday night and a week before Christmas. Most people had already left the city to go home to be with their families. The place smelled of liquor and pine, the former because it is what it is and the latter because of the holiday decorations. The inside of the bar had dark red vinyl booths and a handful of café tables and chairs strewn about. There was wood paneling that went halfway up the walls, with the rest of the place painted a mossy green. The ceiling lamps and wall sconces had fabric lamp shades, which cast a warm, dim glow downward. The floors were checkered with black-and-white tiles. I liked every single imperfection about my perfect little bar.

I scanned the perimeter and stared at portraits of saints hung next to portraits of regular people. A portrait of Saint Catherine of Siena, the patron saint of jurors, was hung next to a portrait of a Supreme Court Justice. Saint Francis of Assisi, the patron saint of the poor and the sick, was next to a porn and reality TV star. Saint Ignatius of Loyola, the patron saint of soldiers, was next to a U.S. General. I wondered how ordinary or extraordinary their lives really were. And whether my life was *actually* special, like their lives had been.

The bartender looked up and called my name from across the room.

"Hey, Mike—the usual?"

"Yeah, but I'll take it neat."

I usually ordered bourbon on the rocks, but because it was so cold outside, I craved the warm sting of the whisky against my throat. While I waited, I gazed at the bursts of light reflecting against the window. If I squinted my eyes a little and forced them out of focus, the bursts of light would draw nearer to my face. I kept squinting and un-squinting, back and forth and back and forth, trying to force the light all the way to my face, to reach out and touch me.

"Cheers to you, Mike. Cheers to life," he said as he placed the glass on my table.

"Yeah," I said. "Cheers to life."

I took a sip, and the alcohol punctured my senses. It felt so good.

One of my favorite songs was playing in the background. I started humming and then singing along faintly, my voice cracking in between lines.

"I am that I am that I am that I am…"

I took another sip and then another and another.

The bartender brought me a second drink even though I had gotten my first only a few minutes ago. *Fuck it*, I thought. I downed the rest of the first drink like it was a shot. Then I reached over to grab the new drink. I stared into the circle created by the rim of the glass, focusing on how still the liquid's surface was while thinking about my life.

I thought about Michelle and the happiness she had made me feel and the love I had tried to give her. I thought about Jud and all the failed friendships that littered my past. I thought about Adam and Matt and how they tried so hard to help me but still disappointed me. I thought about my job and all the stress and anxiety and emotional energy I spent on it. I thought about my mom and sister and hoped they appreciated what I tried to do for them. And I thought about my dad. I wondered where he was and what he'd think of me, of who I had become. I thought about all that had come before me—all the lives lived—and how I fit into the story.

I pulled my phone out of my pocket so I could text Adam.

WHAT IS LIFE

Three gray dots pulsed on the screen. I smirked in anticipation of his response.

> meh. life sux so you should
> just have fun and experience

> everything you can. live like
> theres no tomorrow. get
> drunk and fuck a lot

I felt nothing. It was an answer that no longer appealed to me. I'm not sure he even believed in the advice he always gave me.

I swiped back to my main messages list and scrolled down to Matt's name. I tapped on his face, the screen refreshed to reveal our texting history, and the keyboard popped up. With the blinking cursor ready for me, I typed the same thing.

WHAT IS LIFE

I didn't get an instant response, which made me anxious. My left leg started shaking. I took another sip of my drink, and then another and another.

And then the three dots appeared, replaced with his message two seconds later.

Hey. Is everything OK?

> Yeah, I'm fine. I just want to
> know what life is about.
> What's the point?

Life is light. When you are
facing the light, you are
living. And I want you to
know that you are so alive
right now, Mike! Just pray
about it!!

> Thanks.

I felt something. But his answers were always the same. I was beginning to wonder whether his faith was just surface-level.

I pressed the home button, tapped open Instagram, and scrolled to my Instafamily. Tonight, I didn't feel the usual envy when I gazed at their life. Instead, I felt pride. I was so happy for them, that they existed and that their family was whole. I wished the rest of the world—the rest of my *life*—could be as whole.

The latest picture showed little Sara and Silas eating cupcakes, giggling in laughter at the frosting on the tips of their noses. I closed my eyes and imagined I was there in person, reaching out to them. I imagined walking through their front door and hugging them tight. They would run toward me, their long-lost friend who had been there all along but invisible to them.

I opened my eyes and looked down to find my phone screen dark. In an instant, they were gone. I grabbed my drink and finished what was left. I held my arm up to signal for the bartender to bring me another.

I turned to stare out the window and spotted a couple walking by. They looked so cozy holding each other's hands, bundled up in their coats and scarves and gloves. She had big blonde curls that stuck out from under her red beanie, and she was laughing. He was smiling wide at her and then pulled her in for a kiss. They were so happy.

Clank! The third drink hit the top of the table. I pulled it in by sliding it toward me. I was holding it with both hands like it was a cup of hot cocoa. I leaned over it and breathed in its scent of musk, leather, oak, and spices. The warm notes wafted up and through my nose and created a heady feeling. I closed my eyes again. I liked the feeling of being buzzed. It was like a literal feeling of contentment. You could drink yourself into being content. But I hated that it was ephemeral. When the buzz wore off, real life would show up again.

I looked up and saw a woman walking her dog in front of the window. She was portly, and her legs were bowed. She bounced along the sidewalk just like the boxer she was walking. Her dog stopped to sniff a curbside plant bed, so she stopped, too. Then the dog began a dance, assuming a squatting position and spinning around in a circular motion until he found the exact spot and the perfect angle. As he released his bowels, he made eye contact with me. He had such a look of humiliation in his eyes even though he was doing something so natural and hardwired into his being. He was full of so much shame for no reason at all.

After he finished, he broke eye contact with me and jumped back onto the sidewalk. Then the woman took a bag, wrapped it around her hand, bent over, and picked up the steaming pile of poop. "Good boy!" I saw her mouth as she tied up the bag. The two of them, master and animal, walked away.

My phone screen lit up. I leaned over to read a breaking news alert. But I didn't care anymore. It was always bad news. I grabbed my drink and, bringing the rim to the edge of my lips, tilted my head back and let the liquid drain into my mouth. I tapped the bottom of the glass with my index finger like it was a baby bottle, trying to get every last drop of the bourbon.

Then I stood up and walked to the bar. I leaned forward and put one hand on the edge of the bar top, then I took the palm of my other hand and slapped it down.

"Fuck life. Give me another drink."

The bartender turned around, looked me dead in the eyes, and said, "You got it, boss." He poured me another glass, handed it to me, and said, "Cheers, Mike. And fuck life."

I grabbed the glass and walked back to my booth. I sat down and took a long, deep breath and then let out a long exhale. I could feel the alcohol pulsing through me, the buzz moving through my veins and numbing every part of my body.

I looked across the room and saw two guys walk in. One of them, the taller of the two, tapped the other's butt and then leaned in and kissed his neck. They both giggled. They must have just come from a long dinner because they both looked drunk. And it must have been a date because they both had that look on their faces you get when you are excited by someone else. They ordered their drinks and then walked toward me and sat down two booths away. They kept whispering things to each other and giggling out loud. "I want you to rip my clothes off," said one guy. "I'm going to bend you over tonight," said the other guy.

I smirked and took another sip of my drink. Then I looked out the window and saw a couple pushing a baby in a stroller. The mother was glowing—and not because of the light from the streetlamp. She was staring at her baby with the kind of gaze only a mother has. She was full of so much joy. The father had his arm around his wife, his gaze focused on her. And the baby, who should have been asleep this late at night, was staring at his mother, his gaze focused on his exclusive source of nourishment.

I closed my eyes and pictured my Instafamily in the same situation, a circle of fixed gazes that formed a family: father, mother, children.

My phone lit up again. This time it was a text message from my mom, who had finally gotten a smart phone after I had sent her some extra money.

> Ate good dinner last night.
> Baked chicken. Green beans
> and cauliflower. Wild rice.
> No desert. Getting real
> healthy honeybunch!! Dog
> passed away today. Had to
> work late tonight. Will add
> dog to prayer list at church
> Lv Momma

At the end of her text was a series of emojis: chicken leg, flower bouquet, dog, heart, church, purple cross, information girl. My smile turned to a frown. She went from baked chicken to dead dog. *Oh, my God! My childhood dog is dead!* I couldn't even comprehend it, not this late at night, not this drunk, and not through a text message.

Everyone had gone mad!

I heard a bus horn, and my head jolted up. I looked out the

window and saw a city bus idling at the curb, its lights flashing off and on. The door was open, and the bus driver looked angry, his mouth moving into all sorts of shapes while his hand was using the center of the steering wheel to conduct a symphony of sound. Then he held his hand down on the horn, and a long uninterrupted honk caused all the people in the bar and the passersby on the sidewalks to turn their heads.

I slid across the bench to get up against the window. I could hear the muffled sounds of an argument happening between the bus driver and a passenger. Then one of the voices got louder as a woman walked off the bus in a rage. She turned around, planted her feet on the sidewalk, and yelled, "Baby, you can kiss my big black ass!" And then she stormed off, waving her arms in the air.

I opened my mouth, slack-jawed in disbelief at what I had just witnessed. I laughed out loud, at first under my breath, and then louder and louder because it was all so ridiculous. *What planet am I living on? What is this place? Why must I endure it?*

The world had gone mad!

I slid back to the middle of the bench to get my drink. I picked it up, inspected the amount of liquid left inside, and finished it. I closed my eyes again and took a deep breath. I felt so content. I imagined my bed and how warm and cozy it would be. I wanted to be home to collapse onto it, to melt into its softness, to go to sleep. I wanted to feel safe.

I decided it was time to go. I opened my eyes, grabbed my coat, walked over to pay my tab, and then was on my way. I started walking south on Eleventh Street, slow and steady because I realized I couldn't walk in a straight line. But I felt good. My God, I felt good!

As I was walking, I noticed in my peripheral vision a triangular neon orange flag floating in the air. I turned to my left and focused my eyes on the flag, tracing it down to its pole and then down to whatever moving thing the pole was attached to. Whatever *it* was, it was moving at the same slow pace that I was, either taunting me or challenging me to a race.

As I continued to walk, now half-shuffling sideways to get a good view from across the street, I saw it under the bright light of a streetlamp. It looked like an ice cooler on wheels, but with LEDs lighting its path and a black strip of glass up top that served as its eyes. It was a robot! One of those robots I had read about that delivered food to the McSpecials. *Great*, I thought. *The robots are coming.*

When it got to the street corner, it stopped and then turned left up a hill. I waited for a green light so I could cross the street and then chased after it. When I got halfway up the block, I looked down and said, "You may be smarter than me, but you'll never have a soul, you techno piece of crap!" I laughed as it whirred away.

As I continued my walk home, a smile formed on my face. All of these things were life happening. All of these people were life passing by. But I just felt like a bystander, like some fool who had paid too much money to watch the show and gone home without a souvenir.

I looked up and saw a man standing on the sidewalk in front of an alley, blocking my way. He was dressed in black from head to toe, talking on the phone and pacing back and forth. His dark brown hair, which was combed to the side, blended into a thick beard. The cuffs of his pants were frayed, and his leather shoes were dull and scuffed. The man noticed me, made eye contact with me, and said goodbye to whomever he was talking to. As he turned toward me, I noticed a flash of white in the center of his neck. It was a clerical collar.

"Hi, Father," I said.

I was a little nervous, just like when I was a child at church. Priests had always intimidated me some.

"Good evening, young man. You look like you've had a *very* good night!" he said, too cheery for how late it was.

I stepped forward and realized he was the same priest that had anointed the sick two years ago. And the same guy I had seen at the bookstore when I first got to D.C. I couldn't believe it!

"Yeah, hah, I *did* have a good night. I'm on my way home now—almost there…"

I knew that he knew that I was drunk. I straightened my posture to increase my credibility.

"How did you know I'm a priest?" he said.

"Because your collar is showing a little bit inside your coat."

He looked down, straining to see underneath his chin.

"Ahh, I see," he said with a smile. "You must be Catholic. Very well, I've nothing to hide. It's just so cold out and, sadly, they don't make coats with the collar."

We both stood there in silence, the sound of rustling vines on the side of a row house the only thing filling the gap in conversation.

In a hesitant voice, I said, "Father, ca—can I ask you a question?"

"Yes, of course," he said. "You may ask me anything, anything at all."

I could see a small cloud of his breath, of his words, floating on the cold winter air.

"What's the point of life? Like, not the meaning of life, but what's the point of it all, you know?"

A wide smile formed on his face from cheek to cheek, and then he chuckled.

"My son, looking at you now—having this random, but wonderful, encounter with you—I am confident you already know the answer to your question. The fact that you asked it speaks bounds."

My face contorted into confusion. I did not, in fact, know the answer to my own question. That's why I had asked it of him, a theologian! A man of God!

He opened his mouth to say something but then stopped himself.

"Father?"

He took one of his hands out of his pocket and placed it on my shoulder.

"*Ad majorem Dei gloriam*," he said. "Him! The one. That is your answer."

He gave me a knowing stare.

"But I don't understand," I said. "It can't be that simple. That isn't what they said life would be about!"

"You, son, are already on the path to salvation. I can see it in your eyes," he said. "It is not one that is easy, but it is the one that leads to full life."

Maybe he was right. Maybe I had done it all wrong. The path I was on to find love and purpose had turned out to be a dead end. Maybe I'd need to take a different path.

"But I don't understand!" I said. "How do I get onto that path?"

He looked unsure, like I had said something wrong.

"Son?" he said. "Where are you *really* going?"

"I'm on my way home."

He paused and stared deep into my eyes. I didn't blink.

"Very well," he said. "Would you like to confess before you start your journey?"

He spoke with such confidence. I needed to fight back, to show him I was smart and accomplished and in control.

"I have nothing to confess," I said. "I haven't done anything wrong. I did everything they told me to do."

I was betting he wouldn't be able to counter my confidence. This would all be over before it even began, and soon I'd be under the covers in my bed and fast asleep.

"You are wrong, child," he said. "You have *everything* to confess because you are a human who falls short each and every day. We all hurt other people, whether we intend to or not, because it is the reality of the human condition. We are connected to each other even in our isolation. Whether we like it or not, our speechlessness is speech and our inaction is action. This is why you must examine your conscience."

I couldn't believe it. *Who does this guy think he is, lecturing me this late at night?* It's like he knew about my life.

"Father!" I yelled. "Why do *I* have to do all the work? *I* was the one who was wronged by all these people! *I* was the one who had to suffer!"

"Swallow your pride and surrender," he said. "And then you will receive the grace from God that renews us all over and over and over again—as much grace as we need, given when we need it most."

He spoke in such absolutes. I didn't know what else to say. I was tired of fighting back.

"I want this grace!" I said. "I want to feel it! How do I get it?"

"Do you remember the Act of Contrition?" he said.

I didn't remember it, but I didn't want to disappoint him. "Yeah."

He nodded and then bowed his head. I plunged my hand into my pocket and pulled out my phone. Then I pressed the home button.

"OK," he said. "Now, what would you like to confess?"

I moved my eyes up and stared into the vast expanse of the night sky. The light from the billions of little stars overwhelmed me, and I began to weep.

"Son?"